STAND FAST AND REPLY

BOOKS BY
LAVINIA R. DAVIS

HOBBY HORSE HILL
BUTTONWOOD ISLAND
PONY JUNGLE
PLOW PENNY MYSTERY
STAND FAST AND REPLY

STAND FAST
and
REPLY

by Lavinia R. Davis

DOUBLEDAY, DORAN & COMPANY, INC.

GARDEN CITY, NEW YORK

THIS BOOK IS
COMPLETE AND UNABRIDGED,
MANUFACTURED UNDER WARTIME
CONDITIONS IN CONFORMITY WITH
ALL GOVERNMENT REGULATIONS
CONTROLLING THE USE OF PAPER
AND OTHER MATERIALS.

Contents

v

vi CONTENTS

STAND FAST AND REPLY

~~~~~~~~~~~~~~~~~~~~~~~~~~~~~~~~~~~~~~

Wet Behind the Ears

THE LATE AUGUST SUN glittered on the deep blue of the ocean and in the distance whitecaps scudded before the warm wind. Bitsy hesitated for a moment, her seventeen-year-old body taut, and then hurled herself into the water. She ducked expertly, felt the breaker heave over her legs, and then struck out toward the fish nets with a smile on her wet red lips.

Swimming in strong surf was still fun. After the last two days, it seemed to be the only thing at Sea Cliff that hadn't changed. Once beyond the breakers Bitsy floated on her back, staring up at the sky. It wasn't just that she had been up at Rye all summer and that for the first time in her life the family hadn't rented the Wade cottage on Shore Road that made everything seem queer now that she had come back. It was the cold, snobby way that Mabs Holcombe and Minty Blaine and all the other girls treated her. And the boys were different too. So many of them were away working that the few who were left behind were suddenly high-hat and hard to please.

The sea water began to seep up through Bitsy's cap

and she rolled over on her stomach. The summer visiting Aunt Helen up at Rye had been a flop. Aunt Helen hadn't known any of the younger crowd, and though Bitsy had tried to make friends she had stayed an outsider. She had comforted herself with the thought that at Sea Cliff she was one of the gang, but now, after two days, she wasn't at all sure. Bitsy felt cold and apprehensive as it occurred to her that maybe she was the one who had changed. She had been something of a leader in the old rough-and-tumble, kid days, but maybe from now on she would always be on the outside.

The vast emptiness of the sky made her feel lonelier than ever and she began to tread water, waiting for a wave to ride in to shore. There was no point in just staring into space and getting more and more shaky about joining the crowd around the swimming pool. Bitsy looked over her shoulder and saw the perfect wave, a great green mountain of water slowly building up behind her. She waited half a second and then ducked and kicked at just the right moment.

She had caught the wave perfectly. Her small, neat body was tapered and relaxed as the water rushed her forward. This is it, she thought, feeling somehow befriended by the roar of the water. This is it. I have come home, oh, sea!

In another moment it was over. She was rolled up on shore and picked herself up, breathless, excited, and covered with sand. She rinsed off in a shallow backwater and pulled down the bathing suit that always hiked up in the wrong places.

The beach was nearly deserted except for some sun-tanned babies and a few nurses who clustered under a big beach umbrella. In the distance three little boys in striped jerseys worked like terriers on a sand castle, but there was no one of Bitsy's age in sight. For a moment Bitsy lingered, watching the three little boys. It was awfully safe and comfortable being that age. You went to the beach every morning and again in the afternoon and there wasn't anything to worry about except whether you could win a cup in the tadpole race in the water sports.

Bitsy looked away from the boys and walked reso-lutely up the board steps to the Beach Club. Only some-body who was a failure, a dud, would want to be six again. It meant you were afraid of being grown-up, afraid of not being popular and having the boys ask you to do things, if you wanted to go on being a little kid.

Bitsy hurried over the boardwalk and past the bath-houses toward the pool where the college crowd always congregated in the late afternoon. The Sea Cliff pool was long and blue and the water looked clean and inviting with the sun making little gold barbs on the ripples. Bitsy never noticed it, her eyes searching for Minty Blaine and Mabs Holcombe and the others. She saw them sitting under the green-and-white umbrella nearest the diving boards and hurried toward them.

Mabs Holcombe was knitting an intricate-looking sock, and talking to Minty and the two Warner boys and Josh Asprey. A little hopeful flutter stirred Bitsy as she saw Josh. She felt pretty sure Josh would ask her to the

Labor Day dance at the Yacht Club. Bitsy hadn't been at
Sea Cliff for two days without learning that all the other
girls were dated up, and if there wasn't anybody else
he'd just have to ask her.

Bitsy skidded on the wet boards around the edge of
the pool, collided painfully with the bench, and almost
fell into Minty's lap. "S-sorry," Bitsy got out.

"Oh, it's all right." Minty dried her arm where Bitsy's
bathing suit had wet it and then went right on talking
to Josh Asprey. "What did you say to her then?"

"Why, I just told her that Sea Cliff was getting duller
than ever and that she'd have to have pity on a seagoing
chap and come up."

"Who's coming up to what?" Bitsy asked, trying to
rub the ankle she'd skinned in slipping and at the same
time to fit into the conversation.

"My cousin Buella from Louisville," Mabs drawled in
her new Southern accent that grated on Bitsy's ears.
"You all don't know her. Josh has just asked her up for
the Yacht Club dance and she's going to stay with me."

Bitsy suddenly felt cold. Josh wasn't going to ask her,
and there wasn't another boy left in town. Her ankle
hurt more than ever now and she was desperately afraid
she would cry. "Wh-when is the dance?" she asked, just
to say something.

"Monday, of course." Minty didn't even look at her as
she answered. "It's always on Labor Day."

Bitsy wriggled miserably in her wet bathing suit and
tried to sit on her legs that were scratched and freckled
instead of burned a sleek, even brown. Of course she had

known about the dance, but she just had to say something. If only she could be suddenly bright and amusing so that nobody would know how much she minded not to be asked. If she could make the boys laugh at her the way they did at Minty or angle to sit next to her the way they did with Mabs. "I've—I've just been in the ocean——" she began, but nobody was listening. Josh had started to hold some wool for Mabs, and Minty was launched on a story that seemed to be all about people that Bitsy didn't know.

It wasn't until Bitsy heard the name Em Renfrew that she was on familiar ground again. Em had lived in the house next to the Wade cottage for years. In the cops-and-robbers, collecting-driftwood era she had been Bitsy's best friend, but that seemed ages ago. Bitsy and the other girls all went to private schools in New York while Em went to the high school in Sea Cliff. Em was nice enough, but she hadn't ever fitted in with the crowd since they had grown up. "Well, Byrd asked her if she wanted a coke," Minty went on, "and she looked at him like a dying duck in a thunderstorm and said, 'Oh yes, Lieutenant, *anything* from you!' "

A howl of laughter met Minty's mimicking of Em, and Bitsy wriggled further back into her corner. It wasn't that she was especially fond of Em, but it made her uncomfortable to hear the gang pull anybody apart. She couldn't help wondering what they would say about her the minute she left to get dressed. She was groping in her mind for something to tell them about her swim, her trip down from New York, or her whole summer at

Aunt Helen's that might possibly amuse them, when Mabs stopped knitting and waved in that languid way of hers to somebody across the pool.

"Hi, Byrd," Bill Warner called. "Come on over and join the folks."

Byrd Gaylord dived into the water, hauled himself up on the side of the pool nearest the umbrella, and shook himself like a big Newfoundland dog. Byrd was older than the others, already twenty, and he had just finished his training as a flying cadet. He was only back at Sea Cliff on a week's leave before he was to be sent off to a regular post.

As Bitsy looked at his broad, confident face, a sudden surge of absolutely breathless hope went through her. What if Byrd asked her to go to the dance with him! He was older than the others and much more sure of himself. He was a fine athlete and a finished dancer, and even in the free-and-easy kid days he had been something of a hero to Bitsy and the others. Now that he was a full-fledged pilot he was the undisputed king of Sea Cliff. And he might ask me, Bitsy thought. He might so easily ask me. She half smiled, so blissful was the prospect, but Byrd only nodded to her and started talking to the others.

"Oh yes!" Bitsy began, but now Dave Warner had asked Byrd something about Kelly Field and Byrd had already forgotten that Bitsy was there.

"B-Bits! B-B-BITSY!" The stuttered shout made Bitsy jump and she looked up to see her nine-year-old brother Stanty dog-paddling across the pool and shouting at the same time. "B-Bitsy! Y-you've got to come home right way." Stanty pulled his skinny brown body over the side of the pool and stood in front of Bitsy, shivering and excited. "M-Mum s-says you're to c-c-come!"

"Oh, run away, Stanton," Bitsy said. "You're half frozen."

"Y-you're to come r-right away!" Stanty insisted through blue lips. "I sw-swam almost out to the f-fif-fish nets to f-find you."

"I'll be back at the Inn in plenty of time for supper," Bitsy said, but Stanty wasn't going to be put off like that.

"You'll c-come n-now!" he insisted. "D-Dad's there!"

For the first time Bitsy really looked at her small brother. Dad had been in the Army since March. He was down in Washington at a desk job and that was why they hadn't rented the house at Sea Cliff. There hadn't been any hope of his getting off for the week end. Mother had said so only yesterday. "Are you sure?" Bitsy demanded. "You're not trying to be funny, Stanton Close?"

"C-course n-not, you d-dope!" Stanty exploded, and the gang laughed.

"How're tricks with you, Stanty?" Byrd Gaylord asked him. "You've gotten pretty good at s-sw-swimming!"

Stanty considered Byrd for several minutes before he answered. "O.K.K., *Admiral!*"

Byrd make a good-natured lunge at Stanty, but he escaped and plunged back into the pool, splashing the others. "You c-come on home, Bitsy," he spluttered when he got to the surface. "M-Mum said t-to!"

"I guess I'd better go," Bitsy said, but now the rest of the crowd were moving too. The two girls and the Warner boys were going into the ocean and Josh and Byrd dived into the pool.

Bitsy went into the shower to get the salt water out of her hair and then hurried down the dark, damp corridor to the bathhouses that were kept for guests of the Inn. It wasn't until she was nearly dry that she heard Byrd and Josh come into the bathhouse next to hers.

"She's really something," Josh's voice said, "little and cute-looking and a whale of a line. Even better than Mabs'."

"I'll take a look at her," Byrd promised. "But you've got to produce something better than the local talent if you want me to go to that shindig. Why, that Close kid's still wet behind the ears."

Bitsy jammed a moist foot into her red moccasin. She didn't want to hear, she didn't, she didn't, but the wall of the bathhouse was like paper and it was too late to call out. "Oh, Mabs is O.K., and Minty." Josh's voice was condescending. "And you needn't worry about getting stuck with Bitsy. She won't even be at the party. We do the inviting, and only the smooth dames get a bid."

Bitsy didn't even wait to put on lipstick but fled down the hall and into the dazzling sunlight. Stanty, with his hair slicked down except for one stiff little shoebrush at the back, was already waiting at the edge of the pool. "You g-girls take all d-day," he said. "Let's get going."

Bitsy followed him across the graveled driveway and over toward the Inn. Stanty chattered on about Dad and his new summer uniform and how he was going to get a pistol, but Bitsy didn't hear a word.

The cold, frightened feeling that had haunted her in the ocean was back now, a tight icy vise around her heart. What she had unconsciously dreaded had come to pass. She was a failure, and everybody knew it. She was worse than Em Renfrew because not even the towel boys or the life guards tried to date her. She hadn't been asked to the Yacht Club party, and all the other girls had known she never would be. Josh had gone out of his way to ask a girl from another town, and Byrd, why, Byrd Gaylord thought less of her than he did of Stanty or the babies who built sand castles down on the beach.

~~~~~~

Shifting Winds

W HILE STANTY WAS OUT getting Bitsy, Captain Close walked across the spare, sunny bedroom and stood looking out of the window. "It's the fact that it's all happened at once that makes it so tough," he said. "Losing the money'd be bad enough any time, but now when I can't even try to take care of you——"

Mrs. Close got up and put her hand through her husband's arm. "It's all going to work out for the best," she said. "I'm really convinced of that. Why, for all these years we've been living on—on whipped cream. The best schools for the children, lovely clothes, a big apartment."

"Well, you won't have them now." Kenneth Close's voice was bitter. "And I can't *do* anything."

"But you've done it already! When I think that after only six months in the Army you've been chosen over the heads of all those other men, younger men, and with more army experience, I'm so proud I can hardly see."

For the first time Captain Close looked at his wife. "You're a love," he said gently, and now his naturally young face looked almost boyish again. "You're the most wonderful woman in the world but even so. You'll have the kids and yourself and only a small part of my pay. So much has got to go toward keeping Aunt Marion in that home, and there's nobody else to help. Helen's done more than her share by having the children all summer."

"Everybody's got burdens," Katherine Close told him. "And it's time I shared them again. It's time Bitsy and Stanty did too. Why, I was working my way through art school when I wasn't much older than Bits."

"I know it! Oh God, I know, and that's what I wanted to keep you away from. I wanted you to be free and unburdened and able to paint anything and everything that you wanted."

"Well, I have, haven't I?" Mrs. Close's voice was genuinely cheerful. "And I haven't produced any masterpieces. A little competition's what I need, Ken. Honest competition. The pay or pay not of the market place."

"That's just what I've flopped at!" Kenneth said, and now he turned away from his wife again. "Leaving those investments in Baker's hands when I joined up was—was, well, mental."

"It was not. And besides, no man that's kept his wife and two children just wallowing in luxury for seventeen years can call himself a flop. Especially not a man who's gone into the Army and been picked out for a special mission the way you have."

"Oh, my darling," Kenneth said, but just then there was a scuffle outside the door and the next moment Stanty bounced in.

"I t-t-told her," he said. "B-but she's s-slow."

"I'm coming." Bitsy's young voice sounded down the hotel corridor, and the next moment she was in her father's arms.

"Dad!" she said. "I just didn't believe it when Stanty said you were home. Mother said yesterday you weren't coming."

Captain Close looked down at his daughter's upturned face. "Day before yesterday was just about a year ago, ten years ago, so much has happened since."

"Wh-what?" Stanty perched on the foot of the iron bedstead and swung his brown legs over the edge. "L-let's g-guess!"

"You couldn't," Captain Close said, and the note of bitterness was back again. "None of them are exactly Christmas surprises anyway. Not the kind of things that it's fun to guess about."

"Then you h-haven't g-gotten any m-m-medals?"

"Stanty, you're cracked," Bitsy began, but now Mother was speaking.

"Some of it's almost as impressive as that," she said. "Dad's been chosen from over a hundred other men to go overseas."

"T-to J-Japan?"

"To go *where?*" For the first time since she had left the bathhouse Bitsy thought of something besides what Byrd Gaylord had said.

"I'm not even sure myself," Captain Close said. "And if I did know, I couldn't talk about it."

"C-can I go with you?" Stanty demanded.

Captain Close shook his head, and Mrs. Close moved

over and sat down on the bed behind Stanty. "You've got to stay with me," she said. "And help me move out of the apartment."

"Help m-move?" Even Stanty's ears looked surprised. "W-why?"

"Things can happen awfully quickly about money," Mrs. Close told him. "And we've had some very bad luck with investments. With the money Dad saved up, you know. We aren't even going to live in New York."

"Not live in New York?" Bitsy's voice was shrill with excitement. "You mean I won't go back to graduate at Miss Fair's?"

"That's right," Mrs. Close said. "We're in luck our lease on the apartment is just up."

"B-but where will we l-live?" Stanty persisted. "H-here at S-Sea Cliff? At the Inn?"

"At twelve dollars per?" Captain Close muttered. "Not a chance."

"That's the best part of it," Mrs. Close said. "Dad and I were talking about it just before you came in. We're going out to Ohio. To Bricklow, where I lived when I was your age. And we'll be living on a farm, Stanty, with pigs and chickens and cows and everything. You'll love it."

Bitsy dropped down into the only free chair and looked around her. The faded chintz, the scoured white walls were the same. The painted bureau and the two iron bedsteads looked just the way they had that morning, but Bitsy couldn't have been more stunned if they had suddenly started to waltz. They were not going back to New York where she had spent every winter of her life. She was not going to Miss Fair's where she had started in the primary. "Where will we live?" she asked suddenly. "In what house, I mean?"

"Cousin Bertha's house," Mrs. Close said, and now she avoided her husband's eyes. "She's only my second cousin really, but we grew up together as girls. Great-Uncle Bert left us each an equal interest in his house when he died, and Bertha's said for years that any time we wanted to we could come back. It'll be going home really."

It won't be home to me, Bitsy thought fiercely. Just because Mother had come from Ohio didn't mean she belonged there. And Mother had never been enthusiastic about the farm before. "You—you always hated it," Bitsy burst out. "You always said it was terribly quiet and dull! You've kept rubbing it in how much more fun I had at Miss Fair's than you had at high school."

"There's a new high school," Mrs. Close said, and now her deep violet eyes were pleading. "A big splendid one over in Meudon. You'll get a lot out of that, and Stanty'll go to the little grade school that's right near the farm. He'll be able to go all by himself, without anybody taking him."

"B-boy," Stanty said, but Bitsy hardly heard him.

"When will we be going?" she said. "After Labor Day?"

"I'm afraid that's one of the tough parts of it all, Flopsy Buttons." Captain Close used the old familiar pet name that belonged to the days of pigtails and no front teeth. "We'll be leaving here tomorrow morning. You see I've only got four days before I go off, and Mum and I have a lot of things we've got to get settled in New York. I'd like to be able to fix it up so that you could stay over here, but it'd be pretty expensive and every penny counts."

"But I want to go to New York tomorrow!" The words shot out from Bitsy's lips. Here was a way out! Now she could escape hearing about the Yacht Club dance and being in a place where everyone thought she was a dud! "I—I'm crazy to go right away!"

"Good girl!" Captain Close said, and Mrs. Close smiled, and the look of faith and pride on her lovely face made Bitsy feel like a traitor. The family thought she was just being a good sport! They couldn't guess that after what had happened this afternoon she never even wanted to hear about Sea Cliff again. Bitsy struggled for words, but now Stanty had something on his mind.

"H-ow about G-Ginger?" he asked. "Can I take him to the f-f-farm?"

"You bet you can, son. Bertha wouldn't mind another dog, would she, Katherine?"

Mrs. Close laughed. "From what I remember of the farm," she said, "one more dog wouldn't make the least difference in the world. I don't believe she'd even know he was there."

"G-good!" Stanty rocked back onto the bed with his feet up in the air. "Sw-swell. G-Ginge has j-just hated being in a k-kennel."

"I like my family," Captain Close said suddenly, and

the pride in his voice made Bitsy wince. "If ever a man was blessed with three perfectly wonderful sports, I'm the fella."

"W-will you shoot J-Japs or G-Germans?" Stanty had popped upright on the bed again. "Have you a g-gun?"

Captain Close grinned. "An officer doesn't carry a gun," he said. "But I've been issued side arms, a pistol, you know, and I'll show it to you when we get down to New York."

"M-M-Minnie!" Stanty let out, his squirrel face wrinkled with bliss. "A real pistol!"

Bitsy moved over to the window and let the salt breeze blow on her face. All of Stanty's talk about the pistol had brought home what Dad was about to do. It wasn't a desk job any more but something exciting, dangerous, in which he might be hurt or even killed.

"Dad——" she began, and then bit her lip and said nothing. She looked at her mother, but Mrs. Close's beautiful face was perfectly controlled. It was only her hands that gave her away. The thin white fingers gripped the iron bedstead so that her knuckles stood out like little stones.

Bitsy turned back to the ocean that grew darker and more purple in the fading light. Four figures were walking across the beach. As they climbed up the steps to the Beach Club, Bitsy recognized Minty and Mabs and the two boys. Minty walked a little ahead of the others, her red bathing suit trim and smart looking even now that it was wet. Bitsy leaned outward to see better, and just at that moment Bill Warner hurried forward to take

Minty's arm. I'm glad I'm leaving! Bitsy thought, and the combined emotions that swept her made her feel almost sick.

Dad was going off; something had happened about their money. Mother was being so brave that it hurt to watch her; even Dad, who was usually so cheerful, sounded gruff and queer. It was all terrific, overwhelming. Yet right now nothing, no, not even Mum's face when she thought nobody was looking, mattered so much as the fact that she, Bitsy, wouldn't have to sit all alone like a hopeless goon and listen to the other girls talk about that party.

III

A Coat of Green

FOUR DAYS LATER Bitsy went to bed in her own room in the apartment for the last time. The close air smelled of moth flakes and tar paper, and it was hard to go to sleep. The street lights flooded into the curtainless room and it looked bare and abandoned already. There were big ugly marks where the pictures had been and a trunk took the place of the two chairs. Even the bureau, naked and forlorn without a bureau scarf or any little ornaments, looked different.

Bitsy stretched uneasily, her body listless and tired. The last few days had been hectic and confused, and it was impossible to connect them with any other Labor Day week end she had ever known. Mother had been quick and businesslike about packing up her paints and sketchbook, but she was perfectly vague about storing away the silver and the china and the other things. Mary and Agnes, the two maids they had had before Dad had left for Washington, had always attended to the housekeeping, and Mother was lost without them. She had worked hard sorting and cleaning while Dad and Bitsy did the actual crating with Stanty running to and fro between them like an excited squirrel.

Stanty had been more nuisance than help about the crating, but this morning he had been a lifesaver without even knowing it. They had gone to a Schrafft's down the street for their last breakfast together and it would have been a nightmare without Stanty. Even Mother, who all the other days had been gay and amusing about her own inefficiency, had become suddenly silent and tense. Bitsy had started in on her scrambled eggs, but when she looked at Dad, brown and solid in his uniform and smelling of the clean, familiar odor of shaving soap, it had suddenly come over her that this might be their last meal together for years, forever maybe. Her courage failed, and the eggs tasted like ashes.

Only Stanty had been really cheerful and absolutely uninhibited. He asked Dad just how many people he thought he would shoot, and then before he'd even finished his sentence, dived at his waffles and syrup as though he hadn't eaten for a week.

And on the last aching drive down to the station, where Dad was to take off for an unknown port, Stanty had been a help too. Bitsy turned away from the light and burrowed her face in the pillow. It was bad enough to feel lost and uncertain yourself, but to see Mother, whom you'd always thought of as middle-aged and serene and absolutely sure, obviously racked with a grief that she struggled to hide, was almost unbearable. Bitsy could see her now standing on tiptoes for the last kiss; and then her face white and drawn and suddenly old, looking dumbly after the train as it pulled out of the station.

Stanty had saved the day. He had waved frantically until even the red taillight had been swallowed up in the darkness and then had turned to Mother, his head on one side. "Those w-waffles," he said, "were an awful l-long time ago."

For an instant Mother hadn't heard. She had looked down at him like someone trying to wake up out of a bad dream. "What did you say, darling?"

Stanty had put it more bluntly. "I s-said I w-was h-hungry. The w-waffles didn't last."

Mother had laughed with two big tears glistening on her long lashes and had hugged him right then and there. "You can have anything you want," she said. "I could use a cup of black coffee myself. How about you, Bits?"

But Bitsy hadn't wanted a second breakfast and she had wanted to do a few last errands at Woolworth's. "Good." Mother had pulled a dollar bill out of her purse. "Get anything you want and meet us at the apartment."

Now that Bitsy thought over those next few hours they were as vivid as though they were just happening. It was as though anything you did between two such important things as saying good-by to Dad and leaving New York was underlined forever in your mind. Like that moment when they had walked by Miss Fair's school their second day in New York. Bitsy had walked past the red brick school building for years, but now passing it on a hot Saturday in September was suddenly important.

"We will be back in New York by spring, won't we, Mum?" she'd said, because it seemed too incredible that after all the years in the primary and the lower school she wouldn't ever be there to graduate with her class. "We will come back here to live, I mean?"

"Of course we will." Mother's voice was light with the cheery confidence that was as much a part of her as her dark, wavy hair or her lovely coloring. Then a moment later she had hesitated, as though she were forcing herself to speak. "I hope we'll be back," she said finally. "But I guess these days we can't really be sure."

But in the hours after Dad's train left, Bitsy wasn't thinking about Miss Fair's. It was good to be out alone on the crowded, busy streets. She still enjoyed being allowed to get around by herself after all the years of being taken everywhere. Somehow being alone among so many strangers gave you time and privacy to straighten out your own mind.

Bitsy walked slowly up flag-draped Fifth Avenue. It seemed even brighter and more dazzling than in midwinter, and you could see people better now that they weren't all bundled up in winter clothes. She noticed a girl in black walking with a Marine and watched them until they were out of sight. It was funny how people stood out more, how you noticed them individually when you hadn't been in the city for a long time. She walked on up the glistening pavement and looked in at the shop windows. There were fur coats everywhere and fall dresses and wonderful-looking tweeds.

Bitsy went into one of the big five-and-tens and threaded her way through the bright maze of stationery, knickknacks, and toys until she found the cosmetic counter. She picked out the powder puffs she wanted and waited while a salesgirl, not much older than herself, took care of two other customers. One of them, an elderly woman with a shopping bag, changed her mind three times over a choice of talcum powders, and then lost her temper when the salesgirl had wrapped up her third choice as she settled on a fourth.

Finally she was finished and marched off disgruntled as the girl reached for Bitsy's puffs. "Anything else?" she asked, and Bitsy shook her head, still looking after the angry woman who had stopped at the stocking counter.

"That's all, thanks," Bitsy said, and their eyes met looking after the fat customer.

"There're bound to be some lemons," the girl said matter-of-factly, and handed Bitsy her package.

"I'll bet!" Bitsy said, and the girl smiled.

"It's a big help when we get someone who doesn't kick when they have to wait a few minutes," she said, and Bitsy left the store feeling suddenly more cheerful.

Once back under the bright flags of the Avenue, Bitsy's mind rested for a moment on the girl at the store. It would be pretty awful waiting on crabby people like that all day, but it was better than sitting around Sea Cliff being snooted by Minty and Mabs. Anything would be better than to just have to sit hopeless and useless because the only thing that was expected of you was to look pretty and to have a good line. As she thought of Sea Cliff a little flutter of uncertainty caught at her heart. Suppose Ohio was like that all the year round? Suppose she landed in a close, watertight crowd like the one at Sea Cliff where any extra girl was either a nuisance or a menace?

Bitsy was opposite a big expensive leather store by now and she stopped to look in at the folded frames, the writing cases, the military hair brushes, and other gifts for soldiers. What would it be like to have someone other than your father or your uncle for whom you could buy things like that? To be able to buy that wallet for a young pilot, for instance, and know that he would carry it with him wherever he went just because you had sent it to him? But thinking about any pilot made her remember Byrd's voice through the bathhouse walls, and she hurried on across the street to get away from the thought.

She found herself in front of a big department store, its beautifully arranged windows as colorful and streamlined as a modern painting. She hesitated for a moment, looking at the new tweed coats. Her own winter coat was warm enough but it didn't have any more style than a flour sack. "For Glowing Autumn Days," she read the placard under a lovely green model, and the next moment whisked by it through the revolving doors.

She passed the scented air of the perfume counter and the tempting glitter of the costume jewelry and made straight for the elevators. In a few moments she was out on the Junior Miss floor with a bewildering display of suits and coats all around her.

"May I help you?" A saleswoman with two coats over her arm came up to her.

"Oh, I'm just looking. The green coat in the window downstairs, I just wanted to look at it."

"Right this way, miss." The saleswoman was efficient and impersonal. "You mean our new Troubadour Coat?"

"I guess so. Green with a flared skirt."

"It's a beautiful model," the saleswoman said. "I've got it right here in a 14."

In another moment Bitsy had slipped into the cool, smooth-feeling lining and stood staring at herself in the mirror. Or was it herself? The girl in the trim green coat looked so much older, more assured. Her cheeks were pink from walking and her wavy brown hair was blown back becomingly. Even the freckles looked different against that flattering bluish green.

"You look lovely," the saleswoman said. "It's just your type."

"It's beautiful," Bitsy breathed, and as she looked at herself, flushed and starry-eyed, she knew she did look lovely.

"We have a very smart little felt hat that goes with it," the saleswoman said, but Bitsy wasn't listening.

Two voices were arguing inside of her. It'd just make you out in Ohio, one voice said. Mother said anything, but she meant in the five-and-ten, the other voice said.

"It's a good foundation for any wardrobe," the saleswoman went on. "And it's the best buy in our fall sale. Real imported Harris tweed and only forty-seven fifty. It'll be perfect for college."

"I'll take it," Bitsy said suddenly. If the saleswoman who must see college girls every day thought she looked that old she'd just have to have it. It'll start you off on the right foot in Bricklow, the first voice said. Your allowance won't pay for it, came the second. And now a third voice, gloomy and depressing, crowded out the others. Mother didn't say a word about allowances on the first of September. Maybe there won't be any allowances from now on. I've got to have a certain amount of clothes, Bitsy settled all the voices. And this is a good investment.

"Charge or pay?" The saleswoman had already taken out book and pencil.

"Charge," Bitsy said faintly. "To Mrs. Kenneth Close, 54 East 87th Street, only the address has changed. It's going to be Bricklow, Ohio."

"It's ideal for the country." The saleswoman had already helped Bitsy to take it off, and now her everyday self in the cotton print she had had for two summers stared back at her.

"I'll take it right with me," Bitsy said, and a few moments later she left the store feeling like a cross between a thief, a spendthrift, and a woman of the world.

If she'd only told Mother about it right away and gotten that over with, it would have been so much better. But when she came home, Mother was busy sorting over some sketches to see which ones to keep and which ones to burn.

"Hello, darling," she said without even looking at the

big box in Bitsy's arm. "What do you think of this drawing I did of Dad last winter?"

"It's good," Bitsy said, wondering when the moment
would come.

"Fair." Mrs. Close put it on the "save" pile with a
little sigh. "What an awful lot of junk one does accumu-
late."

So there was the coat still lying in the big gray box
right beside her trunk where she could see it from her
bed. She had opened it just as Mother passed down the
hall, but Mother was busy then finding something for
Stanty and hadn't noticed.

It wasn't until they were all ready to go the following
morning that it finally came out. The other boxes and
bags were already out in the rugless hall and Stanty had
rung for the elevator. "All ready?" Mrs. Close asked, and
then she stared as Bitsy came down the hall with the big
box. "What's that, darling? Something I forgot?"

"It's—it's my coat," Bitsy said, and now as she looked
at her mother she suddenly loathed herself. "I bought
it yesterday at Bonwit's fall sale. I'll take it back if you say
so. Honestly."

For a moment Mrs. Close stood perfectly still. "You
bought it yesterday at a fall sale?" she said. "How?"

"Charged it," Bitsy said, and now she wanted to cry
and to throw herself around Mum's soft neck the way
she had when she was five and had eaten all the cookies
Agnes had made for a dinner party.

But Mother didn't look as though she were waiting for
Bitsy to say she was sorry. She just stared at the box and

held her pocketbook tight, as though she might lose it. "How much did it cost?" she said finally.

"Forty-seven fifty," Bitsy said, and it sounded like forty-seven million. "I—I've got to take it back."

"You can't," Mrs. Close said slowly. "They don't take back things bought at sales."

"Hi, J-Joe's here!" Stanty with Ginger on a leash pounced into the room. "Let's go!"

"Right away, dear." Mrs. Close's eyes were still on the box. "You take the small bundles and ask Joe to help with the big ones."

Stanty and the dog rushed out and Mrs. Close turned to look at Bitsy. "I know you didn't mean to cheat or do anything terrible," she said, "but this just can't happen again. We're broke, darling. We just haven't got the money we've always had before."

"My—my allowances," Bitsy said, and now she was very near tears.

For the first time her mother took a step toward her. "It's a lot my fault," she said. "I should have told you day before yesterday that we couldn't afford any more allowances. Dad and I talked it over, and I meant to tell you and just plain forgot."

"I shouldn't have done it." Bitsy looked away from her mother. "I ought to have guessed about the allowance. I did kind of."

Just then Joe, the elevator man, followed by Stanty, came back to the door. "Anything else, ma'am?" Joe asked, but Mrs. Close shook her head.

"I guess we've got everything," she said, and turned to

look back into the empty living room. "If you'd take that load down and come back for us."

Stanty and Joe disappeared, and Mrs. Close turned quickly to Bitsy. "Darling," she said, "we'll have to manage somehow this time. If I can only get some illustrating right away, it'll be wonderful. But you must understand that we're poor. Really poor compared to what we have been. From now on we don't charge anything. Not even an egg."

"I do understand," Bitsy began, "and, Mum, I'm so terribly sorry——"

"It's all right, dear." Mrs. Close had already left the hall. "If I can only get work fast enough——"

For a moment Bitsy could only stare dumbly after her. Mother had hardly mentioned the wrongness of it, the fact that Bitsy had done a thing that she herself knew was unfair. She had been too worried about the money to think of anything else! So this wasn't like the Depression then, way back the year before Stanty was born. The family had talked awfully poor then, but they had only moved into a smaller apartment and let one of the maids go. Down in the street Stanty honked the horn impatiently, and from the outside hall Bitsy could hear her mother's clear voice calling, "Come on, Bits, Joe's here with the elevator."

Bitsy picked up the coat as though it were hot and collected her hat and purse. So she was going to be really poor, worse off even than Em Renfrew down at Sea Cliff. She walked numbly into the hall, and the months in Ohio yawned ahead of her like an ashen waste.

~~~~~~

IV

Across New Fields

AFTERWARDS whenever Bitsy thought about that drive out to Ohio, the rain and the chilled stiffness of her neck stood out more than anything else. It started to drizzle as they came out of the Holland Tunnel and the dark clouds in the west promised more rain.

Picnicking was out of the question, so they stopped at a roadside stand for lunch. When they got into the car again, Bitsy rearranged the box with her new coat in it between the portable sewing machine and her mother's suitcase. Joe, the elevator man, had packed the car so neatly only a few hours ago, but it was already a mess. Ginger's hairs clung to the thick plush of the back seat and there were scraps and leaves of Stanty's comic books everywhere. "It's my turn to drive," Mrs. Close said after Stanty and the dog had settled down in back among the bundles. "You've driven over a hundred miles."

Bitsy settled back to rest but found that she still watched the road. She looked back and saw that Stanty was asleep, his arm around Ginger's neck. A couple of years ago she wouldn't have been on the alert, but now that she had learned to drive, her eyes were on the road whether she was driving or not.

They stopped in the middle of the afternoon for a cup of tea and to stretch their cramped legs, and then they kept on until they were shooting across the Pennsylvania Turnpike. Bitsy was driving now while Mrs. Close looked anxiously ahead through the steady sheets of rain. "It won't be easy to find a place for the night," Mrs. Close said. "We'd better turn off at the next gateway."

They turned off at Breezewood and stopped at the first tourist camp off the main road. For a moment after they had driven in, Bitsy thought the place was deserted. There were no lights, and the drenching rain made it hard to see more than a few feet ahead. "What shall I do?" she began, when Stanty giggled.

"L-look! B-Billy Wh-Whiskers!"

Bitsy turned as she heard her mother asking into the darkness if they could stay there for the night. Then she saw the long, wagging beard and finally the serious, stolid face above it. The man stood in hip boots and old clothes while the rain dripped from the brim of his black Mennonite hat. "Could we have rooms for the night?" Mrs. Close tried again.

"Wh-why does he w-wear those wh-whiskers?" Stanty's whisper was bugle clear. "H-he looks like a g-goat!"

"Hush!" Bitsy said, and the next minute, as she saw her mother's carefully controlled expression, she knew she was going to laugh.

"Th-there're three of us." Even Mrs. Close's voice faltered as she motioned to Stanty to be quiet.

"Thank you, ma'am, thank you." The man looked at them through thick glasses as though they had come from Mars.

"Could——" Mrs. Close began again, and now Bitsy shook with laughter.

"Bitsy, stop it!" she said, and Bitsy was worse off than ever. She was tired, she was cold, and giggling so that the tears rolled down her cheeks.

Mother began to take the suitcases out of the car as Ginger growled. "D-don't growl," Stanty scolded him loudly. "It's only wh-whiskers. They w-won't hurt!"

Bitsy was off again on an aching wave of laughter that left her leaning helplessly against the driving wheel, choking and coughing.

Somehow they got the bags out and followed the man into a clean, bare little cabin with a flat-looking double bed in each small room. "Would you want hot water?" the man asked them while Stanty stared owl-eyed up at the Biblical texts that were tacked on the wall.

"Yes, please." Mrs. Close didn't trust herself to say more.

"Pint or quart?" The beard waved at them.

"Quart," Mrs. Close said, and then as the door closed she sank down beside Bitsy on the big bed and laughed until the tears came.

They got their quart of water, but a little later, when Bitsy went up to the main house to see about supper, the place was dark and empty-looking and no one answered her knock. "We've got our p-picnic," Stanty said. "The one we didn't eat."

That meal was fun. They ate it using Stanty's small suitcase on their knees as a table. Just as they were finishing up the electric light quite suddenly and firmly went out. This time Mrs. Close went up to the main house, but the proprietor seemed to have left for good. She came back with the flashlight from the car. "He forgot about 'Let thy light so shine,' " she said, pointing to the other Biblical texts, and that was enough to start them all laughing again.

They cleared up by the light of the flashlight and Stanty gave the scraps to Ginger. There was nothing for it but to go to bed, and Bitsy was so tired from driving through the rain that she was entirely ready. She undressed and went in to say good night to Stanty. He was already asleep, looking very small and cherubic in the big bed, with one small brown hand still reaching out toward Ginger.

"It's been a surprisingly good day." Mrs. Close's voice came softly through the darkness when they were finally in the other double bed. "You've both been dears."

"It's been fun." Bitsy rolled over the hump in the mattress to try to find a comfortable place. "That crazy man——" She giggled again and then lay still, listening to the sound of Stanty's breathing in the next room and the low rumble of cars on the roadway far behind them. It wasn't until she was nearly asleep that she thought about her new green coat again. "Mum," she said, but there wasn't any sound from the dark head on the other side of the pillow. Bitsy switched on her flashlight and looked down at her mother.

Mrs. Close lay on her back with her upturned face white and somehow unprotected looking as she slept. She must have been dead tired, Bitsy thought, and again twinges of conscience caught at her as she remembered the coat. From now on I'll just have to have more sense. She rolled over again, gently tugging at the skimpy blanket. When you were off with just Mother and Stanty this way, getting cold together, and tired, and then sometimes laughing so that you cried, such different things seemed important from the ones that mattered so at Rye or Sea Cliff. Mother didn't want to leave New York either, Bitsy realized slowly. I—wonder—what Ohio's going to be like. The next minute she was fast asleep.

The following day was uneventful except for the rain. It continued to pour down so steadily that Stanty asked whether somebody had upset the ocean. It wasn't until they were over the Ohio border that the sky finally lightened, and then as they drove into Columbus the rain really stopped.

They had supper in the capital and then went on again through a wide, fertile countryside that seemed to be tied together with ragged wire fences. Stanty had been asleep for most of the afternoon but he was wide awake now looking out of the window as they rolled along. "Cows, sheep, pigs, chickens, and a big brown horse all in one f-f-field," he chattered excitedly. "I've n-never seen 'em all t-together before."

Bitsy didn't say anything. Mrs. Close was driving the

car down an open road and she had a chance to look around her. The unpretentious clapboard houses were far from beautiful, but they looked comfortable and lived in. Even the wide, flat fields had a rich, opulent charm in the ruddy light. The sun was out for the first time—a golden ball setting in the west ahead of them. It made it hard for the driver, but it cast a lovely mellow light over the fields on either side of the road. The newly cut fields looked neat and garnered and even the dry, standing corn had a parchment sheen to it. Occasionally they passed brighter green fields where tall alfalfa still waited to be cut, and once to the south there was a rise of land where giant elms and buttonwoods stood out darkly against the lighter green.

"Maybe this was what brought the pioneers over the Alleghenies," Mrs. Close said, and Bitsy gave a little grunt of pleased assent. It was good country, open and friendly looking after the rain-swept mountains they had left behind.

By the time they got through the town of Meudon it was dark, and Bitsy took a last turn at the wheel. "You drive now," her mother said, "and then I'll be able to tell you where to turn off. It can't have changed much since the time I was out for Cousin Vin's funeral."

They came to a place where a "road under construction" sign partially blocked the way, but when Bitsy slowed down Mrs. Close motioned her on. "We have to go only a little way along this pike," she said. "I'm sure we'll be able to get through all right."

Bitsy stepped on the gas and they sped on over the

deserted road. They had gone about five miles when a row of red lights right across the road finally blocked them, and Bitsy came to a full stop. "We'll have to turn around," Mrs. Close said. "Better let me get out and see how much space you've got."

"Oh, it's easy," Bitsy said quickly. She was impatient to get there, and it was irritating that Mother wouldn't believe that she could turn in the dark.

There was open ground to the left where the new section of the road was to be laid, and Bitsy turned the car onto that. She began to cramp the wheels when she felt them spin in the slimy mud. "Wait!" Mrs. Close called, but Bitsy had already pressed down on the accelerator as hard as she could.

They skidded forward for a foot or two, and then came to a dead stop, their wheels whirling. Bitsy shifted gears frantically, but it was no use. "Stop!" her mother said again, and now she had the door of the car half open. "You'll just get us in deeper. Let me get out and look."

The racing of the motor shook the car as Mrs. Close jumped out. The next minute Bitsy heard a shout of pain and realized that Mother must have lost her balance and either slid or fallen beside the car.

"Mother, what happened?" Bitsy and Stanton called out at the same moment.

"It's all right. I slipped in the mud, that's all. My foot must have been asleep."

In another instant Bitsy was out of the car. She took a step forward and felt the mud, cold and clinging, surge up over her shoe tops. "Stay in the car," she shouted to Stanty. "And hold Ginge!"

She got around to the other side of the car and found her mother had pulled herself up by the car door. "I'm a fool," Mrs. Close panted. "I've ruined my clothes and given my ankle a rotten wrench."

"Are you sure you're all right?" Bitsy had the flashlight out by this time. "You haven't broken anything?"

"No-o." Mrs. Close eased herself backward into the car. "But I can't walk."

Bitsy lowered the flashlight so that it glowed on the glistening mud and on the spattered wheels of the car. They were in up to the hubcaps and there were no passing cars to help them out. She looked around at the black, forbidding fields on either side of the road and for the first time felt afraid. They might be miles from any help, and Mother was too badly hurt to walk a step.

"Wh-what are w-we g-going to d-do?" Stanty's voice demanded from the darkness.

"I'll have to telephone." Bitsy said the first thing that came into her mind. "You stay here with Mum."

"Good girl," Mrs. Close said cheerfully, but when Bitsy trained the light on her face it looked drawn with pain. "You go right along. Stanty and I'll be perfectly all right."

Bitsy moved carefully, afraid that the sucking mud would pull off her shoes. Fortunately she had on a pair of old saddle shoes that she had nearly outgrown, and she managed to get to the strip of cement still shod. She stamped off as much of the mud as she could, and walked down the narrow strip of road toward a small yellow light that promised some sort of household. She walked for only about ten minutes, but it seemed interminable. She strained her ears for the sound of another car, but all she heard was the distant mooing of a cow and the chorus of grasshoppers and katydids. Finally she came to the front yard of a small house. She walked past a large gray cat that eyed her disdainfully and knocked on the shabby door. She was almost ready to give up and turn away when a stooped old man opened the door. "Could I use your telephone?" Bitsy began. "Our car's stuck in the mud down the road and I want to reach a garage."

"There ain't one." The man looked at her with old, unblinking eyes. "Nur a garage neither. Not nearer n' Meudon."

"You mean you haven't got a telephone?" Bitsy looked at him dumbly. "There—there isn't one here?"

"That's right," the man said. "Nearest one would be over behind Willie French's. That's the house back down the road a piece, but Willie ain't to home. His neighbor's got one though, and you kin reach there by crossin' straight over Willie's 'falfa field."

Bitsy thanked him and hurried back to the car. "I've got to go on this way," she told her mother. "That other house didn't have a phone."

"That's all right," Mrs. Close said, and now Stanty shouted after her. "It's O.K.K. I'll take care of M-Mum."

He's cute, Bitsy thought with a sudden flood of warmth

toward her younger brother. Lots of little kids would have gotten panicked.

She passed a small abandoned-looking cabin and then a house which she decided must be Willie French's. She hesitated as she saw a light across the fields behind it. The light looked more than a "piece" away, it looked miles, and there might be barbed wire or swamps or anything to cut her off. For a moment Bitsy thought of going back to the car to get Ginge. The next moment she forced herself to squat down on the wet grass and crawl under the fence that separated the field from the road. She had gotten Mother and Stanty into this mess. It was up to her to get them out of it as quickly as she could.

~~~~~~

V

Dark Entrance

Bitsy walked as fast as she could without stumbling across the uneven field. Once to her left she saw a circle of light approach and then disappear again and knew it must be a car somewhere to the west of her. She felt lonelier than ever when it was gone and moved on with only the cold little stars for company. Even with the pale circle of light from her flashlight the darkness seemed a solid wall, and it was hard to judge the contours of the field. She half fell over an extra-long hummock of grass and went on again, a tingle of fright chasing up her spine. If she fell and hurt herself so that she couldn't get back to the car, Mother would be frantic.

She stopped once to make sure of her bearings and caught sight of a dark figure moving up behind her. For the first time real panic swept over her. There might be a tramp or a robber coming across the field after her! She began to run wildly, desperately. Her fear of falling, of getting caught in barbed wire was nothing compared to this new terror of human attack. She stumbled and slid over the wet grass and plunged on again, her heart drumming and her throat tight.

She was quite close now to the building where she had seen the light. Her flashlight played full on the white-washed walls before she realized that it was a big barn and not a house at all. "Oh, dear God, make there be someone inside," Bitsy prayed as she fumbled for the door. She found it next to the lighted window and pulled hard on the latch. The door creaked open, and she stepped over the high sill into the barn.

"Shut that door!" Bitsy heard the voice even before she saw the man and the boy working over the horse just ahead of her. She was right under the horse's yellow teeth, and she shrank back against the wall. It seemed to be all teeth and bones, like the skeleton of a dinosaur. She stared up, uncertain where to go, and then saw that the man held the horse's nose screwed by a leather thong and was forcing open its mouth while the boy reached up with an enormous pill. The boy got the pill down, the man let go the thong, and the horse's head dropped, shaking and slobbering. "Shut that door!" The boy's voice was sharp. "Too much cold air."

Bitsy did as she was told, and then moved a step nearer over the concrete floor. "I'm stuck," she panted. "Out in back on the new road. My mother's there, too, and my little brother, and she's hurt and I've got to get to a telephone."

The boy never even looked away from the horse, but the man turned and considered Bitsy with pale, vacant eyes. For one awful moment the thought tore through

Bitsy's mind that they were both stone deaf. "I'm stuck," she shouted, her voice echoing in the gloomy corners of the barn. "I've got to get to a telephone!"

"Where are you going?" The boy threw the words over his shoulder as he rubbed down the horse's sweating flanks.

"To Mrs. Vinton Crane's," Bitsy told him. "They live somewhere near here."

Just at that moment the horse foundered and would have fallen if it hadn't been for the wide belt that was swung underneath its belly. "Easy, Rossy, easy, pet." The boy's voice was soothing as he and the man strained together to hold up the horse's head.

"If you would just tell me where Mrs. Crane lives? Or where there's a telephone?"

The boy had completely dismissed her from his mind as he struggled to ease the sick horse. The man helped for a moment and then turned to look at Bitsy, his square face expressionless. "Crane's?" he said, his accent foreign and guttural. "You near."

"But where? Where is their house? Couldn't you or your son show me the way?"

The man stared at Bitsy with his hands on his hips. Slowly a new queer look came into his face. "My son?" he said, and then put back his big head and laughed. "My son show you way, eh? That good! You hear, Teem? You, my son, to show her way to Crane's!"

Bitsy cowered further against the wall. Was this big, boisterous foreigner really insane? He took a step toward her, and she would have screamed, but he pushed roughly past her and opened a door on the far side of the barn. "Crost yard," he said, and jerked his thumb into the darkness. "Dis Crane's."

Bitsy turned and fled out the back way. So this was Cousin Bertha's. She'd been that near and hadn't even known it. That man and his boy were undoubtedly Cousin Bertha's farm hands. She found herself in a muddy barnyard surrounded by a board fence. She looked around uncertainly, and through some straggling bushes caught the gleam of a lighted window. "It's got to be Cousin Bertha's," Bitsy told herself. "It's just got to."

She raced across the barnyard and arrived breathless at the front door. Before she could even knock it opened and a big woman in a cotton dress looked down at her. "I'm Elizabeth Close," Bitsy panted. "I'm looking for my cousin, Mrs. Crane. My mother's hurt and our car's stuck back on the highway."

"I'm your cousin Bertha." The big woman's deep voice was reassuring. "Come right in, child. You look half dead."

"But the car——" Bitsy was near tears now that she knew she was safe. "Mother's in it and Stanty. Mother's hurt her ankle."

"Is she badly hurt? Were you in a motor accident?"

"No. Only stuck in the mud, and when Mother got out she sprained her ankle. But I had trouble finding you and they've been there just ages."

Cousin Bertha moved quickly for such a large woman. "Margaret," she called to someone who was sitting in

the living room. "Take this poultice over to the barn.
Tim's been waiting for it."

She turned back to Bitsy and reached for a coat from
a hook by the stairs. "We'll get back there right away,"
she promised. "The boys have been drenching the horse
and Bruce is after the vet, but I'll manage with the
Lizzie."

She led the way back across the barnyard to a small
shed, and Bitsy saw a high, rickety-looking old model-T
truck in front of some hay. "But our car's really stuck,"
she protested. "Oughtn't we to call up a garage?"

"There isn't one nearer than Meudon," Cousin Bertha
said firmly. "And Bruce won't be back with the other
car for the best part of an hour."

Before Bitsy could say another word she had found a
long rope in a dim recess near the hay and had gotten
into the Ford with Bitsy beside her. It started with a
consumptive wheeze, and in another moment they were
rattling off down the road.

"I had a fearful time getting to you," Bitsy began.
"There was something behind me in the field, and when
I got to the barn——"

"Your mother should have known better than to come
this way," Cousin Bertha interrupted her. "It's a very
easy turn onto Pike's Lane."

"It was my fault we got stuck in the mud." Bitsy tried
again, but Cousin Bertha didn't seem to be listening.
She was driving the old car as fast as it would go, and the
windows shook so that Bitsy was afraid they might
splinter.

"Just where were you?" Cousin Bertha asked once. "How far down the new pike?"

"There was a house an old man said belonged to some-one called French," Bitsy told her, and a few minutes later Cousin Bertha had rattled up beside the Closes' car.

"What a mess!" Mrs. Close said when she and Cousin Bertha had kissed and she had introduced Stanty. "I was a perfect fool not to know where I was going."

Cousin Bertha said absolutely nothing to help her out but busied herself tying the rope around the bumper of the Closes' car. "Elizabeth, you can get in and cramp the wheel hard," she said. "That is, if you know how to drive."

"I've had a license for over a year," Bitsy protested, and Mrs. Close put in soothingly that she had driven half the way out. By this time Cousin Bertha had gingerly made her way back to her own car and fastened the rope firmly to her own bumper.

"Now when I start, you give your car all the power it's got and turn sharp to the left," Cousin Bertha com-manded.

"Can you manage?" Mother asked, but Bitsy only nodded her head. She'd have to manage. She'd been an ass to get into the mud in the first place, and she wasn't going to make a fool of herself in front of Cousin Bertha again if it was the last thing she did.

Cousin Bertha was in the truck by this time and had started her motor. "Ready?" she shouted, and the next moment the Ford rattled forward.

Bitsy shot the gear into first speed and stepped on the

accelerator. The next moment there was the roar of the engine and the sputter of wheels. The rope tautened, and for a moment Bitsy was sure it was going to break, and then the next instant her own car lurched forward. "Bertha managed," Mrs. Close said under her breath. "You might know it."

With one more pull they had the car safely back on the cement. Bitsy got out to help untie the rope, but Cousin Bertha was ahead of her. "You follow me," she said, jerking the rope free. "And mind you keep on the road."

"Yes, Cousin Bertha," Bitsy said meekly, and got back into the car.

By the time they got back to the farmhouse there were more lights on, and the girl whom Cousin Bertha had called Margaret stood by the front door to welcome them. She looked pale and rather tired in an unbecoming green dress, but she had fine, dark eyes and her handshake was friendly. "This is Bruce's wife," Cousin Bertha introduced her as they helped Mrs. Close into the house.

They had just settled her on the Victorian sofa when Ginger let out a terrific growl and the old toy fox terrier who lay in a basket in one corner of the room barked furiously. "D-do you th-think they're g-going to fight?" Stanty asked.

"Not unless we put them up to it," Cousin Bertha said shortly. "If we leave them alone they'll make friends fast enough."

She turned out to be right, and by the time she came back with hot water for Mrs. Close's ankle, the two dogs were sniffing at each other and hostilities were suspended.

Cousin Bertha had so completely taken charge of caring for Mother that Bitsy hung around useless for a moment and then went out to unload the car. Margaret came with her and took a cardboard hatbox and Bitsy's new coat while Bitsy struggled with her own heavy suitcase. "You're in the hall room," Margaret said, leading the way up the narrow linoleum-covered stairs. "And your mother and Stanty are in the big room over the library."

Bitsy put down her suitcase and looked about the room that was to be hers. There were a narrow iron bed, a bureau that had obviously been painted at home, and a heavy mahogany chair. These and a small painted table were the only pieces of furniture. "I think you'll like this room," Margaret said. "I used to stay in it sometimes before Bruce and I were married. It looks over the forty-four."

Bitsy was too tired to ask or care what the forty-four was, but she recognized the friendliness in Margaret's voice and smiled. "It looks neat," she said, and tried not to think of her own prettily papered room in the apartment in New York.

They went down to the car for another load. This time Bitsy hauled at an old suitcase of her mother's while Margaret went ahead of her with a duffel bag that belonged to Dad. "Margaret, put that down right away," Cousin Bertha said, and Mother, her voice softer and less commanding, suggested that they wait until tomorrow.

For a moment Bitsy stared at Margaret, bewildered. The duffel bag was filled with only Stanty's clothes and wasn't heavy at all. Was Margaret sick or had she hurt herself or something? "I'm having a baby," Margaret said quietly. "Early in March."

"Oh golly, I see," Bitsy said, and could have kicked herself because she could feel her own face getting red. "Let me take that duffel bag."

"Why didn't you get Steve?" Cousin Bertha asked as she came back into the hall.

"He's helping Tim with the horse," Margaret said, and the answer seemed to be satisfactory. Cousin Bertha didn't say another word but just put down her bowl of hot water and marched out to the car. She didn't say anything, but it seemed to Bitsy that the car looked messier and dirtier than ever.

"Ginger's sort of shedding," Bitsy apologized as she tugged at another suitcase. Cousin Bertha didn't answer but led the way back to the house with the biggest bag in one hand and all of Mrs. Close's painting equipment in the other.

They finished unloading, and then they helped Mrs. Close up the stairs. "You might know I'd pull something like this," she said once. "It's like the time we went after quail, Bert, with Vin over by the river."

For the first time since Bitsy had seen her Cousin Bertha really smiled. "I was just thinking of that," she said. "I've still got that sketch of Vin you did when your ankle was mending."

"I'll do a sketch of the boys this time," Mrs. Close

promised. "I don't know how I can wait until breakfast to see them both."

By this time they were in the big square bedroom that was to be Mrs. Close's. There was a double bed on one side and a small cot waited for Stanty on the other. "C-can Ginge stay here too?" Stanty wanted to know.

Cousin Bertha looked at him and for the second time that evening she really smiled. "He's as bad as Tim," she said. "Just mad over animals. Yes, you can keep him any place you want to as long as you'll clean up after him. We don't have a whole houseful of help the way you did in the city."

"They both know that," Mrs. Close said as Cousin Bertha turned to open the windows for the night.

"The sooner you get to sleep the better," she said. "Bitsy's in the hall room and I'm right where I've always been, over the kitchen. If you want anything, send Stanty. He looks as though he'd be good at finding people."

"Sh-she's O.K.K.!" Stanty said when the door had closed and Cousin Bertha's firm footsteps no longer resounded down the hall. "She likes Ginge."

"She likes boys and dogs and all sorts of country things," Mrs. Close said, and ran her hand through Stanty's stiff hair. "You and she will get along beautifully."

"She's awfully kind of firm," Bitsy said in a half whisper. "She scares me."

"I know!" Her mother's light little laugh made Bitsy feel comfortable and companioned for the first time all evening. "But her bark's a lot worse than her bite. She was mad about her husband Vinton Crane, and when he died ten years ago she went back to being the flat-footed, brusque person she was as a girl. He was the only person who ever reached her soft side."

They chatted on for a few minutes, and for the first time Bitsy really had a chance to talk about her trip across the dark field. Mrs. Close was interested in every detail as she always was, but Stanty was so tired that he was cross and had to be put to bed. Finally he was covered and comfortable, and after she had kissed her mother, Bitsy tiptoed out of the room and into her own.

It's all going to be awfully queer, she thought as she brushed her teeth in the old-fashioned bathroom that was used by the whole family. Even this room with the brown toilet seat and the sloping bathtub was unlike anything she had ever seen before. I wonder what Tim and Bruce will be like, she thought, and yawned at her own reflection in the mirror.

Once in bed she lay very still in the darkness of the unfamiliar little room. Far out in the distance she heard the low, muffled hooting of a night owl. She buried her face in the pillow and her eyes smarted with tears. I wish the war were over, she thought fiercely, and that Dad was home and I was going to Miss Fair's. I hate changes!

~~~~~~

VI

The New Order

THAT NIGHT Bitsy had queer, mixed-up dreams about vast, dark fields that roared and hissed like the ocean and then when you tried to swim through them turned into hay. At six o'clock, when the morning train East shrieked through the plains, she was wide awake. She lay still for a moment, listening to the lonely, wailing note of the train whistle. After it had disappeared, she heard the chirrup of the birds in a tree near her window and the scratching and clucking of some larger fowl on the ground. She got up to look out. It was still quite dark, but she could make out the white forms of chickens scurrying across the lawn toward the kitchen.

"Chick! Chick! Here, chick!" The commanding voice was certainly Cousin Bertha's, and Bitsy decided that she might as well get up.

The dining room was empty and so was the living room, and she made her way into the kitchen. Cousin Bertha was nowhere in sight, but a young man in blue jeans was eating a bowl of oatmeal at the kitchen table. "I'm Bruce," he said, getting up. "I'm glad to see you,"

"I'm glad to see you," Bitsy said, and as she smiled up into his thin, intelligent face she meant it. He looks kind of like Byron or the young Shelley, she thought. Sort of fine and poetic-looking.

Right now there was nothing particularly poetic about Bruce Crane. He pushed aside the book on airplane engines that he had had propped up in front of him and ate his oatmeal until the hired man whom Bitsy had seen the night before came in to ask about plans for the day.

"I'm going to cut the forty-four," Bruce said. "And you can rake it with the mule this afternoon. This morning you'd better stick around and help Tim with Rossy."

Steve stared rudely at Bitsy and then disappeared without speaking. Bitsy was still looking after him when Bruce turned to her, laughing. "You mustn't mind Steve," he said. "He's a pretty dumb Pole and he doesn't understand much English. There aren't any other Poles around here and I guess he gets kind of lonely living all by himself in his little shack. He lived in Connecticut before he came to us, but he couldn't stand working in a factory so he moved out here."

"I thought he was feeble-minded last night," Bitsy admitted. "He and I guess it was his son were working over a horse in the barn and I had to ask him three times where the house was."

As Bitsy finished there was a noise at the back and the boy whom she had seen last night put his head in. "Bruce, come on out right away!" he said. "And where's Mum? Rossy's worse."

"Hang it!" Bruce was on his feet before the younger boy had finished talking and together they started for the barn. "Get Mother, will you?" Bruce Crane called over his shoulder. "Tell her to come over to the barn right away."

For a moment Bitsy stood numb while a red, uncomfortable flush spread over her neck and cheeks. The small, wiry-looking farm boy whom she'd seen last night wasn't the hired man's son but her own seventeen-year-old third cousin Tim Crane. She turned slowly toward the door, wondering where she could find Cousin Bertha, when Stanty clattered down the stairs followed by Ginger. "G-Ginge's in a hurry to g-get out," he said, heading for the door.

"Where's Cousin Bertha?" Bitsy called. "Have you seen her?"

"Upstairs. In the room right over this one." The next minute the door slammed behind him so that the potted geraniums on the shelf over the sink rattled.

When Bitsy got upstairs, Cousin Bertha was sweeping out her own already spotless room. "Bruce wants you," Bitsy said. "Right away over at the barn. I think the horse is worse."

Cousin Bertha made a little exclamation of disgust and moved toward the stairs. As she started down she told Bitsy to bring up her mother's breakfast on a tray. She'd be back as soon as she could.

"Yes, Cousin Bertha," Bitsy said, and moved down the narrow hall toward her mother's room. The house was in two distinct parts and Mother's room and her own little cell were in the wing away from the kitchen. Bitsy opened the wrong door once and found herself in a closet where there seemed to be endless piles of old wrapping paper and used cord. They keep everything, Bitsy decided, thinking of the crowded kitchen and the living room with the packed desk and piles of old magazines. In another moment she had her bearings and opened the door to her mother's room.

"How's the ankle?" she asked, and Mrs. Close wrinkled her pretty nose.

"Fair," she said, "but awfully stiff and sore. Still, I'm grateful it wasn't my wrist."

Bitsy looked at the bruised and swollen ankle and then remembered Cousin Bertha's orders about breakfast. "You stay right here," she said as Mrs. Close tried to pull herself up. "Cousin Bertha said I was to bring up breakfast and that you were to stay still until she saw your ankle."

"Bertha'll tell us all right," Mrs. Close grinned. "But some coffee would be wonderful."

Bitsy hurried back to the kitchen, feeling businesslike and efficient, but when she got there the feeling gave way to helplessness. The kitchen was so big and there were so many cupboards and closets. She looked around in the scullery and finally found a tin tray hanging above a sack of potatoes. There were shelves and shelves of Mason jars filled with fruit and vegetables, but she had no idea where the table linen was kept.

Finally she tore off a strip of paper toweling from the roll by the door and covered the tray with that. She found cups and saucers in one of the big cupboards and was just looking around for spoons when Bruce came back from the barn. "Put you to work already, have they?" Bruce said as he helped himself to more oatmeal.

Bitsy nodded, more sure than ever that she was going to like Bruce Crane. He showed her where the spoons were kept and filled a dish with oatmeal to put on the tray. "You'd better take the last of this coffee," he said, pouring out a cup from the pot on the stove, "and then maybe you wouldn't mind making some more. Mother always saves hers until she's through with the dishes and Margaret hasn't come down yet."

As the door shut after Bruce, the lost, helpless feeling swept over Bitsy again. Margaret was asleep, Mother couldn't leave her room, and the rest of the family were all fussing over a sick horse. Here she was all alone, without the faintest idea how to make good coffee on a coal stove in an old-fashioned enameled coffeepot. To make matters worse, Cousin Bert didn't look a bit as though she would appreciate having her precious coffee ration wasted by amateur cooks.

Bitsy picked up the tray and carried it to her mother's room. "What a woman!" Mrs. Close said as she sipped the hot coffee. "How'd you manage?"

"Bruce helped me," Bitsy told her. "He's nice."

"Good. I hope you like Tim too. He's only a few months older than you are."

"I thought he was the hire——" Bitsy began, and then stopped short. Bruce knew already that she'd thought Tim was the Polish laborer's son and so did Steve and

Tim, unless he had been too occupied with the horse. There was no point in having Mother and especially Cousin Bertha know about it if they didn't have to. "Stanty's going to love it here," she said quickly as she caught a glimpse of him through the window. "He and Ginge are running all over the place."

"Yes, he'll have fun," Mrs. Close said as she lay back again among the pillows. "And I think you will, too, darling. Cousin Bertha'll leave you alone, you know, and in a couple of weeks school will be starting."

Bitsy took the tray downstairs, wondering what she ought to do about the coffee, but fortunately Cousin Bertha was already back in front of the stove. "You can go now," she said bluntly. "I see Stanty's been out and around already."

"He hasn't had any breakfast," Bitsy began, wondering whether she ought to bring him in or not.

"He'll come in fast enough when he's hungry," Cousin Bertha said. "Do him a world of good not to have a nursemaid trailing him the way your mother tells me he did in New York."

Bitsy went outside feeling snubbed. It was still early, but the brightness of the sun and the limp look of the trees promised a scorching day. She crossed the uneven little lawn to the barnyard. It had a queer, familiar, yet unfamiliar look now that she was seeing it in daylight for the first time. The great white barn with the iron roof was even bigger than she had thought and there were several small sheds and outhouses around it that she hadn't noticed last night.

She walked through a small apple orchard toward the field that she had crossed on her way to the farm. The space that had stretched out like a black, sinister sea looked tame and surprisingly small in the revealing sunlight. In the middle of the field a black-and-white cow peacefully chewed her cud, and Bitsy realized, chagrined, that this was the dark, menacing figure that had frightened her so as she made for the barn. She grinned to herself, grateful that she hadn't mentioned it to a soul.

She turned back to look at the Cranes' farmhouse behind its frame of sycamores and black walnuts. The way it was situated among the trees reminded her of Connecticut except that the house itself was taller and high-ceilinged and set so far back from the road.

The main part of the house was of brick with a white clapboard addition tacked onto the kitchen end. The lines were not unpleasing, but for years nothing had been done to beautify the outside. At one end, beyond an overgrown truck garden, a patch of spindly saplings shut off the view; at the other end the barnyard came up almost to the kitchen door. It was not exactly untidy, Bitsy realized, but with the gaunt farm tools and the shabby outbuildings it looked somehow like a middle-aged woman who no longer has time to think about her looks.

Bitsy walked past the house to where a green alfalfa field rolled up toward a wide stretch of yellow corn. She saw Bruce running the mowing machine, a light, newly cut swathe in his wake. He looked up from the tractor seat and waved as she rounded the corner, and Bitsy waved back, feeling suddenly befriended. It wasn't until she had started to move on again that she saw that Margaret had come out the back way and that Bruce was waving to her.

"It's a lovely morning, isn't it?" Margaret said. "More like June than September. I hope the rains hold off till they have the old fifty in."

It dawned on Bitsy that Margaret was talking about the different fields on the farm. The forty-four was the field Bruce was cutting now, and perhaps the fifty was the field she had crossed last night. She turned to ask, but Margaret had started up the old model-T Ford and conversation was impossible. Margaret got the car running and then turned down the window to shout to Bitsy. "I'm going down to the library," she said. "I work down there five days a week, but if you want anything just ask Bruce."

Bitsy nodded and waved. No matter what the rest of the people on the farm were like, Bruce and Margaret were definitely nice. She walked back to the barn and found that Tim and Steve were still working over the horse. She felt shy about seeing them when they had tricked her about Tim being Steve's son, but this morning they took no notice of her whatever. She tried not to notice the mixed smell of manure and horse physic and to ask intelligent questions about Rossy. "Is he much worse?" she asked, and now Tim snapped out at her over his shoulder.

"What does it look like? And besides she's a mare. Can't you use your eyes?"

The mare did look terrific; even Bitsy could see that. Her eyes were glazed and sunken and her breath came in and out with a coughing rattle. Tim and Steve worked on silently, the one handing up a sponge as the other reached for it. Bitsy stood the smell as long as she could and then hurried out into the soft, balmy air.

She found Stanty under the apple tree throwing sticks for Ginger. "This place is n-nifty," he told her as he hunted for another stick. "They've got p-pigs and sh-sheep and n-neverything."

"Want to come and see 'em?" Bitsy suggested, but Stanty shook his head.

"I and Ginge are busy. I'm t-training him."

Bitsy started off for a walk, feeling cross and at loose ends. The farm might be all right if you were Stanty's age and content with playing with a dog. But if you were seventeen and grown-up, what was there to do? She kicked a stone aimlessly until it hurt her toes. She might have to stay at the farm for months, even years. The time stretched out endless and hopeless in front of her.

It wasn't until she was off the farm and in a new stretch of country networked by dirt lanes that she was sufficiently aroused out of her gloom to really look around. On one side of her a little cart road led off in the direction of a soft, billowing hill topped by a buttonwood tree. Bitsy started up the rise with a slight stirring of interest. There wasn't anything else to do. She might just as well see what was on the other side of the hill.

The soft, undulating distances of the landscape were

deceptive and Bitsy had to walk much further than she expected. She tore a hole in her dress and scraped her leg getting over a barbed-wire fence, but it was satisfactory to finally reach the brow of the hill that had seemed so far away. On the other side more broad rich acres of grass and corn checkerboarded out toward the horizon. Here and there the pattern of the fields was broken by a group of farm buildings or a herd of white-faced cattle settled around big buttonwood trees. It was peaceful and prosperous, but also uncomfortably hot.

By the time Bitsy started back the sun was straight overhead and she moved more slowly. It would be dull going back the same way so she chose a tractor-scarred lane to the left that led her into unfamiliar country. She had walked on for nearly an hour before she realized that she was quite lost. The cornfields and alfalfa fields seemed to go on forever, but there was no sign of the Cranes' house or the sycamore and walnut trees that surrounded it. She came to an ugly yellow clapboard farmhouse that stuck high up out of a dusty farmyard and saw a boy of about fifteen pumping up a bicycle tire by the kitchen gate. "Could you tell me the way to the Cranes'?" she asked, and the boy turned and considered her before he answered.

"You're Tim Crane's cousin?" he asked finally.

Bitsy nodded. "How'd you know?"

"Tim's in the Four H," he said, as though that were an answer. "He said he had a humdinger cousin coming on from New York. You've walked quite a piece, haven't you?"

Bitsy began to think so herself as she made the last half-mile toward the Cranes'. She passed a newly cut field and then there was a wooded gully with a thin little stream at the bottom of it between herself and the apple orchard. The thickly growing saplings and underbrush had not been cleared, and for the first time all morning she couldn't see far ahead of her. She jumped when something rustled at her feet, and then saw that it was a very small black pig rooting around in the ironweed and goldenrod. She chuckled out loud, but the sound died in her throat as she saw Tim just ahead of her. His back was toward her but the thin, blue-jeaned figure was unmistakable. Something about his shoulders, the way he was standing, kept her from calling out. He half turned and she caught a glimpse of his white, tired face. The tears rolled down his cheeks, and he hit out aimlessly at the tree he was leaning against.

Bitsy moved forward impetuously. The mare had died, that was clear, and Tim felt terrible. "Oh, Tim," she began. "I'm so sorry it happened."

Tim jumped with surprise and then snapped crossly: "Do you have to scare a chap to death? For Pete's sake leave me alone."

Bitsy hurried on up to the house, feeling crushed, and wondering if she had made another mistake. But at lunch time, half an hour later, there was no place set for Tim, and Cousin Bertha said that he felt too badly about the horse to eat. "Was it a good horse?" Mrs. Close asked. "Did he use it for riding?"

"She was a farm mare," Cousin Bertha said, "Came of

a good blood strain, but she had something wrong with her off hind leg so that Tim got her cheap. He always hoped to breed her."

"Wh-what will he do with her n-now?" Stanty asked, his eyes round with curiosity. "Wh-what w-will he do with the b-body?"

His mother would have made up some kind, evasive story for him but Cousin Bertha was painfully direct. "Sell her for fertilizer," she said. "There's a man in Misqua who pays four dollars for dead horses."

Except for the carting off of the dead horse, which Stanty insisted upon seeing, the afternoon was uneventful. Before the fertilizer man's truck turned in at the driveway, Bitsy started out for another long walk, and then, when she came back, helped Mother fix up one side of her big double room as a studio. It wasn't until just before supper that Bitsy went back into her own little room for the first time all day. Her bed, still rumpled and unmade, the way she had left it in the morning, dominated the room. She realized, guiltily, that she had been supposed to make it herself and pulled it together hurriedly, hoping that Cousin Bertha hadn't seen it.

Bitsy wasn't used to making beds, and the sheets and blankets went every which way. Even when she had pulled it all apart and tucked it in again nothing came out straight and the bedspread over the top looked lumpy and untidy.

She left it feeling cross and inadequate and turned to the mirror. The first glance showed her that the day in the sun had given her a whole new crop of freckles and that was the last straw. She jerked off her sticky clothes and pulled a faded cotton print out of the narrow closet. She had thought of putting on the pale, shell-pink silk that she had worn in the evenings at Rye, but it didn't seem worth it. The blue cotton had a round white turnover collar that Minty had called babyish, but it was the most comfortable thing Bitsy owned and she pulled it on grimly. She brushed back her fluffy hair over her ears and banged down the brush. The girls at school had always laughed at her when she had worn her hair like that, but it was cool and clean feeling and right now she wasn't trying to please anybody but herself.

She went downstairs and found Tim reading a Farm Bureau pamphlet. His hair was neatly slicked down for supper but his face was suspiciously blotchy and he looked incredibly young and small to be seventeen. For a moment Bitsy was uncertain whether to speak to him or not. Just then he looked up from his pamphlet. "Boy," he said. "You look nifty."

Bitsy thought perhaps he was kidding her the way Stanty always did when she was dressed for a party, but when she looked over at him, the expression of admiration on his ruddy face was absolutely genuine. It was all too confusing. When she had tried to be nice to Tim about his old horse, he had almost bitten her. Now, when she had gone out of her way just to dress for herself, he acted as though she were a glamour girl. Bitsy started to say something, but just at that moment Cousin Bertha came into the room and Tim turned to her, laughing. "Say, Mom," he said, "Bitsy thought I was Steve's son. What do you think about that?"

Suddenly Bitsy lost her temper at Tim. She no longer cared that he was a boy, a person who might be useful at parties, someone to write the girls at school about. It didn't even matter that Cousin Bertha would undoubtedly take his side. "I think you were both mean about it," she said hotly. "I came in on you in the dark and then Steve just laughed and said you were his son. It's mostly your fault."

She would have said more but now the words choked and she stood waiting for Cousin Bertha or Tim to flare back at her. Tim only looked surprised, but Cousin Bertha actually smiled. "That's right, Bitsy, you just stand up to him," she said, and straightened out the old copies of *Time* and *Life* as she spoke. "That Steve puts him up to too many fool tricks anyhow."

~~~~~~

VII

Poor Old Ginger

THE TROUBLE with September was that you were tired of summer and yet fall didn't really begin. At the end of Bitsy's first week on the farm it was still hot and she felt more in-betweenish and unsettled than ever. Stanty had started in at the grade school that was in the little village of Bricklow beyond the farm, but the opening of the high school in Meudon had been put off for another week because of repairs. For the first time since she was in second grade Bitsy found herself wishing that school would open. It wasn't that she looked forward to studying, but her experiences at Rye and Sea Cliff had left her feeling unsure of herself and she wanted to take the plunge with the new high-school crowd and get it over with.

Life on the farm was less concerned with outside people than anything Bitsy had ever experienced. Once a neighbor had come over to collect some scrap and another time the boy she had met on her walk came over, stared at her curiously, and then went off with Tim to look at the pigs. There had been some talk about a boy called Tracy Larson and his sister, but they hadn't turned up. Tim obviously thought that Tracy was a wonder, and Bitsy had a mental picture of a bronzed, stalwart young farmer whom even Mabs or Minty would recognize as a he-man. If she landed him for a beau it might be something, but right now there was nothing to do on the farm that she couldn't have done at twelve.

Sometimes it felt safe and sort of reassuring to be expected just to do kid things again, but most of the time Bitsy felt as though she had heard the roar and the heave of breakers and then found herself swimming in a backwater. The worst part of it was that everybody else on the farm was so completely occupied. Even Mother was busier than Bitsy had ever remembered seeing her. She'd always painted, of course, but it had usually been in the morning when Bitsy and Stanty were off at school or busy doing something else. Now, even before her ankle was properly healed, she was up and about working on the preliminary sketches for a children's book. In the evenings, when the rest of the family sat around the living room table playing card games or listening to the radio, she worked on alone in Great-Great-Uncle Bert's library.

The library was in the old brick wing furthest away from the kitchen and was the least-used room in the house. Right now, at half-past eleven in the morning, it was absolutely quiet except for the twittering of the birds outside and the gobble, gobble of the turkeys as they stalked past the window. Bitsy, who was perched up on the wide window shelf, looked after the turkeys and wondered vaguely what Tim was doing. She thought of going out to find him but decided that he'd either be off in the fields with Bruce or working over some of the animals. It was amazing how much Tim could find to do with the beef cattle and the sheep and the pigs. Sometimes in the evenings, long after they had been fed and he had had his own supper, Tim would wander out to look at the cattle and Bitsy would find him there an hour later giving them an extra brushing.

"He's a born farmer like his grandfather," Cousin Bert said once, and Bitsy could see that she was right. Bitsy enjoyed the animals herself, though at first it had been hard to realize that they were a bread-and-butter necessity and not just pets like Ginger. Once Bruce had let her run the old tractor. After she had gotten on to it, it had seemed almost as easy as running a car, and she stepped down off the high seat feeling hot and exhilarated. It was only the constant talk of crops and seeds and which field ought to be set in what that she found boring. At first she had put it down as dumb and provincial, but gradually it had dawned on her that none of the Cranes was in the least slow-witted. There was the evening they had played the current-events quiz, for instance, when, except for Stanty, Bitsy had gotten the lowest score. "I should think your fine New York school would have given you current events," Cousin Bertha said, and Bitsy felt her hackles rise as she always did at criticism of her old life.

"They did have good lectures and everything," Bitsy began, and then unexpectedly Margaret came to the rescue.

"It's a lot a matter of what you've just been reading," she said. "And Bitsy's been busy moving out and all." The next moment she asked Cousin Bertha something about the pickle they had had at supper and they launched into a talk about canning that seemed to occupy the women as much as crops occupied the men.

Margaret was almost the most puzzling person on the farm. She wasn't even middle-aged, like Mother or Cousin Bert. She was just twenty, only a few years older than Bitsy herself, and yet there was a quietness, a sort of resignation about her that Bitsy was sure she herself wouldn't feel when she was fifty. She went faithfully to her work at the library, but when Bitsy had asked her about it she had answered vaguely and then changed the subject to ask about Bitsy's old school. It was only when, very rarely, she talked about Bruce that her sallow, rather plain face grew really animated.

One evening Margaret and Bitsy were in the apple orchard when a big plane suddenly swooped by overhead, shattering the quiet. Stanty rushed out to identify the plane. "I b-bet it's a P-P-40," he said excitedly, but Margaret shook her head.

"It's a trainer," she said. "See the way its wings tip forward?"

Stanty had scurried around to the front of the house to get a better look, and Margaret had gone back to the apple tree. "That's the kind of plane Bruce'll start out with if he ever gets in," she said. "He was talking about it last night."

"Is Bruce going into the Air Force?" Bitsy was so surprised that the question blurted out like one of Stanty's. On their very first evening at the farm Cousin Bertha had said flatly that Bruce was needed on the farm and that with the baby coming there was no chance of his being drafted. Since then the subject had never come up, but the way she spoke about running the farm seemed to include Bruce in the plans for years to come.

"He's trying hard," Margaret said. "He was turned down once on account of his health, but he'll have another chance later on. He's got to get in."

"And you want him to?"

For a moment Margaret didn't say anything at all, but when she spoke, her voice was as leisurely as ever. "He's just got to, that's all. It's his life, and living near one of the biggest airfields in the world makes it that much harder. Why, even when we were in the first grade, Bruce was making paper airplanes when the rest of us were playing Indians."

"Does his mother know?" Bitsy was really curious. Cousin Bertha had been so dogmatic about Bruce's staying home and she didn't look like a person who would fool herself about anything.

"I don't honestly think she does. She never comes near our room or Bruce's study behind the barn. It's part of her code of not interfering, and so she never sees the plans and models he's always making."

"But she must know if he's been crazy about engines ever since he was a little boy."

"Maybe." Margaret was doubtful. "But you see Mr. Crane was killed piloting a plane, and I think the only

thing she's never been willing to face was that one of
the boys would have the same interests. Mr. Crane never
really liked farming any more than Bruce does, but Mrs.
Crane can't dream of any other life and she's made herself believe that Bruce is happy."

"Has he always hated it?"

"Well, not hated it exactly, but he feels that he was
meant to do something else. Even Steve understands
that. I guess it's why he likes Tim so much better. Steve
hates machinery."

"He's a queer duck," Bitsy said. "The way he looks at
you without saying anything gives me the creeps."

"You mustn't mind Steve," Margaret said kindly. "He's
as much a part of this farm as the silo. He's queer and a
little feeble-minded, but he's devoted to the family. You
see when Mr. Crane was killed, he was stunting over this
house when his engine failed. Steve was the only one
who saw him and he dragged him out of the burning
plane. He drives Mrs. Crane wild sometimes, but she
wouldn't fire him no matter what he did."

"Where does he live?" Bitsy asked. "He doesn't eat or
sleep in the house."

"In what used to be one of the slave cabins," Margaret
said. "That little bit of a building at the edge of the main
road. He cooks for himself and he never goes out except
Saturday night; when he usually drinks up his wages
for the week."

Bitsy knew the cabin. It was the dark, deserted little
place that she had passed the night she had come to the
farm. She felt glad now that Steve had been up at the

barn with Tim and the sick horse. To have come upon that white, vacant face in the dark would have been really frightening.

Margaret had gone back to picking up the tart little King David apples that Cousin Bert had asked for, but Bitsy was too interested to think of picking. Margaret's words had made her feel as though her plain, workaday cousins and the Pole were people in a play. "Tell me about Tim," she demanded. "What does he want to do?"

Margaret laughed. "Just what you'd think. Farm and raise the best sheep and hogs in Fayne County. Tim's like his mother: he's a very square peg in a square hole."

Bitsy could have gone on asking questions by the hour, but now Margaret had her basket full of apples and started for the kitchen door. She hoped that another chance to ask questions would come up soon, but it never materialized. It wasn't that Margaret avoided her, or seemed to feel that she had said anything that she shouldn't, it was just that work and meals and play were so organized in the Crane house that you seldom got a chance for private conversation with anybody.

But at that Bitsy could see that Margaret was right about Bruce. He did his work on the farm, but the drive and enthusiasm came from Tim and the Pole. It was only once, when Bitsy came upon Bruce tinkering with the tractor motor, that he had been really engrossed. "Good morning," Bitsy said, but the first time he didn't even hear her. When he finally did look up, his face was as rapt and far away as a sleepwalker's.

"What's wrong with the engine?" she asked, and

Bruce had tried to show her just why the spark missed fire. She had listened politely and tried to ask the right questions, but Bruce had suddenly looked down at her and said, "You don't understand a word I'm saying, do you?"

"I guess I'm sort of dumb," Bitsy admitted. "I don't understand much about motors."

"Well, nobody does on this farm," Bruce said, and went back to his tinkering. "Nobody, that is, except Margaret."

Margaret was a good listener, Bitsy could see that, but it wasn't until she visited his study one night that she saw what he meant about her understanding. It was a fixed rule, flatly announced by Cousin Bertha at their first family supper, that Bruce's study was his and Margaret's sitting room and that the rest of the family didn't go there without invitations. Bitsy had been very curious until the evening after the quiz game, when Margaret had asked her over. The old brick shed was snug enough, with bright window curtains and a small iron stove, but somehow it was a letdown. It wasn't just the furniture obviously salvaged from Cousin Bertha's attic, or the feed company calendar, or the cheap clock that Margaret said was a wedding present, that made it look unimpressive. It was that it looked more like any small farm sitting room, than an aviator's study.

And Bruce sitting down holding Margaret's wool was equally a letdown. It was only when he began to show her one of his plans that he acted the part that Bitsy expected of him. He began by tracing the flow of gasoline with a pencil, and then before Bitsy could even get out a question he had gotten interested in a new angle to the gas feed and had forgotten all about her.

Then Margaret took over the explanations and it became clear to Bitsy what Bruce had meant. Margaret understood those plans so thoroughly that she could explain them the way she could have explained a recipe for cake or a new knitting pattern. Her mind was methodical and clear and somehow completely uninterrupted by anything else. When she was half through, Bitsy was floundering, but before she had finished Bitsy had been forced to grasp what she had been trying to explain.

And yet she isn't brilliant. Bitsy had felt almost defensive in her own mind. I bet she isn't as bright as I am.

Right now Bitsy was getting stiff from perching on the window shelf of Great-Great-Uncle Bert's library. She closed the book that she hadn't really been reading and walked over to the glass-doored cases. There was a funny collection of classics that had a faded book plate in the front and neat little comments in a small scholarly hand. There were a few fairly recent novels and then shelves and shelves of things like *Stoddard's Lectures, Farmers' Almanacs,* and *Collected Sermons.* Great-Great-Uncle Bert, the brother of Cousin Bertha and Mother's grandfather, had been something of a scholar, but neither his daughter nor his grandsons had taken after him, and the library had come to a dead end around 1920.

Bitsy went back again to *Wuthering Heights* and pulled a chair closer to the window. *Wuthering Heights* was a story of a farm in a remote countryside and so was Cousin Bertha's, but the resemblance stopped there. The land in the book was wild and spectacular while the view out of the window was so soft and pleasant as to be dull. The people in the book were racked by passionate love affairs while here on the farm they seemed to be entirely concerned with their work and what the Yankees were doing.

As Bitsy looked around the high-ceilinged, oak-paneled room, she wondered if the life here had always been like that. In Great-Great-Uncle Bert's time the house had been something of a showplace. This musty room still had an air of distinction about it and so did the heavy brick gateposts with the name Bricklow worked into them, but for the rest, the place was a working farm and looked it.

Even the front lawn which Cousin Bert said had once run to the turnpike was small now and open to the chickens who strayed across it looking for worms. To the north of the library, the land sloped gently to the ravine and the fields beyond. At one time there might have been an extensive view, but now it was choked with wild cherries, sumac, and maple saplings that no one had bothered to cut back.

Bitsy had just really started to read when she heard a bicycle bell and saw Stanty rounding the corner of the house with Ginger galloping after him like the oversized tail of a kite. Bitsy got up reluctantly and went upstairs to wash her hands. She knew the routine of the household well enough by this time to know that when Stanty came home from school she and Mother were supposed to have the table set.

Cousin Bertha was an immensely capable worker who didn't like to be interfered with when she was cleaning the downstairs rooms or doing the cooking, but she did expect Bitsy to set the table and to take her turn at drying the dishes. Bitsy made a face to herself, but she set the table carefully so that Cousin Bert wouldn't complain.

Lunch was uneventful, though Bitsy was still surprised at the slices of apple pie that Tim could get down after two helpings of roast beef and potatoes and five ears of corn. Tim wasn't much taller than she was and thin, but he ate like a truck horse. Right now he was watching Stanty turn the pedal of his bicycle as he got ready to ride back to school. "You oughtn't to take Ginger," Tim called out to him. "I had a dog run over once following me to school."

Stanty didn't listen, and when Tim told him a second time he only shrugged his small shoulders and said that Ginge was "t-trained."

Tim might have said more, but just then Steve called to him to hitch up the mule and he went off. "He'll be sorry," he said over his shoulder to Bitsy. "That turn beyond the school's a bad place for any pup."

Nothing more was said about the dog following Stanty to school until the following Thursday when Stanty came home for lunch without him. Tim had just gone out to feed Rip, the old fox terrier, and he missed him immediately. "Where's Ginge?" Tim asked, but Stanty was busy playing with a picture puzzle and said he didn't know.

"Where'd you see him last?" Tim insisted.

"Oh, he's around," Stanty began, and then was suddenly indefinite. "I s-saw him by the turn in the h-hill."

"Were there cars on the road?" Tim asked, but Stanty couldn't remember.

"Maybe he'll come back later," Bitsy suggested, who was hungry for lunch.

"S-sure," Stanty said, his eyes on his puzzle. "G-Ginge always comes back."

For a moment Tim stood frowning at Rip and then disappeared in the barn and got out his bicycle.

"Where you going?" Stanty asked.

"Crazy," Tim snubbed him. "Want to come?"

Stanty went back to his puzzle, but Bitsy hesitated for a moment and then started down the road after Tim. He hadn't said anything. Tim seldom did say anything when it wasn't necessary, but she had a hunch that if he had gone off this way just before lunch it had something to do with Ginger.

Tim made better time than she did, but by the time Bitsy had reached the hill by the schoolhouse, she knew she was right. There was a good deal of traffic because of the detour from the turnpike and twice she had to step into the gutter to get out of the way of cars that were trying to make up speed on the back road.

By the time Bitsy reached Tim, he had gotten off his bicycle and was leaning over something on the road. The next instant she saw it was the dog. Poor old Ginger. He lay on his side, his four legs stiff and his eyes shut.

"Is he dead?" Bitsy got out.

Tim didn't answer but kneeled down beside the dog and tried to find his heart. "What'll we tell Stanty?" he asked suddenly. "It'll half kill him, won't it?"

Bitsy nodded as she touched the dog's soft black-and-tan ear. "Poor old Ginge," she said. "I hope it was quick."

"Probably the wheel knocked him behind the head and killed him instantly," Tim said. "There isn't a mark anywhere." He got up dusting his hands on his blue jeans and looked at Bitsy. "We've got to move him further away from the road so that Stanty won't see him on his way back to school," he said decidedly. "And then in the afternoon I'll bury him."

"And then tell Stanty?"

"I don't know." Tim avoided Bitsy's eyes. "Couldn't he just think he'd gone off visiting and maybe found some other dogs he wanted to stay with? If it happened gradually, it wouldn't be quite so awful."

Bitsy agreed, thinking of Tim's face the day Rossy had died. He was like Cousin Bertha in some ways, but she doubted if Cousin Bertha had ever been as gentle as that. "I'll help you move him," she said, and together they lifted the dog's limp body to a shaded grassy spot beyond the wire fence.

They were late for lunch, and Cousin Bertha looked firmly at Bitsy and said that unless there were a staff of servants with nothing better to do than wait, it was important to be on time. It was the kind of remark that irritated Bitsy more than anything else, but now that she and Tim were conspirators, she didn't mind. "Bitsy was helping me." Tim looked his mother straight in the eye as he spoke. "It was something that couldn't be put off."

When Stanty had gone off again, Tim pulled an old express wagon out of the barn. "I've got a box that'd be just the right size," he said as he and Bitsy started off. "I'd hate to just stick him in a hole."

Bitsy felt the same way, but she hadn't expected any-thing like that from Tim. It was clear that he liked ani-mals, but he was also intensely practical about their ulti-mate purpose. Even as he brushed off the black Angus calves, he and Steve talked about which packing house would offer them the best price for the beef, and she had seen him kill and pluck a chicken without turning a hair.

Now she followed after the rattling little cart without a word. She remembered the exact day seven years ago when Dad had brought home the small black-and-tan puppy to the rented house on the Shore Road. She had been only a little kid then to whom a dog was the most important thing in the world. It was only in the last few years that other things like the gang around the swim-ming pool had become suddenly more important and she had ceded her share in Ginge to Stanty.

Tim reached the place where they had left the dog ahead of her and turned with a sudden exclamation. "Bitsy," he called. "Come here quick!"

Bitsy hurried forward, and the next moment she was staring down at the grotesque figure of the dog. He had been propped up into an absurd, impossible position.

There was an old straw hat on his head and a dead rat lay across his crossed paws!

"Who did it?" Bitsy got out.

"Steve," Tim said shortly, and kicked the rat into a hole and threw the straw hat toward the scarecrow from which it had been taken. "His idea of being funny."

"How rotten!" Bitsy began, and then sprang forward as the dog's head lolled against Tim's arm. She had seen Ginger's eyes open! There was absolutely no doubt about it. "He isn't dead!" she said, and Tim felt some movement at the same moment.

They managed to get Ginger to the cart, and then Tim stared down at him more closely. "I couldn't feel his heart," he said. "But maybe there was just too much hair."

"We've got to get him away from here," Bitsy said, but Tim was already loading him onto the cart.

"He may just have been knocked out," he said. "Or he may be badly hurt inside."

"We'll have to get a vet," Bitsy suggested, but Tim shook his head.

"We can't. He charges ten dollars, and besides he isn't much good. I'll go over on my bike and get old Pete Glendon, who raises the pointers. He knows more about dogs than anybody in the county."

Bitsy was busy trying to support Ginger's head so that he wouldn't be too badly shaken by the old cart. The dog's eyes opened once more and his tail wagged feebly. "Good boy," she whispered. "Good old Ginge." Suddenly Ginger, the old homely dog who was as familiar and as uninteresting as a bit of carpet, had become a symbol, a sort of touchstone to her new life in Ohio. If he lived, it was going to be all right. If he didn't——

"He's going to be O.K.," Tim said suddenly. "I've just got a hunch."

VIII

While the Sun Shines

T IM WAS RIGHT about Ginger. He did live, although for several days he was a very sick old dog. When Peter Glendon came over to look at him that first afternoon, Bitsy's heart sank. Glendon with his old straw hat and faded blue jeans looked more like a caricature of a farmer than like Hobson the kennel man at Sea Cliff or the veterinarian they had once called in in New York.

He talked endlessly in his slow, drawling voice about the cattle and the weather. Bitsy thought he would never really get down to prescribing for Ginger, who lay limp and pitiful in front of them on the barn floor. But when he finally got around to it his suggestions made a lot of sense. "The wheel probably just glanced him off the road," he drawled. "Most likely gave him a concussion. Best thing you can do is to keep him quiet and warm and keep cold compresses round his haid."

When Stanty came home from school and found out what had happened, his honest, pointed little face grew red with fright and shame. "I—I guess it was my f-fault," he gulped. "I'll j-just have to take the best care of him."

He meant well, but it was really Bitsy who nursed the

sick old dog. Stanty had to go to bed too early to be of much use and Tim had too many regular chores to take on anything new. Bitsy hurried through supper and then went back to the barn to wring out more wet compresses to put on Ginger's head. It was nearly eleven when he finally feebly lapped up a little water. Bitsy watched him, feeling as grateful as though he had done a trick to please her. She covered him with an old piece of horse blanket and then stole through the dark house to her own bed.

The next morning he seemed really better, and when she had changed his water she went out to find Tim. He was in the pasture nearest the house putting new corn stover into the feeding bins for the sheep. Bitsy opened the gate and went into the sheep pasture. When she came up to Tim the sheep nudged her gently with soft, curious noses. There must have been fifty of them, and their thick gray coats streaked with dirt seemed like a curly tweed sea lapping around her knees. For a moment she was nervous of so many loose animals milling around her at will. "Do they ever butt or anything?" she asked, but Tim shook his head.

"Only the bucks," he said, "and that's usually because they were abused. Our Old Judah's as tame as a kitten."

Bitsy helped him pull the corn out of the back of the truck and into the outdoor bins. She liked the soft nuzzling and the cheerful tinkle of the bells that the largest ewes wore around their necks. "Those are meant to keep off dogs," Tim said when she questioned him. "But they're not much help."

A few moments later Bitsy heard Cousin Bertha calling her from the house. She started down but paused on her way to look over her shoulder at Tim and the flock. Most of the sheep were busily eating at the bins, but a few, apparently hoping for choicer tidbits, had followed Tim to the rise in the middle of the field. There was something about the little scene—the soft green field, the gray clumps of sheep, and Tim's thin blue figure above them —that was at once new to Bitsy and yet curiously familiar. "I like this place," she thought to herself. "It looks the way a farm ought to look."

By the end of the week Ginger was nearly well again, though now he seemed like a really old dog. Bitsy had taken to feeding both Ginger and Rip, the old fox terrier, and sweeping out the corner of the barn in which they slept. She did it at the same time each morning until Sunday, when she overslept and was late for breakfast. She hurried into her seat, apologizing as she took the napkin out of the blue-and-white ring. "We'll have to make allowances," Cousin Bert said resignedly. "But remember this cook likes to go to church the same as anyone else."

That was bad enough, but it was even worse when it turned out after breakfast that Bitsy had used up all the hot water in her bath. Cousin Bertha put water on to heat for washing the dishes before she turned to Bitsy. "You know this isn't a city apartment," she said frigidly. "And there isn't a lot of help just hired to make you comfortable."

Bitsy hurried over to the barn feeling cross at herself

and even crosser at Cousin Bert. She had just finished feeding the dogs when Tim came up to her with seven goslings in a shoe box. "These are yours if you want 'em," he said, and put the box in Bitsy's hands.

Bitsy looked doubtfully at the little puffballs. Chickens and turkeys and geese were the kind of things you had as pets when you were Stanty's age. Still, if Tim was giving them to her that might make a difference. "A new boy friend of mine gave me some awfully cute pets," she began a letter to Minty in her mind. As Minty didn't know that Tim was her third cousin and looked about fourteen it sounded quite impressive.

"You'll get a decent price for 'em later on," Tim said casually. "But it'll be work raising 'em at this time of year and I haven't got time. Their mother got run over yesterday."

"How'd it happen?" Bitsy asked, trying to cover her irritation at Tim's giving them to her as a convenience rather than a tribute.

"Steve did it when he was drunk," Tim said with his mother's bluntness. "He's apt to go on a loop whenever Bruce pays him."

"Well, why don't you do something about it?" Bitsy asked. "He's your servant, isn't he?"

Tim's look was withering. "He's our *hired man*," he said. "We don't have servants on this farm or slaves either. He didn't mean to run over the turkey. And what he does in his spare time is his business."

Bitsy's whole body stiffened with annoyance. The way Cousin Bert and the others carried on you'd think that anyone who'd ever had a servant was a Simon Legree. She started to answer, but now Cousin Bert's voice calling from one of the upper windows interrupted them.

"Time to get ready for church, children! Better not dawdle, or you'll keep us all waiting."

Bitsy looked rebelliously at the second-floor window. Cousin Bertha expected everybody to do a man's work and at the same time she acted as though they were all Stanty's age.

"I don't know that I'll go to church," Bitsy said. "Mother probably won't be going, and I might just stay with her."

She went up to her mother's room to find her wearing a hat and the blue-and-white print dress that she used to wear in New York in summer. Her paints were neatly put away; she had made her own and Stanty's bed and was now helping him into a clean shirt.

"Are you really going to church?" Bitsy asked, and Mrs. Close nodded.

"You'd better hurry and get ready too," she said, and went on helping Stanty.

Bitsy went into her own room feeling snubbed. Since they had come out to the farm Mother seemed like an entirely different person. She, who had always been so vague and dependent upon the maids at home, had suddenly turned into an automaton. A few weeks ago she had gotten her first order to illustrate a children's book, and ever since then she had worked on her drawings with a grim concentration. At the necessary times she did her share of the housework, and then went back to her drawing again.

"She hasn't got any time for me any more. She's just living for her work," Bitsy sympathized with her own reflection in the bathroom mirror.

By the time Bitsy was dressed, she could see Stanty with the others out in front of the old family sedan. "Mum," Bitsy said, as she burst into her mother's room, "if we've got to go let's take our own car. I've just got to talk to you."

Mrs. Close blotted the letter she had been addressing when Bitsy had come into the room. "Listen, darling," she said. "I've decided to sell the car. A man who might want to buy called up late last night and Steve's going to show it to him this morning."

"Sell our car? You mean we're going to get a new one —or go without?"

"Just sell it, dear. Stanty doesn't need it and neither will you going to school on the bus. My work's all right here, and when I have to go into town, I can go in with Margaret or Cousin Bert. It won't be a bit bad."

"But—but everybody has a car," Bitsy protested. "Unless they're terribly poor."

"Well, we aren't going to have one now," Mother said. "This crash of ours came so suddenly that we've started under a handicap. I need the price of the car to meet August and September bills."

"You mean things like that coat I bought?" Bitsy said, and now embarrassment and shame made her feel crosser than ever. She could feel her face getting red and she tried to avoid Mother's deep violet eyes. Mother was on the spot, too, a much worse one really than her own, but somehow this Sunday morning everything seemed to have come together to make her feel cross. Suddenly Mrs. Close put her arms around Bitsy and held her close for a moment. "You're all right, Bitsy," she said. "Don't forget that for a moment. You're doing a first-class job, and it's going to get much easier as you go on."

The sudden, unexpected praise broke down Bitsy's reserve. She wanted terribly to cry and to throw her arms around Mother's neck, but suddenly Mother was all business again. "Coming, Bertha," she called. The next minute she had twitched a cover over some drawings that were being ruffled by the breeze and hurried downstairs.

The man came to look at the car while they were at church and decided to buy it. The next morning Mrs. Close drove it over to his farm beyond Meudon. He took her home again and dropped her at the end of the lane just as the mail carrier was stuffing letters into the farm box. A few moments later Bitsy saw her hurrying up the lane with a franked letter in her hand. "It's from Dad!" she called out. "He's safe! In Africa!"

"B-boy!" Stanty shot out of the house at the sound of his mother's voice and squatted beside her on the broad porch steps.

"What does he say? Did he have a good trip?" Bitsy asked, and now her mother looked up from the letter, her face radiant.

"He's been made the administrative officer at a base

hospital," she said. "Bitsy, Bitsy darling, that means he'll be kept back from the front lines."

Bitsy sat down on the other side of her mother. "Go on," she said as Stanty sputtered questions. "What else does he say?"

"The trip took only five days." Mrs. Close talked as she read. "They flew all the way in a bomber. He was actually at work a week after he left Washington." She read on to herself, forgetting Stanty and Bitsy and everything except the closely written sheet in front of her.

"Wh-what did he eat on the b-bomber? Did they s-see any G-Germans? Wh-who d-drove it?" Stanty demanded.

"Darling, wait. Just a second till I finish." Mrs. Close patted Stanty's knee vaguely and went right on reading.

For the first time in years Bitsy remembered the feeling she had had once ages ago in the Wade cottage in Sea Cliff when Dad had just come home from a long business trip. She and Stanty had pounded him with questions until he had finally chased them from the room so that he and Mother could have a moment alone. Bitsy remembered every detail of that sensation. She had felt safe and secure, of course, but for once conscious of being outside the circle of Mother's and Dad's feeling for each other. She turned back to her Mother and saw her completely concentrated on the letter. Mother was alone with Dad now, Bitsy realized. For the first time since the awful morning when he had left, this letter had brought him home.

"Stanty, we ought to go feed Ginge," Bitsy said

suddenly. "He hasn't had a single bite since last night."

Stanty was easily distracted and he trotted off to the kitchen as Mrs. Close gave Bitsy's arm a little pat. "Darling, you're a marvel," she said. "I'll read it to you—later ——" Her voice trailed off as she turned to a new page.

After Ginge was fed, Bitsy wandered out to the barn and found that Steve and Tim were harnessing the mules to a hay wagon. For the first time in days Bitsy really wanted to work herself. Dad was doing a wonderful job in the Army. Mother was working harder than she had ever worked in her life before. Bitsy wished that she were old enough to go into the WACs or the motor corps, but that was impossible. She felt a sudden restless urge to do something, anything, as long as she could get her teeth into it. "Can I help you haying?" she said, and to her surprise Tim looked pleased.

"You bet," he said, and even Steve nodded approval.

"You make load," Steve said. "That some help."

Bitsy wasn't at all sure what "making" the load was, but at least it was nice they really wanted her. She dashed back to the house, pulled on a pair of old blue jeans, and clambered onto the wagon just as Steve turned it toward the hayfield.

Steve had already raked the hay and it lay before them in the hot midmorning sun like a sea of dry, immobile waves.

"Think you can drive the team?" Tim asked, and Bitsy nodded with more confidence than she felt. She took over the reins and after the first few minutes realized that the mules were almost driving themselves. They stood perfectly still just a little ahead of each ridge while Tim and Steve speared the hay into huge forkfuls and threw it up on the wagon.

By the time they came to the fourth ridge, the hay was all crowded into the back of the wagon while the front boards were empty. Bitsy wound the reins around the front seat and started to spread it more evenly with the extra pitchfork. "That's good," Tim grunted as he pushed an extra-large forkful up toward her. "If you make we can put on speed."

Bitsy grinned to herself. So now she knew without having had to ask questions what it was like to make a load. She shoved awkwardly at the hay and half her forkful fell off. She looked up to see Steve's mocking blue eyes and waited for a moment to see how he and Tim managed. They worked the hay into a mound, poked their forks into the middle of it, and then gave it a hard twist as though they were spearing macaroni. She shoved and twisted, imitating their action, and found that she could carry twice as much as she had before.

By the time the wagon was covered with a small mountain of sweet-smelling grass, Bitsy felt that she was pretty well onto the system. "We're going great guns," she said, looking back over the newly cleared stubble. "We've got a lot done."

Steve said nothing, but Tim stopped long enough to take off his hat and squint up at the sky. "Weather breeder," he said as he went back to loading. "We'll be racing a storm before evening or I'm a monkey's uncle."

They brought in two loads before noon, but when Bitsy crawled down from the hayloft after the second, she felt as though it had been ten. The work in the hayfield was hard and hot, but the top of the hayloft was purgatory. There was no stir of air and the hayseed choked in her nose and mouth. The sweat poured from her face, but even before she could manage to wipe it off Steve pushed another huge forkful relentlessly upward.

Tim, who was up beside Bitsy, did more than his share. He clawed furiously at the forkfuls Steve shot toward him and at the same time managed to take over a good many of Bitsy's. "We won't ever be able to get more hay in today," Bitsy panted when they were nearly through the second load.

"Got to." Timmy wiped his dripping forehead on his sleeve. "We've got to get every spear of grass we can or we'll have to buy hay in March and we can't afford to."

It hadn't really occurred to Bitsy to go on haying after lunch, but just as Mother had finished reading her the end of Dad's letter, she saw Tim hurrying toward the empty hay wagon. "Are you going to start now?" she asked, and Tim nodded, pulling his big hat down over his forehead.

"You bet," he said. "Every five minutes counts when there's a storm coming. I don't suppose you want any more though?"

"Oh, Bitsy, you look half dead," Mrs. Close protested, but Bitsy was already halfway across the barnyard. She was more than half dead, she decided, she was three quarters dead, but she was going to finish haying if it killed her completely.

The first afternoon load seemed endless. Bitsy's back and shoulders ached and her arms felt numb. The day had grown hotter and more humid, and it seemed to Bitsy that now after they had had a few clear, crisp days, she felt the heat more than she had all summer. By the time they came down after storing the first load, Bitsy was actually staggering, but somehow she forced herself to go out after the last load.

Tim and Steve pitched hay like madmen. A few big drops of rain had spattered down on them and the leaves of the buttonwood tree at the edge of the field looked white. Bitsy, looking to the west, saw that the farmhouse had a strange electric brightness about it that was intensified by the dark, moving clouds. While she was still looking at it, an unfamiliar car drove up to the kitchen door and Tim called out that it was Tracy Larson.

"Want to stop?" he asked, but Bitsy shook her head and went on working. Now that each remaining ridge of hay was a personal challenge, no mere visitor could interrupt her.

"Good," Tim grunted as he staggered forward under an extra-heavy mound. "I'd have to stick it out anyway."

Bitsy didn't look up again. For the moment there didn't seem to be a thing in the world except ridges of hay lying in dwindling rows ahead of them. Four rows to go; three. As they rounded the corner for the last row, the sudden burst of wind lifted Bitsy's hot hair and blew through her drenched cotton shirt. One, two, three, shove, twist, lift! Bitsy worked furiously, forced on as much by the urgency of the weather as the mute example of Tim and the Pole.

Somehow they got the last piles onto the wagon. Bitsy reached for the reins, but now Tim scrambled up beside her and took them out of her hands. "Gidiyap!" he shouted, and the mules, scared by the first crack of thunder, bolted for the barn.

Bitsy caught a glimpse of Steve running for his own little cabin. The next instant the rain lashed down at them, and she bent her head as they rumbled into the barn.

"Boy, we made it!" Bitsy said, and wiped her wet face. She sprawled back over the top of the load. Now that they had the hay in, she just wanted to lie back, and rest, and talk over how much they had done. Tim was still too busy to celebrate. He had slid off the load and was busily unharnessing the mules.

After a few minutes, Bitsy got herself up and moved off to the house. She went in through the library and straight up to her own room. If Tim didn't want to tell her that she had done a good job, she didn't care. She ached in every muscle, and it would probably be worse tomorrow, but they had the hay in! Each of those apparently endless ridges was gone, and she felt as though she had personally beaten an old enemy.

She turned on a bath and dropped in the last of some bath salts that she had been given for Christmas. Now, if ever, she had earned them. She was just luxuriating in the warm, scented water when Cousin Bertha knocked at the door. For a moment Bitsy was afraid she had used up too much hot water, but Cousin Bertha only wanted to tell her that Tracy Larson was anxious to meet her.

Bitsy growled to herself as she pulled on a clean cotton dress and skinned back her hair. She was too tired even to care about a blond Visigoth from a neighboring farm. All she wanted was to get some food and go straight off to bed.

She went downstairs, and as she turned toward the living room, she had a good view of Tracy Larson without being seen herself. He looked more like a bookworm than a farmer. He was tall and weedy-looking, with silver-rimmed glasses on his homely, studious face. Even his clothes were not what Bitsy had expected. He wasn't in blue jeans but wore some kind of tan sport suit with a loose shirt open at his thin neck.

She stared at him, hardly believing that he could be so different from the person that she had imagined. He looks like a mess, she thought, and the next instant it dawned on her that Timmy was talking, and about her!

"Wait until you meet my cousin Bitsy," he said proudly. "She's some looker and she works like a man."

~~~~~~

IX

Gray Goose in a Green Field

A WEEK AFTER the thunderstorm, the weather
turned cold, and on the Sunday before school opened
they had a real frost. It was good to go to bed in the
cold after the breathless, sticky nights they had been
having, and Bitsy slept better than she had for weeks.
She woke up to Cousin Bertha's sharp knock and
wrinkled her cold nose over the patchwork quilt.
"Quarter of eight," Cousin Bertha called. "I guess you've
had your beauty sleep."

Bitsy pushed back the warm covers and jumped out of
bed feeling lighter and friskier than she had for a long
time. She sniffed the mixed smells of coffee and frying
fat and decided that Cousin Bertha must have started on
a batch of pancakes. She hurried into the green sweater
and plaid skirt that she had had last winter. After months
of cotton clothes they looked smart and new. She pulled
on her new moccasins and hurried down the hall, almost
colliding with Tim.

Tim was dressed in his farm clothes which he began to

94

pull off as he made for his own room. "Save plenty of johnnycakes for me," he said. "I've worked up an appetite."

For the first time Bitsy realized that Tim had farm chores to do even when he went to school. She hesitated for a moment, looking out of the hall window. Probably she, too, was expected to take care of her geese before she left. She went out into the cold air and hurried over to the barn. The weather was really chilly, and as she let the goslings out into their small coop and gave them fresh water her hands were stiff with cold. She brought them some fresh grain and then dashed back across the yard to the house, the crisp air making her feel almost as though she had been in a cold, invigorating shower.

She had felt a bit cross and put-upon on her way out, but now with breakfast just ahead of her she was exhilarated and cheerful, as though she had accomplished something important. She stopped for a moment on the kitchen steps to take a deep breath of the tangy air and then realized for the first time that she was very hungry.

She went into the kitchen and found Cousin Bertha busily scalding the milk pail. "Squaw winter," Cousin Bertha said, nodding out of the window. "All my dahlias gone in one night."

The big Jane Cowl dahlias that had glowed beside the kitchen door only yesterday were black and limp. They looked actually burned, their thick stalks dark and waxen and the heavy heads bent. Bitsy turned away from the window and saw that Cousin Bertha was still looking out at her flowers. For once she didn't bustle on with her work but just stood there, her usually placid face suddenly sad. She became conscious that Bitsy was watching her and turned away from the window and back to the kitchen table. "The first frost always makes me kind of sad," she admitted unexpectedly. "All those months of growing killed in one night." She looked as though she were going to say something more, but the next minute she was beating vigorously at the batter in her big bowl.

"It's a shame," Bitsy said, suddenly liking Cousin Bertha better than she ever had before. "Those dahlias were beautiful."

By this time Tim was in the kitchen eating a big pile of pancakes while his mother filled his lunch box with sandwiches and fruit. "You'll have to manage with a paper bag today," Cousin Bertha told Bitsy. "But I don't think much of the school cafeteria."

"Shall I buy a lunch box?"

Cousin Bertha shook her head. "I'll find one up in the attic," she said. "There must be an old one of Bruce's around somewhere."

Bitsy went upstairs to say good-by to her mother and when she came down Tim had already gotten his bicycle out of the barn. "You ride in back," he said. "And I'll leave you at the bus corner."

"Aren't you going to take it?" Bitsy was really surprised, and Tim shook his head.

"Too slow," he said. "It stops so often that I save a half-hour either way. I always bike except when it's too cold or raining."

Bitsy straddled the carrier on the back of the bicycle and they rolled down the long lane toward the road. Riding like a little kid on the back of your cousin's bicycle was the sort of thing that would make Minty's plucked eyebrows arch disapprovingly, but right now that didn't seem important. Bitsy glanced at the cornfield behind the barn and saw that there were several newly husked piles of golden corn. "Has Steve done all that already?" she asked as she saw the farm hand walking toward a new stack.

"I did most of it," Tim said as he pedaled toward the main road. "After I finished the chores and before breakfast."

They were nearly at the bus stop now, and Tim stopped to let Bitsy get off. For a moment Bitsy had a lost, frightened feeling that she hadn't had about school since first grade. There were going to be both boys and girls at this school. It was the only way you met people, apparently, and that made it awfully important. "How about waiting until the bus comes?" she suggested, but Tim shook his head.

"Got to pick up some feed sacks before school starts," he told her. "If I do it afterwards, the store'll be crowded and I'll be late getting home."

Bitsy said nothing more and waved cheerfully as Tim pedaled off down the flat white road that led toward Meudon. Working time and money were equally precious on the farm. You thought and planned before you spent an unnecessary cent or an extra hour. If Tim bicycled three miles to school and back every day to save time for work, you couldn't blame him for not wanting to waste time just being companionable.

The air was still chilly, and Bitsy did a little dance step to keep warm. The farm life was a world in itself. Maybe all farms were like that or maybe it was just Cousin Bertha's. At all events, high school would be a part of the real world again and entirely different. It probably wouldn't be much like Miss Fair's, Bitsy thought, except for the actual lessons. With both boys and girls around, it would be sure to be more like Rye or Sea Cliff. At the thought of those communities Bitsy's confidence leaked away and a wave of hopelessness and inadequacy swept over her. By the time the big school bus pulled up beside her her hands and feet were really cold and she felt fidgety with apprehension.

She had barely time to get on the bus before the driver moved off again. "Hello, Bitsy," a voice said in her ear. "I was looking for you."

Bitsy half fell into a seat directly across from Tracy and Flossie Larson. Flossie, with her flat, tow-colored hair and too bright lipstick, was just as uninteresting looking as her brother, but right now Bitsy was delighted to see them both. "Hello," she said. "It's really cold, isn't it?"

Before the Larsons had time to answer, a small dark girl in a pink sweater had come across the lurching aisle. "Are you Bitsy Close?" she said. "I'm Rose Pesky. I've heard a lot about you."

As Bitsy wondered what she could have heard, another girl, with pretty red hair, smiled over at her from her seat behind the Larsons. "Are you the girl who helped Tim pitch the hay?" she said. "Gee, I've certainly heard about you all right."

By the time the bus had stopped to pick up three more people Bitsy's head was in a whirl.

All the people on the bus seemed to be calling her Bitsy and all of them seemed to have heard about the haying. Tracy Larson was talking to a boy in blue jeans about it as though Bitsy had just won a downhill skiing race. "It was some stunt," he finished, "for a girl from New York and all."

Bitsy started to say something, but as the bus stopped with a lurch, her lunch fell off her lap and she hurried to pick up the crumby-looking brown paper package. The red-haired girl and Rose Pesky had already stooped for it, and as the bus started again, Bitsy bumped into them. She apologized, but they had already straightened up, laughing and good-natured.

The bus was hot and crowded now as it eased its way past the hash houses and the gas stations on the outskirts of Meudon. Bitsy held onto her lunch bag and looked around. There were groups of boys in sweaters and pants, then a block of girls with here and there a boy and a girl sitting together, who paid no attention to the rest of the bus load.

It was all so different from anything that Bitsy was accustomed to or had expected! It wasn't just that there were both boys and girls and all strangers to her. Even the girls looked less of a piece and sort of uniform and patterned than the ones at Miss Fair's. Full-blown Rose

Pesky looked older than Margaret Crane, and the plain, scrubbed little girl who had gotten on at one of the farms looked as though she ought to be in the fifth grade.

Everybody was talking now and several of them mentioned her haying. Slowly it dawned on Bitsy that for a girl from New York to actually work hard out in the fields was as surprising to them as though she had taken to studying a Bible on the Beach Club porch at Sea Cliff. The only difference was the way her act was received. There it would have been cruelly teased, but here they treated her effort with respect. "I helped with the haying for the Victory Club," the red-haired girl told Rose Pesky. "But I didn't think a New Yorker would do it." The chatter went on, and Bitsy had time to look around her.

They talked to one another and now and then someone made a remark to the driver, who answered it in a good-natured drawl. "It's just a bus ride," Bitsy thought, "but they're all having a wonderful time." Suddenly, for no good reason, she thought of Mabs Holcombe's bored expression and the shrewd, worried look that came into Minty's eyes when she thought no one was looking.

She turned to see the back of the bus and dropped her lunch again. Once more Rose and two other people stooped to pick it up. "I'm a dope," Bitsy apologized, but Tracy Larson only grinned and fitted her package in between himself and his sister where she saw he had already stowed his own.

"You've got to get used to Davy's driving," Tracy said.

"He's practicing for the Rocky Road to Dublin. Isn't that right, Dave?"

"That's what you-all think," the driver drawled, and swerved around a pair of small children that were having a fight in the middle of the street.

They're really friendly, Bitsy thought, feeling suddenly warmer and more at ease. Minty'd probably say their accents were corny and their clothes weren't just right, but they're a lot kinder and politer than she is.

By this time they had pulled in behind three other busses that were already disgorging their passengers in front of an enormous school building. The great red-brick pile took up most of a city block and people seemed to be streaming toward it from every direction. It was bigger than anything Bitsy had ever associated with a school before and more impersonal. The boys and girls hurried up the steps and spilled into the bare school hall. Bitsy hesitated for a moment, bewildered by the unfamiliar building, the thundering of feet, and the size and strangeness of it all. She was just wondering which way to turn when she heard Rose Pesky and Flossie Larson on either side of her. "You were too quick for us," Flossie said, and now for the first time Bitsy saw that the broad mouth under the thick lipstick was generous and kind. "We stopped to register, and by the time we looked for you you'd gone."

"I'm lost," Bitsy admitted, which she never would have done to the girls at Miss Fair's. "Where do you go first?"

"You come with us," Rose said, and as Flossie led the

way down the hall she tucked her arm into Bitsy's and urged her along. "Flossie's in Home Ec., but I'm taking Academic so you come with me."

They left Flossie at a big room furnished with Bunsen burners, iceboxes, and a long kitchen table. A young teacher was already writing an assignment on the blackboard and Flossie had time only to wave good-by as she scurried inside.

A few minutes later Bitsy had been through the registrar's office and had filled out some forms and been given a class schedule. As she hurried after Rose through the packed corridors she heard a battery of typewriters. "What's that?" she asked, shouting to make herself heard above the racket of the hundreds of boys and girls who swarmed through the hall.

"Steno class," Rose said. "Don't they have one in your school?"

Bitsy thought of the small, highly academic classes at Miss Fair's and shook her head. This place wasn't her idea of a school. It was more like a small factory with boys working over machines and drafting boards on one side while just beyond them an equally large class was at work in what seemed to be a science lab. "Did they all get here extra early?" she asked, but Rose shook her head.

"Early session," she said. "The school's overcrowded even with the new wing. They've over 1,500 students this year."

"But where do they come from?" Bitsy asked. After

the weeks on the farm, it didn't seem as though there could be that many people in the whole state.

Meudon, Rose told her, and Misqua and all the outlying villages. The town was packed now because of defense factories and all the vocational courses were filled. "We're lucky we're in Ac," Rose finished. "We've got the best teachers and the classes are tiny."

The classes that ran from twenty to forty pupils didn't seem small to Bitsy. They seemed enormous and very noisy with so many people in a fairly small room and the clicking of typewriters floating in through the open door.

Once the work began the Math. and Science courses didn't seem so very different from the ones at Miss Fair's though it felt strange to be doing schoolwork with a lot of boys. The Latin class was much like the one at home though it was ever so much easier than the one Bitsy had had last year with Miss Merryweather, who never let you forget that she had taught Latin at Oxford before she had come to America.

Bitsy followed the others to English feeling sure that that would be the easiest of all. At Miss Fair's they prided themselves on their English courses, and this would probably seem simple.

Miss Swigenberg, the English teacher, gave out homework assignments and then asked for short, factual reports on summer reading. Bitsy was so engrossed with looking around the class that she hardly heard the question. A boy in a red sweater got up and said that he had read the *Forsyte Saga*. It was a very good book about an

English family by a writer called John Galsworthy. When he had said that much the boy sat down.

Three or four others volunteered the names of books they had read and then a girl in a fuzzy yellow sweater got up and said that she had read a little book about a dog called Flush by Virginia Woolf. *Flush* was a favorite of Bitsy's and for the first time she paid attention.

The girl in yellow faced the class and gave the date the book was written and when Virginia Woolf was born and when she died. Even before she had finished speaking Bitsy's hand was in the air.

"And what else can you tell us about?" Miss Swigenberg asked when the girl in yellow was back in her seat. She meant the names of other books read during the summer but Bitsy had been too absorbed by the newness and strangeness of the school to hear her original question.

Bitsy launched into an enthusiastic résumé of *Flush* and the author's probable place in English letters. Virginia Woolf's interest in the well-bred little dog was part of her interest in all genuine aristocracy. Bitsy had often heard her parents discussing Virginia Woolf and she warmed to her subject. "She isn't just one more writer," Bitsy finished finally. "She's probably the greatest woman writer who's lived in our generation."

Bitsy knew that what she had said had made sense. Discussing a book, getting at the heart of it, was one of the things they started you doing as soon as you could read at all at Miss Fair's. She looked around the class for approval, but they seemed restless and unimpressed. She turned to Miss Swigenberg, but for a moment the teacher said nothing. "That was all true and interesting," she said kindly. "But you see I only asked for the names and essential facts about the books read. We'll have time for discussions later."

Bitsy's face was a hot pink as she sat down. Why hadn't she listened to the question in the beginning? Just then the bell rang and Bitsy half expected that somebody would tease her for talking her head off the way they would have done at Miss Fair's. It was the noon bell, and the students clattered into the hall without giving the class another thought. Even Miss Swigenberg was hurrying toward the doorway. Bitsy followed, relieved that she hadn't been made fun of. She wondered if they always just gave the dates of books and imagined they probably gave fuller accounts later on. She would find out about that tomorrow. Right now she was more interested in finding the gymnasium where those who didn't lunch in the cafeteria were supposed to eat their sandwiches.

She was just biting into one of Cousin Bertha's sandwiches of pink roast beef and homemade bread when she saw Tim, looking scrubbed and unfamiliar in his school clothes, coming toward her. "How you getting along?" he asked, and made a place for himself and his lunch basket next to Bitsy.

"It's awfully different," she said. "But easier, and the people are more friendly. Flossie Larson was swell this morning."

"Floss is O.K.," Tim said through an enormous mouthful. "But I can't stand the fellow she goes with. Name of Blitz."

"Goes with?" Bitsy looked confused. "You mean he's a beau of hers?"

Tim shrugged his shoulders. "She's been walking out with him steady for over a year. I don't know about this beau stuff. You know what? Tracy Larson just told me he got eighty bushels an acre from his hybrid seed corn. I didn't plant hybrid and we're only getting fifty bushels per acre, but I don't know how we'll get all of that husked without any help. Bruce's going to be busy with the fall plowing, and you can't get extra hands no matter what you pay them."

Bitsy would have tried to switch him back to the subject of "steadies" and "walking out" but just then the school bell rang and they had to separate, as Tim was taking the agricultural course and they didn't have any of the same classes.

The rest of the day went by without anything outstanding happening. There was no one she knew or knew of in any of her afternoon classes and she found that when she wasn't actually engaged in her work, her mind was back on the farm. She would change her clothes as soon as she got home, feed her geese, make sure Ginger was all right, and then see what Tim was doing.

It wasn't until school was over and she was hurrying down to the basement for some books that she realized that the close, cliquy group feeling that she had been dreading didn't even exist. There were couples who went together and groups who came from the same district or went out for the same sports, but there wasn't anything resembling the make-you-or-break-you crowds that ruled Sea Cliff and Rye. It was a relief, Bitsy decided, but at the same time it left her feeling a little flat. All day yesterday she had felt as tense as a swimmer before the gun, and now it was suddenly clear that there wasn't going to be any race.

There was such a line of people waiting for books that she missed the bus going out past Bricklow. She found that there was another one at half-past four after football practice, but she didn't want to wait around for an hour and a half and so decided to walk.

It turned out to be a dull, tiring walk through the outskirts of Meudon. The houses were ugly and nondescript and there were only a few stores. Once Bitsy stopped to look into the window of a live chicken market. She knew the little ones were Bantams, the whites were Leghorns, and the barred black-and-gray ones were Plymouth Rocks. She moved on, feeling pleased with herself at having identified them so easily. She hadn't thought she would get interested in farming, but it had sort of caught up with her before she knew what was happening. Even the talk of rotation of crops no longer seemed so boring after she had worked on several of the fields herself and knew what they had produced.

The next store she passed was a bicycle store, and she stopped to look at a secondhand bicycle that was for sale for twenty-three dollars. If she had that bicycle she wouldn't have to take the long, jolting ride on the bus every day and she would have an extra half-hour at either end on the farm. For a moment Bitsy thought of asking her mother to buy it. Then with a pang of remorse she remembered the new green coat. There just isn't enough money for extras, she thought miserably. I can't ask her for a thing. She looked back at the store and suddenly a new, a marvelous idea struck her. She would earn enough money for that bicycle and to pay for the coat too. It was a knockout idea. Why hadn't she thought about it long ago?

Bitsy walked along more quickly, thinking over the things she could do to make money. She might be able to sell subscriptions to magazines, or if there were some small children near Cousin Bertha's she might be able to watch them on evenings when their mothers wanted to go out. These things sounded dull, but there would be more exciting jobs too.

By this time she had left the uninteresting suburbs of the town behind her and was in the open country. A farmer driving his truck back from town stopped to ask her if she wanted a ride. She thanked him but shook her head. She really wanted to walk now that she had so much to think about.

A woman in an old sedan stopped, too, but Bitsy only smiled, refused, and went on walking. She wanted to walk, but she felt grateful for the kindliness behind the offers of a ride. It was like Rose Pesky's showing her around school and Tracy Larson's picking up her luncheon parcel in the bus. People are just plain nice out here, she thought, feeling suddenly expansive. And a lot friendlier than at Sea Cliff.

She had walked for a long time now and the wide,

white road seemed hot and glaring. She was just wishing she had taken one of the offered rides when she saw a country lane leading off to the left and guessed it would be a short cut to Bricklow.

She turned into the lane and went down a short hill that led her onto a long, covered bridge. She liked the worn old planks of the bridge and it was delicious to be out of the glare. She shut her eyes for a moment, and then when she opened them again felt as though she were looking at something in a dream. After the flat yellow cornfields and the hard white road, the view through the far end of the bridge was refreshingly green and pleasing. The bridge covered a small brook, and the bank running down to the far side of it was soft and lush with water cress. Bitsy was still looking out from under cover of the bridge when three gray majestic geese waddled onto the green strip in front of her. Oh, how pretty, Bitsy thought, forgetting the heat and her own tiredness. The small scene framed by the gray wood of the covered bridge was really charming, and as separate and unexpected as the picture in an Easter egg.

She walked out of the bridge, and it seemed to her that the geese and the small square of green around them were even more perfect and complete than she had thought. The geese looked as though they were posed for a picture, or as though they had been placed there for some sort of a sign and a portent like Kim's red bull in a green field.

She hurried on up the rise at the far side of the gully and then paused for a moment to look back at the little oasis. As she turned, a thought that had been forming in the back of her mind for some time became suddenly whole. She could earn that bicycle by helping Tim husk corn. He had said only at lunch time that he was badly in need of help. She looked down at the gray geese standing silent and perfect at the edge of the water. "Gray geese on a green field." She said the words aloud and they sounded like the beginning of a poem. Gray geese on a green field—— Why, of course, they were going to bring her good luck.

~~~~~~

X

Pigs in the Corn

THAT EVENING Bitsy borrowed Margaret's alarm clock and set it for six o'clock. Mother had said that she wouldn't have to earn money for the coat now that it was paid for, but she was still determined to earn the money for the bicycle. It was black when she crept downstairs the next morning, but Tim was already in the kitchen waiting for her. "I haven't got a real husker," he said, "but you use this."

Bitsy took the small rubber strap with the big nail stuck through it and followed him out to the cornfield. She helped Tim topple over the first big sheaf and he showed her how to jerk off the corn, tear the husk with the big nail, rip it off, and throw the ripe ear to one side. "It's good corn," Tim said, "but we'd have gotten a lot better crop if Bruce had let me get hybrid seed corn."

Bitsy wasn't even interested. It was warmer than it had been yesterday, but even so her hands felt cold and stiff in the morning air. It was still dark, and they worked by the light of an old-fashioned oil lantern that Tim had picked up at Steve's cottage. She watched Tim's quick, expert flip of the wrist as he wrenched the corn free and tossed it to one side. When he did it, it looked easy, but when she tried to imitate him, she felt all thumbs.

He moved on to attack another sheaf and left Bitsy alone. She squatted down and pulled the corn toward her. As she ripped awkwardly on her first ear, the corn turned in her grasp and she scraped her hand with the nail. She tried again, holding the ear more firmly, and this time she was successful. By the time she had husked a dozen or so ears, she had gotten onto some sort of system. Her thin fingers were strong and dextrous like her mother's, and once she really understood how it was done, she managed very well. Husking was tough on your hands, Bitsy decided, but not really exhausting like the haying. Besides, there was real satisfaction in watching the clean yellow ears mount up into a respectable pile beside you.

She had just finished her first sheaf when Tim came back to see how she was getting on. "You're good," he said, gathering the husked stalks and tying them with a string he had fastened to his belt. "Most people don't get the hang of it so quickly."

Bitsy worked harder than ever after hearing praise from Tim. She undid the string that held the next sheaf and throwing all her weight against it managed to topple it to the ground. It looked and felt awkward, but it wasn't impossible. "I'll race you," she called, pulling the dry stalks into her lap.

They worked for several minutes without speaking. There was no sound except the rattle of the dry corn leaves and the thud of the hard ears as they fell to the ground. "Bruce wanted to rent a corn harvester," Tim said once, "but we finally argued him out of it. They cost an awful lot to rent and somebody's got to go over the field after 'em to pick up all the ears they miss. They're all right on a really big farm, but not for this."

It occurred to Bitsy that Bruce hadn't done much of the menial work on either the haying or the husking, but she said nothing. There was something winning and appealing about Bruce that you felt the first time you saw him. He was physically lazy, she knew that now, and sort of evaporated when he didn't want to be bothered with something. Still, if the fact that he didn't want to husk corn gave her a chance to make money, that was her good luck. He had promised to pay her fifteen cents for every bushel she husked and had been glad to have her help. Bitsy jerked off her last ear with a flourish. "Finished," she called, and Tim pushed back his canvas cap to stare at her.

"Say, what is this?" he demanded. "You've never done this before in your life and you're faster than I am. I'm on my last stalk."

Bitsy felt warm and glowing with achievement and praise. Her eyes were no longer sticky with sleep, and the sun was beginning to rise over the east side of the barn. The air was clear and bracing, and in the distance she heard the muffled quacking of a duck. "I saw some wonderful-looking geese yesterday in the prettiest little field," she began, and wondered if she could make Tim understand how private and delightful that little space beyond the bridge had seemed.

"You mean down at Shank's Lane?" Tim asked as he helped her restack her husked stalks.

"That's right. Just over the covered bridge. It's like something out of a picture book."

"Always makes me think of Kim," Tim said. "You know the way they were looking for a red bull on a green field. I don't know why except it's such a very little patch in among all that corn."

"Timothy Crane!" Bitsy began. "I just don't believe you. I thought about Kim the minute I saw it!"

Tim looked up at her and grinned. "I like that place," he said, and went on with his husking. "It used to be part of this farm when Great-Great-Uncle Bert was alive, and I'd like to get it back someday."

Bitsy's fingers flew, but she was too surprised to say anything more. It was strange how when you *tried* to make conversation the way she had with Byrd Gaylord and the others at the Sea Cliff pool it was almost always a flop. And yet here, working out in a cold cornfield before breakfast, she had mentioned something she really cared about and Tim had taken the words out of her mouth and echoed what she had felt in her heart.

By the time they had finished their tenth stack of corn it was quite late, and they could hear Steve rattling the milk pails in the barn. "I've got to stop," Tim said abruptly. "Time I got at my chores."

"I'll help you," Bitsy said, straightening out her stiff legs. "I'll mix the pig feed while you take the milk down to the house."

"You won't get paid," Tim said, looking at her with

the blunt expression that was so like his mother. "And if you stayed here you could get another stack done easily before breakfast."

"That's O.K.," Bitsy said, and hurried after him toward the barn. "If I get in an hour this afternoon, I ought to be able to make sixty cents, and that's pretty good for the first day."

Tim said no words of thanks, but Bitsy no longer minded. He was grateful for any help, she knew that now. Hadn't he gone out of his way to tell all his friends how she had helped with the haying? If he didn't want to pass out gratitude and compliments to her face that was his business. "It was funny you thinking about Kim," she said, but Tim was too busy now to exchange ideas.

"You mix the big pail full of middlings with the small pail full of corn," he told her. "And then get Steve to put out that light. It's kind of tricky."

"All right," Bitsy said, and found that she had to shout to make herself heard above the grunts and squeals of the pigs whose noise increased as their chances of food grew greater. She mixed the food as she had been told and poured it into the troughs. The barn was warm and smelly, but after an hour and a half in the open cornfield, even that close warmth was welcome. Steve clumped past to feed the mules, and she asked him about the lantern. "That easy," he said, and wrenching the top loose blew out the flame. "What matter with you and Timmy? He can't light lamp. Always brings over to me."

Bitsy thanked him and put the lantern away. It was comforting to find something that Tim couldn't do. She knew that he wasn't a student of mechanics the way Bruce was, but she hadn't known before that he found it hard to manage some small mechanical device like the top of that lantern.

After Bitsy's early start, the school day seemed very long, and when it was time to go home, she was tired out. She would have taken the bus, but she remembered that Mother had asked her to buy a small bottle of turpentine. For a moment Bitsy thought of asking Tim to buy it for her tomorrow, but she knew Mother really needed it right away for her brushes and went down to the drugstore herself.

The store was crowded with high-school students and a number of soldiers from Blaine Field, the big air depot the other side of Bricklow Village. Bitsy finally succeeded in getting what she wanted and was just counting her change when she heard someone shout her name across the store. She turned, half expecting to see Tracy Larson or one of the other boys in her class, but she found herself face to face with Byrd Gaylord!

"Byrd!" she got out. "Where'd you come from?"

"Blaine Field," he said, and now he had both her hands in his. "I was ordered up here last week from Alabama. The point is, where'd you come from?"

"Home," Bitsy said. "That is, Cousin Bert's farm. You see Mother and Stant and I came to live out here when Dad was sent overseas."

"Well, what d'you know about that?" Byrd said, his hands still holding Bitsy's and his eyes on her face. "Why don't you keep a fellow posted? Boy, I'd have been glad to know that when I got ordered away from Alabama. I didn't think I knew a soul in this state."

A quick answer flashed through Bitsy's mind. Byrd hadn't been so glad to see her in Sea Cliff. "That Close kid." His words to Josh Asprey rang in her ears. "She's still wet behind the ears." She tried to say something, but now Byrd was pulling her toward the soda fountain.

"This is really swell," he said, and the enthusiasm in his voice was obviously genuine. "We've got to celebrate with a Coke or something."

For a second Bitsy hesitated. She could see that two or three high-school girls at the soda counter were watching her and the tall young pilot who had greeted her like a long-lost friend. No matter what Byrd had said or thought, it would be fun to have a soda with him now. She turned toward him, but as she caught a glimpse of the clock she stopped short. Quarter past four! If she walked her fastest now she wouldn't be able to get back to the farm until after five, and that meant she would have only a half-hour before supper in which to husk corn and feed the geese.

"I can't," she said suddenly. "I've got some husking to do. I've got to get back to the farm."

"Husking?" Byrd laughed down at her. "What is this, a husking bee or something?"

Bitsy wanted to lie, to cover it up so that he wouldn't laugh at her, but it was too late for that. "It's just plain work," she said aggressively. "I'm getting paid by the stack and I'm going to buy a bicycle."

"Good girl," Byrd said; "but if you haven't got the

bicycle yet I'm taking you home. I don't have to be at the Field until five and I've borrowed a car."

It was fun to roll over the bright cement road that seemed so long in the jolting bus and even longer when you were walking over it alone. And it was fun talking to Byrd now that none of the Sea Cliff crowd were around to make you feel frozen and blockheaded. He was really glad to see her too. He had been crazy about Alabama and had been disgusted when he had been transferred to an entirely new outfit at Blaine Field. He didn't know a soul in the place and it was good to see an old friend again.

They were nearly back at the farm when Bitsy saw the little pigs scampering along the side of the road. There were six of them, not over two months old and without the sow. They must have slipped out through that hole in the fence by the mailbox. Bruce had talked about mending it yesterday, but he had probably forgotten it or put it off as he so often did.

"Stop!" she said, and Byrd stepped on the brake. "Tim's pigs! They oughtn't to be out here."

Byrd looked first at Bitsy and then at the pigs and put back his head and laughed. "Listen," he said. "Pigs is pigs and this state's infested with 'em. You can't tell me you know these personally and that they belong to your cousin. They might have come from the farm across the way, from any one of a dozen farms."

The little pigs were almost out of sight by now, the small, long-legged runt galloping desperately behind as he tried to keep up with his brothers. If they got to the crossroads where the traffic was heavy, they would surely get run over. "Of course they're Tim's," Bitsy snapped. "He's the only one near here that has Chester Reds. Everybody else has Hampshires."

"Quite the farmer, aren't you?" Byrd said, but by now Bitsy was out of the car.

"You turn around and cut after them," she ordered. "Keep 'em headed back until I get down there."

Chuckling to himself, Byrd did as he was told. They caught up with the pigs, but even then their work was cut out for them. The biggest pig dashed straight ahead while the two smaller ones squeezed under a fence and ran squealing toward a strange barn. "You stop that one," Bitsy ordered, and the next moment she had crawled under the fence and was chasing full tilt across the newly harrowed field.

It was heavy going over the muddy field, and the pigs were quicker than they looked. Finally she caught up with them and herded them back toward the fence. She could see Byrd, neat and immaculate, in the middle of the road chasing the rest of the pigs toward the farm. "I stopped 'em," he said. "Must be the football player in me."

He looked over at her, laughing, and for the first time Bitsy was aware of how she must look. Her skirt was stiff with burrs, her hair was all over the place, and she could see the shine on her own nose. "I've got to get them back," she said, and trotted along the road while Byrd got into his car and followed after her. It wasn't until the pigs were finally headed down the lane toward

Bricklow that she turned toward Byrd. He was pushing on his horn now and beckoning madly. She tried to pull down her sweater and straighten her hair as she went over to him, but he didn't seem to have noticed how she looked. "I've got to get back to the Field," he said. "But I want to know when I can come to see you again."

"Come for supper on Sunday," Bitsy said, and the minute the words were out of her mouth she wished that she hadn't spoken. Tracy and Flossie Larson and some of Bruce's friends were coming over for a buffet supper. Cousin Bert had said she was to ask anyone she wanted, but how could Byrd possibly be expected to enjoy a party like that? "That is, come if you want——" she began, but Byrd had already stepped on the accelerator.

"I'll be there," he said, and saluted crisply. "Yes ma'am, Father Brown, I'll be there, and I'm coming early."

~~~~~~

XI

Words Left Unsaid

THE FOLLOWING SUNDAY MORNING Bitsy realized even before she was fully awake that something important was happening. She pushed down the homemade patchwork quilt, and as she heard the busy clatter of pots and pans in the kitchen she remembered what it was. Today was the day they were having the supper party and Byrd Gaylord was coming to it.

Bitsy hurried through dressing and went downstairs. Sunday mornings they had breakfast in the dining room instead of the kitchen. Usually they lingered over the good crisp waffles and the small farm sausages, but this morning was different. Both the boys were outside already and Margaret was helping Cousin Bertha shred cabbage in the kitchen. "Plenty of work to a buffaye supper," Cousin Bertha said pleasantly. "At least if you want all the men to feel well fed."

Bitsy nodded and felt like a snob because she couldn't help wincing inwardly at the way Cousin Bert said "buffet." She helped herself to the crisp, buttery waffles and went in to join her mother, who was the only person left

121

in the dining room. "Bert certainly wants you to have a good time," Mrs. Close said. "She's been up since half-past five baking ham and making cream puffs and heaven knows what all."

Margaret came over just then to clear the extra dishes and heard Mrs. Close's last sentence. "It's going to be the spread of the year," she said. "Only Mrs. Crane's Thanksgiving dinner could beat it."

"Do they still have a square dance at the firehouse before Thanksgiving?" Mrs. Close asked. "It used to be a wonderful way to work up an appetite for turkey."

"They still have it," Margaret said. "Tim was talking about it just the other day. He wants to take Bitsy."

Tim hadn't mentioned it to her, but Bitsy felt pleased anyway. Tim never said or did anything particularly complimentary, but it was plain that he liked her and that all the rest of the family knew it. In fact, from that first evening when she had put on the old blue cotton and Tim had liked it they had all acted as though she were some sort of glamour girl. Even Cousin Bert, who scolded her for being late and seemed to make a point of showing her how spoiled she was, had gone out of her way to tell her that she had heard that all the boys in her class wanted to date her.

Right now, when Bitsy went out to the barn to feed her geese, Tim was waiting for her. He stood looking down at the small pen in which they kept the young pigs that Bitsy had found along the road. Five of them had been turned out but one of them was left behind.

"He sprained his leg," Tim said. "I guess when he was getting under those fences."

"The poor little fellow," Bitsy said, watching the small pig run three-legged toward the trough. The little pig was still plump and round, but his straight tail and awkward leg made him look crestfallen and pathetic.

"Would you like to have him?" Tim said suddenly. "He'll need to be fed separately from the others or they won't give him a chance at the trough. He'll be some trouble now, but he'll be worth money by spring. I owe you that for getting them all back."

"You're a peach," Bitsy said. "You don't owe me anything, but I'd love to have the pig if you're sure it's all right."

Tim said nothing more, but as he moved the pig into an unused stall where it could be by itself, his sunburned face looked pleased.

As Bitsy saw his expression she felt a pang of remorse at the way she had accepted the geese from him a few weeks before. At first it had seemed a nuisance to care for them, but gradually it had become as routine as brushing her teeth. Right now those geese were a lot more than just a chore. They were a business venture that would pay for part of the bicycle!

From the barn Bitsy went straight up to her own room to get ready for church. The weather was crisp and cold now and every morning the ground was white and hard with frost. Fall weather had come and fall clothes. She knew what to wear now and what was expected of her on the farm and at school.

She liked the big high school since that first strangeness had worn off, but what she did there never seemed so important as what she did on the farm. It was partly because she had started in the senior year that she felt rootless and slightly homesick for Miss Fair's, but it was even more because what she did after school was so absorbing.

Tim used a lot of the things on the farm that he had learned in his agricultural course at school, and his Four-H Club met there on Friday afternoons. The science teacher was the one who had first interested both Tim and Tracy Larson in hybrid corn, but to Bitsy the school and farm stayed as two entirely separate worlds, with the farm world infinitely newer and more enthralling.

She smiled to herself as she thought of her lonely walk that first day when she couldn't imagine what she could ever find to do at Bricklow. Why, now that she was earning money and caring for some of the animals she felt more completely occupied than she had ever been before in her life.

The warm, secure feeling of really belonging grew as the day wore on. Bitsy felt it especially at church. They began with the hymn *Once to Every Man and Nation,* which was one of her favorites. She had always liked singing hymns but found that now that the prayers and the service were really familiar they were equally enjoyable. She looked around her, trying to decide why this service seemed so much more moving and genuine than any she had attended in New York. Perhaps it was the

simple red-brick building or the sincerity of the quiet,
weather-beaten minister.

As they bent down for the second prayer, Bitsy caught
a glimpse of her mother's face, sad and lovely, and once
more utterly unguarded, the way it had been when she
had seen her asleep in the tourist cabin. "She's just plain
good," Bitsy thought, and a lump caught at the back of
her throat. "Oh, dear God, make Dad come home all
right and make me decent and brave and honest in the
meantime."

The congregation was singing again now. *"Dear Lord
and Father of Mankind, forgive our fev'rish ways!"* Bitsy
looked over the congregation as she sang. They were
farming people mostly: big weathered men with sunburned necks that stood out mahogany red over their
white collars. Beside them were their neat, hard-working
wives and a surprisingly large sprinkling of children.

> *"In simple trust, like theirs who heard,
>   Beside the Syrian sea,"*

The voice behind Bitsy was a full, clear alto, and she
knew it was Margaret's.

> *"The gracious calling of the Lord,
>   Let us, like them, without a word,
>   Rise up and follow Thee."*

The disciples were just this sort of people, Bitsy
thought, suddenly transfixed. That's why it makes so
much sense. Farmers, fishermen. People close to the earth.
But after luncheon there was nothing simple or un-

complicated about the farm. Cousin Bertha worked in the kitchen calling out orders through the window like a drum major. "Bruce, I want a really good-sized pumpkin. Tim, you haven't brought in nearly enough wood. Stanty, there's no need of getting your Sunday clothes that dirty."

Bitsy ran upstairs giggling, but a little shiver of apprehension touched her spine. They were all good people on the farm. She liked Bruce and Margaret and even Cousin Bert in her mail-order cotton dress, but she wondered how Byrd would feel about them. Mother was the only one who could be counted on to do the right thing, and she was working so hard that she mightn't even come to the party.

When the time came it went off a thousand times better than Bitsy could have expected, and she had to admit that it was largely Byrd's doing. He hadn't been able to borrow a car and he came in later than the others. The Bateses and the Bauers, two young farm couples who were friends of Margaret's, were already there. The girls sat talking to Cousin Bert while their husbands, scrubbed and uncomfortable looking, stood silent beside Bruce. Tracy Larson had come without Flossie, who had a cold, and in a few minutes he and Tim had disappeared into the barn. It's going to be a dud, Bitsy decided after she had tried vainly to get one of the farmers to talk. It's never going to jell at all.

Then Byrd had arrived, handsomer, jollier than ever, and more sure of a good welcome. "I hope you don't disapprove of hitchhikers, Mrs. Crane," he told Cousin

Bertha when they went into the dining room. "But I missed out on lunch and I was just too hungry to walk all the way."

Hungry boys were balm to Cousin Bertha's soul, and she melted instantly. "I like to see young men eat well," she said approvingly as Byrd held out his plate for more of her home-cured ham and potato salad. "Except for Tim most boys nowadays don't do more than pick. Now when my father was a young man people really had appetites."

Byrd was equally successful with Mrs. Close. He had remembered that she was an artist, and his questions were so flattering and sensible that she quite forgot to go back to the library to work. "They're quite a few painters over at the Field," he said once. "Doing animated cartoons for the rookie pilots and mechanics."

The next moment Joe Bates asked how they made the cartoons. His wife turned to tell Bruce about a movie they had seen last night, and from then on the conversation buzzed over the table like a drove of contented bees.

They talked about the Field, the war, the shortage of farm labor. Bitsy chattered to Bruce and Joe Bates while she passed the thick brown muffins and made sure they had enough of Cousin Bertha's best relish. "This has everything on the farm in it except the mules," she said; "and Cousin Bert couldn't catch them." The men roared, and when Byrd looked around at the sound Bitsy had the assured, comfortable feeling of being a wit.

"When are you going to talk to me?" Byrd demanded when she passed him the rich, heavily frosted cake.

"There's a time for everything," Bitsy said, "and yours will come." It was funny how much easier it was to talk to people in snatches when you had to see that they were fed and the empty plates cleared than when you were just sitting around a table with nothing to do but be amusing.

When they went into the living room after supper, the conversation changed. Cousin Bertha said something about the sermon that morning and it turned out that young Mrs. Gates taught in the Sunday school. Bitsy went out to help Margaret wash the dishes, and a few minutes later Byrd followed her into the kitchen. When Margaret left to show the Bauers Bruce's study they were alone for the first time all evening. "Can't fit into the conversation in the living room," Byrd said. "It's a long time since I've had a go at the gospel, and I bet it isn't in your line either."

It was on the tip of Bitsy's tongue to say that she had been to church only that morning, but she squelched the idea. "Let's leave them to their Sunday meeting," Byrd said. "Come on out and show me the farm."

" 'Then lettest thou thy servant depart in peace,' " Bitsy quoted as Byrd took the plates out of her hand and ushered her toward the door.

"You imp," Byrd grinned approvingly. "I knew you weren't the psalm-singing kind."

Bitsy felt suddenly mean and disloyal. The church that these people went to made sense. It filled an immensely important part in their lives, and she had felt the power and the glory of it only that morning. She wanted to say something, to explain, to defend, but when she looked up into Byrd's good-looking face above the smart uniform, she lost her courage.

"Hi, Admiral!" Stanty shouted, and he pounced out from the corncrib to join them.

Bitsy switched on the barn lights. She was glad Stanty was with them. With him around there was no point in trying to say anything about the church, and she was relieved. They passed the fragrant banks of hay and the piles of yellow corn. "This took some work," she said, but now Byrd had gone off hand in hand with Stanty to see the pigs.

He's sweet with kids, Bitsy told herself, as though she were defending him in front of Cousin Bert. He's natural and kind and really thoughtful with them.

"Th-this is Bitsy's pig." Stanty's voice carried through the high-ceilinged barn. "Her geese are over there. If you married her I bet she'd give 'em to you."

"Stanty!" Bitsy called, her face red. She knew she was a fool to mind, but she felt almost weak with confusion.

Byrd was perfectly equal to the situation. "Young Stanty's got a good practical approach," he said, taking her arm. "Always like to see a man standing up for another man's rights. What else is there?"

Bitsy took him over to the loaded corncribs that were built into the side of the barn. "Four hundred and eight bushels," she said, and there was pride in her voice. "It took us all of October, but Tim and I did almost all of it. It isn't hybrid, but it's good dry corn. Trace Larson had some of it tested and it was only 17 per cent moisture."

"That right?" Byrd said, and stifled a yawn. Bitsy led the way back to where the two mules were munching their hay. Now that she had been on the farm for two months every detail of the barn, the fat Hereford cattle, the two milking cows, and even the fowl, were tied up with something that she and Tim had done. It was all fascinating to her, but it didn't thrill Byrd. She could feel his interest slipping away like a fish from a hook and led him back to the house.

The rest of the guests were just leaving, and Bruce and Mary Gates were talking about the Thanksgiving square dance.

Byrd brightened visibly. "A party?" he said. "Sounds like fun. When does it come off?"

Bruce told him about it while Tim went to get the guests' hats and coats. "How about your going with me?" Byrd said, and seemed to take it for granted that Bitsy would.

Bitsy was just starting to answer when Tim reappeared from the depths of the hall closet. His hair had been rumpled reaching for the coats and he looked younger and gawkier than ever. "Bitsy's going with me," he said sturdily. "I bought two tickets yesterday."

Byrd laughed, and for one terrible moment Bitsy was afraid he was going to run his hand through Tim's hair the way he did through Stanty's. "O.K.," he said good-naturedly. "You got there first. Any objection to my going stag?"

~~~~~~

XII

Peppery and Cute

THE WEEKS before Thanksgiving were the busiest Bitsy ever remembered. The second of November it turned really cold, and the countryside that had been so green and rich only a few days ago had a new bare look to it. Houses on the way to school that Bitsy hadn't noticed before suddenly appeared now that the trees were whittled down to skeletons.

They had the corn all in and Bruce had paid her five dollars and forty-five cents for her work. She was wondering where she could possibly make the rest of the money for the bicycle when Margaret came home with a suggestion. Mrs. Larson had come into the library only that morning and had said that Flossie needed help with her Latin. She had a condition to make up for the freshman course she had flunked before switching to the Home Economics Department. If Bitsy wanted to take it on she could probably make a few dollars at that.

Flossie turned out to be a dull but docile pupil. She had no particular grounding, and Bitsy found that they spent most of their time going over the grammar and vocabulary that she had missed last year. It was uninteresting work in itself, but Bitsy discovered that it made her own Latin, which had always been her best subject, living and real. One evening as she was walking home from a session with Flossie she looked over the broad, barren sweep of wintry fields and a line from Vergil's *Georgics* suddenly came into her head: "Then winter shuts up the fields with frost."

For the first time she appreciated how perfect the description was. Those fields were indeed "shut" by winter. It was queer how many things like the church service, the Bible, the Lang translation of Theocritus they had read last year at Miss Fair's had seemed dull and obscure in New York and now, in the country, were suddenly poignant and clear.

It was bitter cold, and she ran down the frosty lane with her hands stuffed in her pockets. She was tempted to go straight to the house, but Tim was teaching her to milk now and there was no point missing an evening, so she jogged across the yard to the barn. It was even later than she had thought. Steve had already gone home, and Tim had just finished milking. He put down the pail when he saw her and hurried forward, his face shining. "I bought the bull calf," he said. "The one I told you about."

For a moment Bitsy was nonplused, but finally she remembered that on one of the cold, pale mornings when they had been working over the corn Tim had said that he was going to invest all his savings in a pure-bred

Hereford calf. Bruce had tried to urge him to buy a new secondhand tractor on the installment plan, but Tim had been adamant. "The bull's half the herd," he had said. "If we want better beef cattle, the quickest way to do it is to buy a better bull."

Right now, as Bitsy stared over the high pen at the young bull, he didn't seem very impressive. He was still quite young and amazingly chunky and solid. His coat was glossy and his white masked head was a handsome shape, but other than that he didn't seem very distinguished.

"He's kind of squat-looking," she said. "Sort of like Steve sitting down."

Tim chuckled as he led the bull out to show him off. "He's good and cobby built," he said. "That's his best point. Legs never get shorter, and a long-legged, rangy bull's no good. He cost fifty dollars."

"Fifty dollars!" The words shot from Bitsy's lips. It seemed years since the time when forty or fifty dollars had been an amount you charged on the family's bill and forgot. It had taken her the better part of two months to make fifteen dollars, and she knew Tim earned money almost as slowly as she did. Besides that, most of his savings had been wiped out by his share of the mule they had bought to replace Rossy. "Fifty dollars! How're you ever going to get that back?"

"Two years from this spring," Tim said briskly. "You wait and see the calves we'll get. And three years from now I'll show him at the cattle show at Meudon. That is,

I will," he said, and now his voice was suddenly less confident, "if I'm not in the Army and they still have the show."

Bitsy helped him feed the hogs and then fed her own geese and the young pig before she went into the house. Your ideas about lots of things changed on the farm, but your attitude toward ready cash changed the most of all. She went upstairs and putting down her schoolbooks counted out the crumpled dollars and the pieces of silver. She still needed five dollars to get the bicycle, and that seemed almost as far away as the whole sum had been six weeks ago. She had just given Flossie her last Latin lesson that afternoon. Unless somebody else turned up with a bright idea, she was just going to have to wait until spring brought back more work for everyone.

The next afternoon was still bitter cold, and she came home directly on the school bus. Stanty had stayed late at school. Mother had gone over to have supper with some friends who had just been stationed at the Field, and Cousin Bertha and Margaret were working out in the kitchen. The barn seemed empty and dull without Tim, so that Bitsy drifted into the kitchen to see what was going on.

Cousin Bertha was making fruit cake for the holidays. She stirred busily at the stove while Margaret cut up lemon peel at the kitchen table. Margaret's face looked whiter than usual and her full, gentle mouth was unnaturally set. Bitsy had the uncomfortable feeling that she had interrupted something important. She helped herself to a cookie out of the cookie jar and was just about to go upstairs when Cousin Bertha left to go down cellar. The moment she was out of the room Margaret pushed the lemon peel away from her with a little gesture of impatience. "I wish I had my own kitchen," she said fiercely.

"But can't you?" Bitsy asked, surprised at the vehemence in her voice. "Cousin Bertha's always talking about how you and Bruce are going to add on to his study, and he's had a good year. He said only last night that he'd made a hundred dollars more on the hogs than he expected."

"Priorities," Margaret said bitterly. "It's the war. Like everything else. We used up the building allowance on a s-silo."

The next moment, to Bitsy's horror, her head was down on the kitchen table and she was crying like a tired child. "Oh, Margaret." Bitsy's voice was quick with sympathy. "Margaret dear, don't do that."

Margaret looked up, and the big tears rolled down her cheeks unnoticed. "Bruce got another notice from the draft board. He's to report for another physical next month."

"Does Cousin Bert know?" Bitsy asked, suddenly remembering the strained atmosphere she had felt when she first had come into the kitchen.

"That's the whole trouble," Margaret said. "She won't face the idea that he'll ever have to go. She just thinks I've gotten nervous and jittery because of the baby. And Bruce won't talk about it because he's so afraid of being turned down!"

Margaret was crying again, her shoulders shaking and her dark head down. If only Mum were home, Bitsy thought miserably, but she knew there was no chance of her getting home until after supper.

They heard Cousin Bertha's firm step on the stairs, and Margaret turned around like a trapped animal. "I can't just sit here and talk about the things Bruce is going to do next spring and the spring after," she said fiercely, "when I know he won't be here. I just can't bear it!"

"Come on upstairs," Bitsy said quickly. Cousin Bertha wasn't such a difficult person to live with, but her blindness to Margaret's gnawing fear was making real trouble. "You look awfully tired. Come on up and rest before Bruce gets home. I'll help Cousin Bert."

It was almost like comforting Stanty, Bitsy thought as she led Margaret upstairs. Margaret, who usually seemed so much older, so much surer than any of them, was suddenly as limp and helpless as a hurt child. She looked very woebegone as she lay alone on the big, old-fashioned bed. "Maybe Bruce could fix things up," Bitsy suggested. "If he talked it out with his mother she'd just have to understand."

"Bruce mustn't be bothered!" Margaret said, and some of her old assurance came back again. "It's bad enough his wanting to get into the Army and not knowing if he can and being worried about me and the baby at the same time. He hates discussing things with his mother."

Bruce is a pig, Bitsy thought, but she said nothing and leaned down and kissed her cousin-in-law's face. "Everything will be O.K.," she said, without having much conviction that it would be. "Maybe Mum could talk to her."

She went back to the kitchen to finish cutting up the lemon that Margaret had begun. Cousin Bert was more fidgety and bossy than usual. She had apparently settled in her mind that Bitsy was a success socially and that, surprising though it was, she had learned how to be useful on the farm. Once Bitsy was inside the kitchen, though, she seemed determined to show her how woefully little she knew. "Your mother never was much of a housekeeper either," she said once. "Even as a girl she wasn't interested in cooking."

For a moment Bitsy was tempted to answer back: to say that Mother had a reputation all over the country as an artist, that after not having worked professionally for years she had gotten orders for illustrations on her first try. When she looked at Cousin Bertha's worried face, she thought better of it. She just won't admit that Bruce is likely to be a pilot, Bitsy realized. She knows it just as well as Margaret does, but it keeps her courage up to act as though it couldn't happen.

When they had finished drying the last mixing bowls and the spoons, Bitsy was glad that she had held her tongue. Cousin Bert had just been scolding her for not drying the pots and pans thoroughly enough when suddenly she interrupted herself to ask how much more money Bitsy needed for her bicycle.

"Five dollars and twenty-three cents," Bitsy said. "Why?"

"I'll give you the money today," Cousin Bert said, "and take four of your geese when they're big enough. That'll pay for their feed, too, and everything'll be settled. I'm glad you were nice to Margaret."

Bitsy was so stunned she could hardly speak. Cousin Bert marched over to the kitchen clock where she kept her money and counted the five dollars and twenty-three cents into Bitsy's hand. "There," she said. "Get the bicycle tomorrow. But you'd better be sure it's a good one before you spend that much."

"Thanks!" Bitsy got out. "Oh, thanks loads."

It wasn't until she was halfway upstairs that she thought again about Cousin Bert's unexpected, "I'm glad you were nice to Margaret." She wants to be kind, Bitsy realized uncomfortably. She'd really like to be the way Mum is, who just sort of lets off kindness, but she's afraid of letting down the mask that keeps up her nerve. Bitsy put away the money with a little sigh. Life was complicated and people were complicated and the war was making it all more complicated than ever.

She felt uneasy about supper, but it went off quite smoothly. Margaret still looked suspiciously red about the eyes, but now that Bruce was back she seemed to draw an almost physical confidence from his presence. He was more absent-minded than ever with his mother and Tim, but to Margaret he was gentle and amusing. Once, as Margaret passed him the muffins, Bitsy saw him give her hand a quick, reassuring little grip, and she looked away, feeling as guilty as though she had read someone else's love letter.

Cousin Bert was more than ever concerned with the food and everybody's eating enough. The conversation was mostly between her and Tim about rationing and shortages, and Bitsy was glad when the meal was over. "Don't forget the square dance is on Wednesday," Tim said as he and Bitsy separated after supper to do their homework. "You've got to be all set to step out lively. The Larsons and Pete and Jeff and the Pesky girls'll make a pretty good eight."

Bitsy nodded, but she didn't really put her mind on the party until she was getting dressed for it two evenings later. It was funny when she remembered how at Miss Fair's the girls had talked and thought about the subscription dances they were going to until when the day actually came she was so afraid of being a failure that her legs would hardly take her into the ballroom. People had talked about this party and she had looked forward to it, but sort of the way you did to a Christmas tree or a children's party where there wasn't any chance of being a wallflower. Maybe I've just gotten overconfident, Bitsy thought, looking at her own reflecton in the bathroom mirror. She had on her bright green skirt and a peasant blouse that belonged to her mother. She tied a matching scarf over her ruddy hair. It really was becoming, but you couldn't always tell. Sometimes you looked razzy in your own room, she thought, and then when you were actually at the party and saw the other girls, you looked like a gawk.

She went downstairs and Tim stared at her open-mouthed. "You look swell," he said, but Bitsy knew now that that didn't mean much. He was like his mother. He had settled in his own mind the first day that Bitsy was a smoothie and nothing she said or did would change him. But what would the others think? And how about Byrd, who had looked down even on the Sea Cliff girls, would he think she was up to snuff?

"You look O.K. yourself," she said, and it was certainly true. Tim had left off his stiff Sunday suit that was so outgrown and was wearing a pair of brown corduroy trousers and a bright plaid shirt that really fitted. He pulled on a heavy sweater and put his hunting cap on the side of his head. It wasn't the way Bitsy was used to seeing boys dressed for parties in New York but it was certainly becoming. Tim's got style, she thought, looking at her cousin appraisingly. He's got an eye for things you wouldn't suspect his caring about.

They passed the small gilt-framed portrait of Great-Great-Uncle Crane in his bottle-green coat and white stock as they went through the hall. He had style, too, Bitsy thought, thinking of the handsome library and the spacious lines of the brick part of the house. Tim's style's different, but it's part of the same thing.

Twenty minutes after Bitsy got to the party she knew that she needn't have worried an instant about being a dud. For the first time in her life she had the warm, delirious sensation of being the undisputed belle of the ball. The very first set Tim and Tracy Larson had words as to who was to be her partner, and when she said a little later that she didn't know one of the calls, three boys, one of whom she hadn't even met, offered to teach her.

She was even aware of it during the intermission. Tim took her back to the row of seats that had been placed around the firehouse wall, and boys seemed to spring up from everywhere. They grouped themselves around her in twos and threes. Tim made some quip about there not being enough seats. "Oh, get back the fire horses," Bitsy said; "let's all sit on those."

Laughter greeted her words as though they had been the last thing in wit and humor. It isn't what you say, Bitsy thought suddenly, remembering the moments around the Sea Cliff pool, it's when you say them. Once you're a wow you can say any dumb thing and everybody thinks it's a knockout.

At ten o'clock she went into the back part of the firehouse that served as a ladies' room and there she tasted the full measure of her success. Her conquest was so complete, so entirely apart from just having an ordinarily good time, that the other girls treated her almost as though she were Greta Garbo or Hedy Lamarr. "You do look cute," Rose Pesky said enviously, and made room for her in front of the cracked mirror that had been set up on one of the chemical fire extinguishers. Bitsy smiled at Rose in the mirror and Rose smiled back. The girls were aware of her success, Bitsy realized, but they didn't really resent her the way she would have been resented in Sea Cliff because here there were plenty of boys to go around.

"Bitsy certainly panics the men," Flossie said, and sighed with the hopeless admiration she had shown when Bitsy had easily translated some passage of Caesar that was beyond her.

"I guess that's what you get from living in New York,"

a small, fair-haired girl called Dot Kramer put in. "I'm glad you don't make any passes at my Jimmy."

Bitsy giggled and put her compact back into her purse. Dot Kramer and Jimmy Blum were one of the things that made this party as different from a New York subscription dance as the firehouse was from the Ritz-Carlton. They were "going together," were engaged really, and their status was as definite and settled as though they had been married for years. You could dance with Jimmy or talk to him, but it was almost like talking to your brother or somebody else's husband.

"You girls going to prink all night?" Tim poked his head in around the big door. "They're just starting up *Pull Her Away and Yank Her Back.*"

"Oh boy," Bitsy said, and led the chattering group back into the main hall. "That's the best call of all."

"Another set! Another set! Room for one more set," the caller shouted. Tim took her hand to pull her into the square and just then she saw Byrd!

He looked more tailored and military than ever next to all these high-school boys in sweaters and pants. He was taller than most of them and older and much more assured. "I guess this is my dance," he said airily, and moved toward Bitsy without so much as looking at Tim.

For a moment Tim said nothing. He looked suddenly like a tough, wiry little fox terrier next to a sleek setter. "Look here," he began, but suddenly Bitsy settled it.

"I'm dancing this with Tim," she said. "You should have gotten here earlier, Lieutenant Gaylord."

"Bitsy, you're a peach," Tim said as they swung to the call of "Promenade!" "Promenade!"

Bitsy answered the quick squeeze of his rough hands, but her eyes were on Byrd standing watching them from the side of the room. It's just what he needed, she thought triumphantly. It's just exactly right. The trouble at Sea Cliff was that I'd have given anything even to have him speak to me.

They finished that square and there was an interlude of round dances. Tim and some of the other boys who didn't know how to waltz stood over in a corner all together. Byrd swung Bitsy off with quick, skillful steps, but before they had reached the corner of the room Tracy Larson had cut in on them and Jeff soon cut in on him.

Byrd cut back again, looking slightly annoyed. "I had something I wanted to tell you," he said. "There's just a chance of my being sent down to Washington for a month on a very important——"

He had no chance to finish because now Jimmy Blum had cut in and was whirling Bitsy back into the center of the room. Bitsy had the last square dance with her original set and then went to put on her coat while Tim went out with Tracy to get the Larsons' car. The green coat felt as warm and smart as it had that first reckless day in September. Bitsy felt almost breathless when she thought of how far that much money would go on the farm. She went outside and stood by the front door with the welcome coolness of the fresh night air on her cheeks. She was still thinking about the day when Dad had left to go overseas when Byrd suddenly appeared out of the darkness and stood beside her. "Listen," he said. "Don't you ever give a soldier any time any more?"

"You should have come earlier."

"But I couldn't!" Byrd said, his voice suddenly serious. "I was on late duty. I had to take over some of Oakes' work for tomorrow to get here at all."

"That's your tough luck, not mine," Bitsy said pertly, and Byrd took a step forward.

"You've gotten awfully peppery since you've been out in Ohio," he said, looking down at her by the flickering yellow lamplight. She looked up at him, laughing, and suddenly he put his arms around her and his strong young face came down to hers. "Awfully peppery and awfully cute," he said, and kissed her on the mouth.

~~~~~~~~~~~~~~~~~~~~~~~~~~~~~~~~~~~~~~

XIII

He Loves Me

Aʟʟ ᴛʜᴇ ɴᴇxᴛ ᴅᴀʏ Bitsy went around feeling like a person in a dream. She had gone to sleep with the thought of Byrd's eager face leaning down toward her and she woke with the sound of his husky voice still in her ears. "You've gotten awfully peppery since you've been in Ohio. Awfully peppery and awfully cute."

For a moment, as she pulled on her clothes in the cold, unattractive bathroom, she wondered if she had made a mistake. Maybe he had kissed her because he kissed any girl who would let him. She felt suddenly sick at the thought that she might be cheapened in his eyes. But I couldn't help it, she thought, pulling on her last pair of silk stockings, and now a giggle of reassurance bubbled up within her. It was too quick, and besides I meant it.

She had only just finished breakfast when the telephone rang and Stanty ran in to say that it was Byrd. "Hello," Bitsy began, and the next moment as she heard Byrd's deep voice she knew everything was all right.

"Listen, darling," he said, and she felt as though she were in his arms again in the clear, cold night outside the firehouse. "When am I going to see you?"

"When can you come over?" she asked, her voice suddenly teasing. "Stanty'd love to see you any time."

"I can't get a car," Byrd fumed. "But there's a chance I could borrow a bicycle. Anyway, if you're going to be home I'll get there this evening if I have to crawl."

He loves me! Bitsy thought as she hung up. He loves me, her heart echoed. He loves me, her whole tingling body danced with the knowledge. And I love him. I do so love him.

She wondered if being loved by the right person even changed and improved the way you looked. When she brushed her light-brown hair in front of the old mirror it seemed to curl in just the right places, and the freckles that had irked her so had entirely disappeared. Even the way the family acted toward her seemed new and different.

Tim was no longer blunt and friendly but openly adoring. He admired her and counted on her, she realized, with a quick, uneasy stir at her heart. Something was said about driving the hogs over to a Victory Hog Sale to be held at the Larsons' farm the following week. Cousin Bertha asked Tim how he was going to manage as Steve was to have that day off and Bruce was coming down with a bad cold. "Bitsy'll help," Tim said, and the pride and confidence in his voice made Bitsy feel as though she had already let him down.

She would have said something, but now Cousin Bertha, who never paid compliments, suddenly turned to her and said that she had heard that Bitsy was the belle of the party last night. Bitsy laughed and shook her head, but Margaret nodded approvingly across the table. "You panicked the town," she said. "Why, Bruce heard about it down at the gas station when he ran into Jeff Pflomm."

Even Mrs. Close, who was apt to be too preoccupied to know what was really going on, was definitely impressed. "You seem to be making local history," she said when they had a moment alone in the living room. "Why, Mrs. Larson called up Cousin Bert and they talked about you for five minutes straight."

"The party was fun," Bitsy said, and wondered if Mother guessed just how wonderful it really had been. "Byrd was there toward the end and he wants to come over this evening."

"Too bad he can't come and have some of Bert's turkey," Mother said. "She likes him, and so do I. And all the officers over at the Field spoke so well of him when I went over for lunch with General Harris. He's a nice boy."

He's more than that, Bitsy thought. He's the best-looking, bravest, most attractive man on earth, and he's in love with me.

She was still thinking about it as she sat next to Cousin Bertha at the short Thanksgiving service at ten o'clock. So much had happened, and so quickly. Just three months ago she'd felt like a washout at the Sea Cliff pool. She would have given anything just to have Josh Asprey, whom she didn't even like, ask her to a party. Now every boy she met wanted her to do things and Byrd, the same Byrd Gaylord who was the smoothest man in Sea Cliff, was in love with her.

" 'For he that hath, to him shall be given,' " Mr. Miller's deep voice boomed from the pulpit, and Bitsy raised startled eyes.

" 'For he that hath, to him shall be given; and he that hath not, from him shall be taken even that which he hath.' " It was true! Even about things like beaux and parties. Here in Ohio she hadn't thought about social life but had put her mind on farm work, and just as she was succeeding with that she found herself a belle. And as soon as she was a belle, Byrd, who hadn't even noticed her at home, was in love with her.

The spell lasted all through the day. She and Tim went on a long walk before their big Thanksgiving dinner. "You were swell not to let that guy Gaylord cut in last night," Tim said once, but she brushed him aside and started talking about the pig, Caesar, that had almost entirely gotten over his lameness.

Somehow the only imperfect moments in the day were when she thought of Tim and Byrd at the same time. Tim's only a kid, she told herself. He's six months younger than I am and my third cousin. Anything I do with him doesn't matter. He's just as much of a kid as Stanty.

When they got back to the house, there was a message that Jeff Pflomm had called up and there was a package that had been left for Bitsy by Tracy Larson. It was a homemade corsage of oak leaves and one big chrysanthemum. "I wish I'd thought of it," Tim said humbly. "But I've never bothered much about girls before."

"You've done a lot nicer things than that," Bitsy said, and touched him lightly on the shoulder. "Giving me the pig and all sorts of things."

Tim's open face was suddenly as radiant as a small boy's who had just gotten the present he had given up hoping for. All through the long Thanksgiving dinner he was so lighthearted and amusing that the whole family laughed at him. It was a tremendous meal, with all of Cousin Bert's best cooking and canning. Besides the family, there were some quiet farming cousins from the far side of Meudon; Great-Uncle Benjamin whom Bitsy had never seen before; and two officers stationed at the Field whom Mrs. Close had known in New York.

One of them, a Major French, had been a fashionable portrait painter until he had been commissioned in the Army Air Force and found himself working on animated cartoons intended to teach rookies to fly. With his long white face and drooping walrus mustache he still looked effeminate and out of place in uniform. He was apparently amused at himself in the role of soldier and kept them in gales of laughter at his description of his difficulties. "This business of being saluted is bad enough," he said in his high, precise voice, "but when you have to remember to salute your superiors as well, it's most confusing."

He went on to tell them of his experiences the first time he met General Harris, the commandant of the field. Harris was a West Pointer, a career soldier, and a martinet. He was a bachelor and, though undeniably an able leader, his formal mannerisms were just meat to a mimic like French.

"Harris knows planes," Bruce said once, and Bitsy realized that it was the first time either he or Margaret had spoken.

"Of course, of course," French agreed instantly. "An exceptionally able man. It's just that in Paris or Greenwich Village I never ran into anyone who looked as though he were about to ask if I'd changed my underwear and remembered to brush my teeth."

During the laugh that followed Bitsy had time to look at both Margaret and Bruce. Bruce really did have a bad cold and was obviously feeling miserable. He didn't even try to listen any more but sat staring moodily out at the bare apple trees through the dining-room window. Margaret was equally silent, though she was as ready as ever to pass anything that anyone wanted or help take the empty plates off the table.

Once, as she passed Bitsy's chair, Bitsy realized with a start how much she had changed since she had first seen her. Then it had been impossible to guess about the baby, and now Margaret's swollen and ponderous figure was very obvious. "She's a good big girl," Byrd had said lightly the night of the supper party, but she was even larger now. Her body was very heavy and her white, drained face looked as though it were an effort for her to move.

The guests ate even to Cousin Bertha's satisfaction,

and when they finally left around half-past five she fairly purred with pleasure. "A good Thanksgiving," she said, and for once made no move toward the kitchen. "I'm glad Mr. Roosevelt went back to the old date."

Byrd didn't appear until about half-past seven, after they had all the dishes cleared away and the house in order. His cheeks were red with cold and he was hungry after his bicycle ride. None of the rest of the family even wanted to think about food so Bitsy took him out into the kitchen to get him some supper.

"You're a lot handier than most girls," he said when she set a big plate of cold turkey and warmed-up yams in front of him.

"You should hear Cousin Bert," Bitsy said, and giggled as she gave him a glass of milk and the last of the pumpkin pie. "She thinks I'm mentally deficient around the kitchen."

"Rats!" Byrd said with his mouth full. "You're wonderful. I guess it's because you're more grown-up than most girls your age. You really have something on your mind besides parties."

"How about the time you said——" Bitsy began, her mind on that awful moment when she had heard Byrd and Josh Asprey through the bathhouse wall. The next minute, as she looked at Byrd happily munching away on the food she had given him, she changed her mind. You oughtn't to listen to anything you overheard and besides it didn't seem to matter any more. The Bitsy who had sat frozen around the Sea Cliff pool was so completely gone that she didn't even owe her the loyalty of feeling uncomfortable. "How about another biscuit?" Bitsy said. "I could heat one for you in a minute."

"It'd be swell," Byrd said. "I've been working all day trying out a new plane. In case you're interested this is my Thanksgiving dinner."

Half an hour later they were still in the kitchen talking about a party that was to be given at the officers' club when Tim came into the room. "I wish I could borrow a car to take you," Byrd said, without noticing Tim. "But with the rubber and all, it's darn near impossible."

"How about bicycling over?" Bitsy said. "I got my bike last week and if you could borrow one again, we could bike over."

"Bitsy, you're a knockout," Byrd said. "I don't know another girl who'd suggest that."

Bitsy felt surprised and decidedly smug at Byrd's enthusiasm. Actually she liked the idea of the ride with Byrd before the party, but there wasn't any point of making too much of it. "Of course it's a pretty long ride," she began coyly.

"Bitsy, you darling," Byrd said, and moved toward her when Tim spoke up for the first time since he had come into the room.

"Don't let her kid you," he said. "She goes that far to school every day and eats it up."

"Well, I think it's very decent of her," Byrd began, but Bitsy hardly heard him. She faced Tim, and a dull, angry red had spread over her face.

"Tim Crane——" she began, but she couldn't go on. Tim was absolutely right, and they both knew it!

It was one of the refreshing things about Tim Crane that when he had something to say he said it and there was no bad taste left afterward. He had caught Bitsy short, called her bluff, and, as far as he was concerned, the matter was closed.

Bitsy was irritated for several days, but it was hard to be cross to Tim. He was so hard-working and concentrated around the farm that it wasn't easy to find time to scold him. Somehow she couldn't stop him in the middle of feeding the pigs, or milking the cows, or cleaning out the stable, to tell him that she still felt angry. And then he was so really thoughtful and generous about the things that meant something to him. It was a week after Thanksgiving that he came home one night with a brand-new light for Bitsy's bicycle. "You'll need it going over to that shindig at the Field," he said, "and on dark mornings going to school."

"Tim, you're a peach," Bitsy said, but Tim had already started to brush the two black Angus calves that were to be sold that week and wasn't listening. He had little time for thanks and compliments himself and he didn't seem to expect them from other people.

The first two weeks in December it was bitingly cold. Bitsy's hands nearly froze on the handlebar of her bike and even the loose woolen mittens that Margaret had given her didn't do much good. Finally the weather broke a little, but the thaw was followed by a heavy snowstorm that made any bicycling impossible.

The first morning of the snow Bitsy woke up when Stanty rushed into her room in his pajamas. "L-look," he sputtered, "out of the window. Isn't it s-s-swell?"

Bitsy blinked in the reflected brightness of her room and looked out of the window onto a white, silent world. "Looks good," she said, and reluctantly pushed back the warm blankets and charged toward her clothes.

She didn't realize just how good it was until a few minutes later when she went over to the barn to feed the animals. Tim was late that morning and there were no tracks in the soft snow ahead of her. Bitsy sniffed the cold, damp air and walked around the barn. She had hardly ever been in the country in winter before and the wonderful, Daniel Boone, exploring feeling that walking through the unbroken whiteness gave her was new and intoxicating.

She saw the crisscross prints of turkey feet and a little further on the small four-footed marks that might have been a chipmunk and grinned to herself. The snow brought a silent spell to the familiar barnyard, as though the whole earth were holding its breath. When she went back to the house, she felt as thrilled and exhilarated as though she had been for a swim in stiff surf, but after the first couple of days the thrill wore off.

The snow didn't get filthy and depressing the way it did in New York, but it made it awfully hard to get around. The roads were rutted and hard, and even the little paths to the chicken coops were slippery and treacherous. A high wind came up, and the small drifts made the barn doors difficult to open. "If it stays like this

you won't be able to go over to the officers' club," Tim
said as they fought their way into the barn one evening.
"Even Admiral Byrd Gaylord couldn't pedal through
a snowdrift."

Bitsy felt cross at Tim's using Stanty's old nickname,
but her irritation about that was as nothing compared
to her numb, frustrated anger about the weather. "Byrd'll
just have to borrow a car," she said. "Or arrange something."

"Four gallons are four gallons," Tim said, and left it at
that.

Now that the biting wind made it impossible to stay
outdoors with any comfort, they were all drawn more
closely together within the walls of the big farmhouse.
Bruce had been down with a really bad cold and fever,
but he was up and around again now and spent most of
his time working over a drawing board. Margaret had
been counting on going to Meudon to see *Mrs. Miniver,*
but when the weather turned too bad for Bruce to go out,
she gave it up without a word. They're used to being
resigned, Bitsy fumed. Weather, or stock dying, or anything else just hits them as something that can't be
helped. They don't even try to find a way out.

But the week before Christmas it turned suddenly
warm and balmy and the snow disappeared almost as
quickly as it had come. For a day or two the roads were
muddy, but a southerly wind cleared up the last of the
wetness. "You're in luck over the weather," Tim told
Bitsy at supper. "Tomorrow'll be as good for bicycling
over to the Field as October."

"Green Christmas makes a full graveyard," Cousin Bert said gloomily. "I like a good, cold December better."

The next morning when Bitsy got up it seemed to be the most perfect day that had ever been. The wind was gone and the sunshine was really warm. The air was soft and springlike and she felt like dancing as she got dressed for the party.

She and Byrd had an easy ride over to the Field and found the party in full swing when they got there. For a moment Bitsy hesitated as Byrd ushered her into the big smoke-filled room. She wouldn't know a soul there, she thought, and wished suddenly that she were back with Tim and Jeff and the high-school crowd.

She was hardly in the room before Major French and the captain who had spent Thanksgiving with them rushed over to shake hands. A few minutes later they and several of Byrd's new friends, tall young officers with wings on their blouses, sat clustered around her. Success was so easy once you had a good start, Bitsy thought. It didn't matter if the first people who went for you were children like Tim or old men like Major French. As long as there was a crowd of males around you, you could say anything that came into your head and people thought you were wonderful.

When it was time to leave, Bitsy felt heady with success. Once outside, the darkness was as soft and enveloping as a spring evening. "You sweet." Byrd took her arm as they walked toward their bicycles. "They were all just crazy about you."

"Boo to you," Bitsy said, and got on her bicycle. "I'll race you down to the main road."

They streaked down the long driveway past the officers' brick quarters, but once they had passed the guard at the gate and turned onto the main road it was hard going. Their bicycle lamps seemed suddenly pale and inadequate in the blinding headlights of the cars that rushed past them. "We've got to get off this," Byrd said, and headed down a narrow country road that ran parallel to the main motor route.

There was no moon, and the warm December evening was utterly black. The road was curving and narrow, and they went along single file with Bitsy in the lead. She had just turned to ask Byrd a question when she saw the blinding flash of motor headlights coming around the next curve!

She swerved to get out of the way and her front wheel skidded on the loose gravel! She struggled to get her balance. She heard the grinding of brakes and Byrd's shout of warning. The next moment she had pitched over into the gutter with Byrd on top of her!

She felt the impact of his body and a tearing pain as his pedal tore into the fleshy part of her leg. A minute later he was up, pulling the bicycle away, his scared face peering down at her. "Bitsy," he got out. "Bitsy, are you all right?"

The driver of the car had roared on, unheeding, and as Bitsy pulled herself up, she saw the red taillight disappear around a bend. She was badly bruised and shaken, but except for the ugly gash in her leg she was unhurt.

"I—I'm all right," she panted, still struggling for the breath that had been knocked out of her. "Were you hurt?"

Byrd shook his head. "I must have landed on you," he said unsteadily. "Oh, my God, Bits, if you'd been badly hurt or—or killed."

Bitsy wasn't badly hurt, but now that it was all over, the sudden fright and shock had left her weak and shivering. "Byrd," she said. "Byrd!" The next minute his strong, reassuring arms were around her and he was kissing her upturned face.

She looked up at him in the circle of the light from the bicycle lamps and kissed his smooth, clean cheeks and his hard young mouth. He was strong, he was safe, and his arms held her from any other harm.

They sat at the edge of the road for a moment without speaking while Bitsy dabbed at the cut on her leg with a handkerchief. Finally Byrd broke the silence. "I've loved you ever since that day in the drugstore," he said. "Ever since I've known you really. But I didn't understand how much it meant until that party at the firehouse. Bitsy, Bitsy, tell me that you love me a little."

"Oh, darling," Bitsy said, and her hand touching the crisp waves of his hair was answer enough.

"I may be transferred any day now," he said, and his face suddenly hardened. "They're pretty sure to send us overseas very soon. But when I get back, Bits, when this mess is all over, we'll plan about getting married."

Byrd's big, capable hand gripped hers, but for the first time she felt no reassurance from his touch. The thought of the war, like a sudden icy draft through a warm room, had chilled her heart. No matter what you did or were planning to do, the menace of it overshadowed the future. Margaret and Bruce were racked by the shadow. Even Tim felt it. "I'll show him, that is if I'm not in the Army and they still have the show." The uncertainty in his voice rang in her ears.

"Oh, Byrd," she whispered, and now every fiber in her body yearned toward him for comfort. "It's all so awful!"

"You darling!" Byrd said, and once more he held her in his arms. "Nothing will happen to me. I'm a fool for luck."

Bitsy moved away from his embrace and together they pulled the bicycles back onto the road. Bitsy's leg had stopped bleeding but she let Byrd tie one of his handkerchiefs around it before they started off. The ride was without further incident, but her aching leg made it seem very long. Byrd would have stayed on after they got to the farmhouse, but Cousin Bert sent him off while Mrs. Close was helping Bitsy to bed. Bitsy gave a little sigh of relief when she heard the front door close behind him. She loved him, he was wonderful, but right now, when she ached all over, it was cozy just to be alone with Mother and Cousin Bert.

Mother bathed her and fussed over her while Cousin Bert dressed her leg. It was only after she was in bed and Mother had turned out the light that Bitsy thought again about Byrd's, "Nothing will happen to me. I'm a fool for luck." She turned over uncomfortably and buried her throbbing head in the pillow. She hadn't meant just that. She hadn't even been thinking of Byrd. It was just as much for Bruce, Margaret, Tim, Trace Larson, even, that she had been afraid. For all of the simple, decent people of her own age who had no idea where the twisted, terrifying future would take them.

~~~~~~

XIV

Country Christmas

THE MORNING AFTER the bicycle accident
Bitsy woke up late. Her leg was stiff and sore and there
was a dull ache in the back of her head. She was just
wondering if she ought to get up when Mother came into
the room with a tray in her hands. "Tim's done your
chores," she said. "And even Cousin Bert thinks you
ought to have breakfast in bed."

Bitsy grinned up at her mother as she nestled back
into the pillows. "Cousin Bert must have been really
worried last night," she said. "I'm not that badly hurt."

Still it was good to be able to lie back in bed and watch
the barnyard without having anything you had to do yourself. Steve passed with a gigantic load of wood on his
shoulders to repair the mangers in the main barn. In a few
minutes Margaret went out to the old Ford, and at exactly
five minutes of nine Stanty flew by on his bicycle.

She knew the pattern of farm life now, and it was all
as familiar and reassuring as pulling on an old coat. She
turned away from the window, her eyes on the flowered
wallpaper and her mind on Byrd. "Byrd. Lieutenant
Byrd Gaylord." Bitsy whispered the name softly aloud.

"Mrs. Byrd Gaylord!" Bitsy closed her eyes with the image of Byrd's handsome young face in front of her.

By the time Mrs. Close came back for the tray Bitsy was fast asleep with her tumbled hair dark against the pillow and a smile on her lips. "Sweet dreams, love," Mrs. Close whispered, and pulled the door softly shut.

It was nearly four o'clock when Bitsy finally woke up. She felt completely made over now, rested and renewed by her long sleep. She got up humming a little tune as she pulled on her clothes. When she got down to the kitchen, Stanty was making paper chains for the Christmas tree while Cousin Bertha put the finishing touches on an apple pie. She looked up and smiled when she saw Bitsy. "Your mother and I decided the only thing you needed was a long sleep," she said. "She's gone over to the library to do some work."

"It was wonderful," Bitsy said, and sat down to the hot broth and the homemade bread that Cousin Bertha set in front of her. "I never slept so long in my life before." She had had no dreams, but now that she was fully awake her mind was on Byrd again. She glanced over at the telephone shelf where Cousin Bertha wrote down messages on scraps of used notepaper. "Did Byr——" she began, but Cousin Bertha interrupted with a firm slam of the oven door.

"He's called up three times," she said, without even looking around. "Maybe he thought you were never going to wake up."

Bitsy laughed. Even Cousin Bertha's little digs seemed

flattering and pleasant. Everything was good now that she knew that Byrd loved her. The very walls of the kitchen seemed brighter and gayer.

"I've finished all my Christmas presents," Stanty announced suddenly. "I've m-made Mums and Grandma Close's and everybody's. All I've got to do is to get 'em wrapped up."

Bitsy's heart gave a little upward beat as she thought of getting a present for Byrd. She had bought some handkerchiefs weeks ago to send in the box Mum had sent out to Dad, but other than that she hadn't even thought about Christmas.

Bitsy sat down opposite Stanty and began to help him make the chains of red and green paper. She had made chains like these years ago when she was six or seven in New York. Since then she had thought it was rather silly except for a little kid. Now, like so many other simple things on the farm, it suddenly made sense. Bought decorations for Christmas were expensive, and it was fun and cheap to make them. Bitsy's fingers flew until Stanty complained that she was using up too much of the green and red paper. She compromised on a sheet of royal purple and set to work again. When you stopped to think about it people shut themselves off from a lot of fun just by having money. On the farm nobody laughed at any kind of work you might do because so much needed to be done. There weren't any servants or hired people to do it perfectly so even amateur efforts were gratefully accepted. The things that would have been called childish in Sea Cliff, such as feeding animals or haying and even making Christmas things, took on a new dignity when they were necessary.

Bitsy loved the farm more each week, but for the first time this afternoon she wished that she could be in New York with plenty of money in her pocketbook. It would be wonderful to walk down Fifth Avenue and to know that behind the gay shop windows she could find the absolutely perfect present for Byrd.

Half an hour later Byrd called up again to talk to Bitsy himself. After she had spoken to him Bitsy knew that she didn't really want to be in New York at all. The best present she could find in Meudon would have to do. Being as far away from Byrd as New York City even for a few days would be a nightmare.

At that her Christmas finances worked out better than she had dared hope. The next day at school Flossie Larson told her that her little cousin Mary Lou needed tutoring and that her aunt wanted to know if Bitsy would take it on for the eight afternoons before the holidays. Bitsy took it on joyfully, but the work proved to be incredibly boring. Mary Lou Swenson was eleven and even blonder and duller than Flossie. She was in the sixth grade and having trouble with arithmetic. Bitsy had never particularly liked numbers, and the struggles of getting decimals through Mary Lou's tow head were paralyzing.

For the next week Bitsy biked home from school and then went the extra mile and three quarters to the Swensons' tall, clapboard farmhouse. By the time she left, around half-past five, she was really tired out. The last long slope that led up to Bricklow was hard work against the wind, but on the last evening, as Bitsy ped-aled through the dark and cold, she felt happier than she had ever been before. She was doing this for Byrd. She was earning money to get something that Byrd would really like. The hard bicycle ride was not enough. She longed to do something physically exhausting like that last hour of haying before the thunderstorm. To work like that for Byrd, to strain every muscle and sinew would be perfect bliss.

That evening the whole household went down on a cheerful, bustling shopping trip to Meudon. Bitsy went with them and bought a block of good drawing paper for her mother, a new pastry cutter for Cousin Bertha, and a Boy-Scout game for Stanty. She hesitated over her pres-ent for Tim. There was a *Farmer's Cyclopedia* that cost nearly three dollars and then there was a jackknife that she could get for fifty cents. Tim had one knife, but still he could always use another, and she knew in her heart that he would treasure anything she gave him. For a moment she wavered and then on an upsurge of Christ-mas spirit bought him the *Cyclopedia*.

She made a separate trip to Meudon on her bicycle to get Byrd's present. That was too precious a purchase to make when some member of the family was likely to look over your shoulder and give you advice on what you were buying. She went straight to a small leather shop, but as she looked around her, she realized for the first time she didn't have any idea of what Byrd's interests were or what he would really like.

She hesitated for several moments over the folding picture frames. Byrd had asked for a picture of her, but she didn't have one she wanted to give him. There was the one she had had taken for Dad just before he left but it looked scrubbed and little-girlish. Then there was a snapshot of her in blue jeans that Tim had taken, but she didn't want to give him that either—it belonged too completely to the farm to be right for Byrd. She finally settled on a brown leather cigarette case and went off with it in her pocket.

On Christmas morning Bitsy was as eager as Stanty to wake up early. Byrd had been on night duty Christmas Eve and he had promised to call her up before he went back to his quarters to sleep. The telephone tinkled at half-past six and Bitsy shot out of bed and into the hall. She collided with Stanty, who had gone into the living room in his pajamas to find his stocking. "Go back to bed," Bitsy said as she reached for the receiver. "Go on back to bed." She frowned at the small tousled boy, but no matter how she tried, she couldn't make her voice sound cross.

"Hello," she said, her heart pounding. "Hello!"

"Number, please?" The operator's question came over the line.

"But—but the phone rang," Bitsy said. "I'm expecting a very important call."

"There's no one calling you now," the operator said briskly. "Excuse it, please."

Bitsy hung up the receiver with a thud. There was no

way she could call Byrd at the Field. She would just have to wait and see if he called again. It was sickening. She turned and saw Stanty staring at her. "Go to bed," she said furiously. "Don't you know it's too early to be up?"

"M-M-Merry Christmas," Stanty stuttered, and sped down the hall with his full stocking clutched tight to his striped pajama top.

Even the Christmas breakfast that Bitsy had been looking forward to all week seemed flat. Cousin Bertha's waffles and country sausage were browned to perfection. The sweet, piny fragrance of the Christmas tree and the princess pine wafted in from the living room, which fairly bulged with the presents and bundles laid out last night. Even the weather outside was co-operating, and a new fall of snow had turned the rough outline of the barnyard into a Currier and Ives print. The reflected whiteness outside seemed to affect the rest of the family like wine. They joked and laughed, but when Bitsy found that there was no message from Byrd she sat silent and dumb beside Margaret and Tim.

It wasn't until they were finally in the living room opening their presents that Bitsy forgot Byrd enough to have a good time. She gave Tim his present and watched as he tore off the wrapping. He looked at the photographs and the clear type, and his face changed from tan to red and down to a dull peach again. "Oh, Bits," he said, and his voice was husky with feeling. "Golly, Bits. This is swell of you. I've wanted it for ages."

Bitsy turned back to her own presents with a little thrill of pleasure. Giving people something they really wanted was the point of Christmas. The Christmas tree, the greens which they had picked and hung, even the gingerbread men lining the mantel, were window dressing for that special feeling of wanting to give pleasure.

She looked over her own pile, and her heart leaped as she saw a square box with Byrd's handwriting on the tag. She put it aside to open alone. It was fun to save the best for the last. She opened her other presents and found that there were silk stockings, real silk, in the shade she liked best, from Mother. There was a string of sealing-wax beads from Stanty, beautifully made sport socks from Cousin Bert, and a knitted cap from Margaret. She pulled off the paper from Tim's present and her breath came out in a little gasp of delight. It was a pair of wooden bookends with a gray goose in proud relief on each one. The carving and painting of the geese and of the green fields on which they stood were as expertly done as though they had come from an expensive sport store. "Tim made them himself," Cousin Bert said proudly. "His father always was a great hand at making decoys."

"These aren't decoys though," Tim said, and his eyes sought Bitsy's. "It's a gray goose on a green field."

Bitsy thanked him, and for once Tim stayed to listen, his face as pleased as when he had opened the book. "I thought you'd like 'em," he said. "It was fun making them."

"This is a s-swell Christmas," Stanty said suddenly, and for the first time since very early in the morning Bitsy agreed that it was. She looked over at her mother. Her lovely face was calm and serene as she helped Stanty set up his new lead soldiers. Mother had had a good Christmas too. Yesterday, in the very last mail, there had been a packet of letters and a small package from Dad.

The package had contained a small, rudely carved African fetish, the ugly little figure of an old man with a letter, saying that it had been the only thing Captain Close had been able to buy. As Bitsy watched, her mother, not realizing that she was looking, reached over and gave the idol a little loving tap. She's crazy about it, Bitsy realized. It means more to her than the string of pearls Dad gave her a couple of years ago. It was funny when you came to think of it, when you were Stanty's age you judged a Christmas by what you got, and when you were older you judged it by whom the presents came from. Bitsy's hands pressed Byrd's package tight. No matter what this is, she thought, I'll keep it always.

She was just starting up to her own room when Stanty shouted across to her. "Say, are you asleep?" he demanded. "I've called you t-twice to tell you the Admiral was on the phone."

Bitsy tore across the room. "Hello," she got out. "Merry Christmas!"

"Merry Christmas!" Byrd's voice came back to her. "I'd almost forgotten about it until I got your cute present. Listen, honey, the swellest thing's happened. I've been ordered down to Washington on that job. I'll be gone for a month, leaving tonight."

"Oh, Byrd," Bitsy said, but he was still talking. It was a wonderful chance. He was being entrusted with a mission of a kind that was usually given only to older men. It was the most marvelous break in the world. He had been hoping for it for weeks. Bitsy would remember that he had told her about it at the square dance.

"That's great," Bitsy said, groping in her memory for what he had said. He had mentioned his work just when one of the high-school boys had cut in on them. Right now her mind was an absolute blank. "It's hard on you, darling." Byrd's voice sounded like a stranger's. "I know just how badly you feel. But I'll be back in a month, and it's a great chance."

They talked for a few minutes more and then Byrd had to hang up. Bitsy turned away from the phone with a puzzled frown on her face. Byrd had been so excited about his new job that he hadn't really thought about her or her Christmas present. She knew this trip was impor-tant, but for the life of her she couldn't remember what Byrd had said about it. "Byrd's been ordered off," she said as she came into the living room; "leaving tonight."

"Overseas?" Mrs. Close asked, and her deep violet eyes sought Bitsy's over Stanty's head.

"Washington," Bitsy said, and she felt suddenly let down and cross. "Just for a month, and then he'll be back here again. I wish he'd told me earlier."

She started for the stairs to go to her own room. Even Mother's quick sympathy rubbed her the wrong way. She wanted to be alone, but Tim's voice, brusque and direct the way it had been when she first came to the farm, stopped her at the landing. "What sort of a farmer are you anyway?" he demanded. "That pig of yours is squealing his head off. You forgot to feed him this morning."

It wasn't until after lunch that Bitsy finally had a moment alone in her own room. She took up Byrd's present and broke the string. It was a small square box, perhaps a picture in one of those leather frames she had thought of buying herself. She pulled off the bright paper and there in front of her was a small box of chocolates. For a moment Bitsy just stared at it, numb with disappointment. She thought of Mother, her eyes soft with love as she looked at the homely little idol, and shame and disappointment fought for first place. It wasn't the present that mattered but the thought. But candy! The only thing in the world she couldn't treasure and keep. The most obvious, the most impersonal present he could have sent. The kind of thing you brought to your week-end hostess, to someone you hardly knew.

Bitsy walked blindly across the room and lay down on the bed, her eyes hot with tears. She was still lying there when Stanty bounced into the room. "Go way!" she said, but Stanty wasn't to be put off that easily.

"Tim wants you," he said. "Right away quick in the barn. He s-said it's very important."

Bitsy got up, fuming, and pulled on her old farm clothes. She might just as well do the evening chores at the same time, and she no longer cared how she looked.

She had hardly gotten into the close-smelling barn before she knew something was wrong. Tim's face was wet with sweat and there were worried lines beneath his eyes.

"Boy, I'm glad it's you," he said, and turned back to the big gray ewe that lay on the straw in one of the pens.

"What d'you want?" Bitsy asked shortly. "And what's so important?"

"She's sick." Tim jerked a thumb toward the foundering ewe. "I want to call the vet if I can and you can stay with her. Stanty's too young."

"What's the matter?" Bitsy asked, and let herself into the pen. She would have gone over to the sheep, but Tim moved in front of her.

"Can't you see she's lambing?" he got out. "Move quietly, or you'll get her excited."

Bitsy stood back, her heart beating faster. The ewe's sides were laboring now and her breath came raucously. She tried to rise and then half fell onto the clean straw. "She needs help," Tim said. "Steady her head. Move quietly!"

With trembling hands, Bitsy did as she was told. She was terrified of doing the wrong thing, but even more afraid of disobeying Tim. He seemed to be in three places at once. He had piled up more clean straw, scrubbed his hands, and was back at the ewe's side before Bitsy really had a grasp of the black woolly head. "Poor old girl," he whispered. "You're having a rotten time."

The ewe strained and heaved grotesquely. Her head jerked out of Bitsy's frightened fingers. The next instant Tim gave a little cry of triumph and the small limp lamb was in his hands. With one step he motioned Bitsy back and put the lamb directly by the ewe's head. "Get back," he ordered. "If we get her worried, she won't recognize it."

Tim waited silently as the ewe snuffed the round bullet head. The seconds dragged by like hours. So this is what birth is like, Bitsy thought, and scolded herself because her knees were shaking. Slow and painful and messy. Tim had already cleaned up the membrane and blood from the straw and spread out new, but the pen still reeked with the hot smell.

The ewe had lifted her head now and feebly licked the cellophane-like film that covered her baby. "It's O.K.," Tim got out, and there was relief in his voice. "She's going to nurse it. Sometimes they won't when they've had a hard time."

Bitsy said nothing but followed Tim out of the barn into the silent white world outside. "That's Steve's fault," Tim said bitterly as they started toward the house. "He came home drunk a couple of months ago and turned the ram in with her when she was in season."

"Does it matter?" Bitsy asked, and Tim turned on her.

"Matter? Of course it matters. We want all the lambs the same size so that we can sell them together. Besides, they're a lot harder to raise when they're born so early."

Bitsy followed him into the kitchen and they washed up together at the worn sink.

It wasn't until nearly suppertime that Bitsy had another look at the lamb. Tim had gone straight back to the barn but had told her not to follow him until he called her for fear of upsetting the ewe.

He came back just as Bitsy had finished laying the supper table. "Everything's O.K.," he said. "She's nursing it beautifully. Bring Stanty down to see the Christmas surprise."

Stanty in his new Christmas boots followed Bitsy across the snow. Once inside the barn, he stared at the lamb and would have picked it up if Tim hadn't stopped him. "Golly, it's cute," he got out, and Bitsy agreed. The lamb, still damp and weak, stood up on its own absurd legs. It was coal black and the youngest, most appealing little creature Bitsy had ever seen.

When Stanty had rushed off to tell Mrs. Close the great news, Bitsy still stood there looking down at the little lamb. Now that the actual birth was over, she had time to appreciate how sheltered and complete the barn seemed. There was the soft stomping of the mules and the cattle; the sleepy grunts of the pigs in the dark shadows; and over it all the smell of hay and clean straw. It was in a place like this that Mary and Joseph found refuge, Bitsy thought, and the words of the Christmas story flooded through her mind with new significance. "She wrapped him in swaddling clothes and laid him in a manger."

She turned toward Tim, wondering how to explain what she felt. He must have been watching her because as she looked up at him his hazel eyes smiled into hers. "Makes you think of the first Christmas, doesn't it?" he said lightly. "I'm glad it's a ewe lamb so we can keep it. It'd seem kind of rotten to kill a lamb born Christmas night."

Bitsy said nothing, but when she was undressing that night she looked at Tim's carefully carved geese for a long time. Once again Tim had understood something important before she had been able to explain.

XV

Winter Days

THE WEEK after Christmas the thermometer dropped and there was skating on the Larsons' pond. Bitsy had skated in New York in a rink, but this kind of skating, where the whole community turned out, was a new experience. She had brought out her skates and Cousin Bert unearthed an old pair of Bruce's from the attic for Stanty so that he could go skating with Tim and herself after school.

Everyone from the village and the surrounding farms was there. At one end of the pond a crowd of little boys of Stanty's age scuttled around a big fire that Tracy Larson had built at the edge of the pond. Further on a few of the high-school boys played hockey, and over at one side Tracy himself was practicing figure eights. He stopped with a rink turn that threw up a spray of ice when he saw Bitsy. "Hi, there!" he shouted. "It's the best ice we've had in years."

"B-boy, can he skate!" Stanty got out as Tracy dashed toward them.

Bitsy nodded, but she was not surprised. She knew

now why early in the fall Tim had talked of Tracy Larson with such enthusiasm. He was not good-looking and his small talk would not have passed muster at Sea Cliff, but when Tracy knew something he knew it. Whether it was geometry at school, or planting his father's acres of hybrid corn, or the step of a square dance, if Tracy did it at all, he did it with an easy-going competence that you couldn't help but respect.

Right now he was interested only in getting Bitsy and the others on the ice. "Get going!" he said, and actually jumped up and down on his skates. "It's too cold to stand watching."

It was cold all right! The breath stiffened in Bitsy's nose and her hands felt numb as she pulled off her mittens and laced up her skates. "I'm ready," Tim called, and a moment later she was beside him on the ice. Stanty had already made for his cronies around the fire, his red muffler flying out like a small sail behind him.

"Small fry," Tim said, grinning toward Stanty's bent back and flailing hands. Stanty didn't know much about skating but he wasn't letting that stop him. He flopped down once but was up again before either Bitsy or the two boys could reach him.

Bitsy took a few trial turns around the pond while Tracy and Tim raced ahead of her. Skating was like swimming: you never forgot it. Her skates clicked rhythmically over the black ice and her hands were no longer numb. This is fine, she thought, and now Tracy was on one side of her and Tim on the other. It's the best feeling there is. Like dancing, like flying.

The thought of flying brought Byrd back to her mind. She had been bitterly disappointed that there had been no letters from him since he left on Christmas Day. Still, he hadn't had much time, and he was undoubtedly very busy. Right now it was hard to feel badly about anything with Tracy taking her arm while Tim clowned on the ice in front of them. Tim, who was so serious, so businesslike on the farm, was lightheaded on the ice. He skated beautifully, his neat, compact body under perfect control. Right now he did a crazy imitation of fat Mrs. Larson learning how to skate. He bent and gestured, grabbed at the air, and started to fall.

"You're crazy," Bitsy giggled, but now Tim had straightened up with a neat click of his skates.

"Tag," he said, touching Bitsy on the collar of her skiing jacket. "Bitsy's it."

Bitsy raced after Tim, her face scarlet with exertion. She heard the sharp cut-cut of skates behind her and thought that Tracy was probably chasing Tim too. She skated until she was out of breath and her ankles ached, but still Tim was ahead of her. He was fooling again, pretending to fall and then swooping up as he darted in and out of a crowd of skaters. "You get him, Trace," Bitsy panted over her shoulder. "He's too fast for me."

A dark figure flashed past her and she saw that it was Reverend Miller, the Presbyterian minister, whom she had heard each Sunday. Reverend Miller came from Vermont and he hadn't forgotten a thing about winter sports. His long, gangling form looked strangely out of place in the old-fashioned green toque and huge muffler.

He shot past the crowd of boys who had started after
Tim, and a moment later he had him collared.

"Hey, you're too good!" Tim protested, but by this
time the whole pond was in the game. First Tim was it,
then Spud Jackson, the silent pimpled clerk who worked
in the I.G.A., and finally Reverend Miller. He started
out over the ice, stopped with a neat turn, picked up his
small daughter, and forged on ahead of the others with
the little girl shouting on his shoulders. Even with that
handicap, he was too fast for any of them.

It was dark by the time Tim and the two Closes took
off their skates in front of the fire. At the top of the little
hill that led back to the farm Bitsy stopped to look back
at the pond. There were still plenty of people flying over
the dark surface and standing around the cheerful red-
and-yellow blaze of the bonfire. At one end of the pond
Bitsy caught sight of Reverend Miller humming over his
scarf as he taught Mary Lou Larson to waltz. Little Mary
Lou might be dumb at numbers, but she was a whiz on
the ice. Her fat, red-stockinged legs slid neatly through
the steps the lank clergyman showed her.

A little smile came to Bitsy's lips. It was good somehow to know that Reverend Miller could skate like that
and that he had even forgotten choir practice in order to
teach little Mary Lou to waltz. "That was fun," Bitsy
began, and Tim nodded his head.

"Best part of skating is you see people in kind of a
new light," he said. "Like Reverend Miller and Spud
Jackson and all."

Bitsy turned to stare at Tim's friendly, honest face.

He had done it again, saying just what was in her mind. She started to tell him, but now Stanty rushed back to them like a small breathless terrier. "Aw, for Pete's s-sake hurry up," he panted. "Cousin Bert promised us pancakes and sausage meat for supper."

The skating lasted for a whole glorious week. By the following Monday the ice was as white and soft as cooked fat and by Tuesday there was a warm melting rain which finished it. Tim and Bitsy came home together on the school bus since bicycling was impossible over the slippery roads. They left their books, changed their clothes, and headed straight for the barn.

Bruce and Steve had been working all day rebuilding the sheep and cattle pens inside the main barn. Now that they all worked inside, Bitsy saw more of Steve and realized why in spite of his eccentricities the Pole was invaluable. Although he took his orders and his pay from Bruce, his dumb, doglike devotion was all for Tim. He acted as though the farm not only belonged to Tim but were actually a physical part of him. He would say about one of the weedier fields, "This spring I make heem better," or about one of the rutted lanes, "Steve smooth heem with ashes," and Bitsy had the feeling that he felt he was serving Tim as directly as though he had blacked his boots or carried his bundles.

Bruce and Tim were good carpenters, but in his way Steve was better than either of them. He was strong enough to move the heaviest timbers unaided and he seemed to know by instinct just what size piece of wood would be needed. He would watch Bruce figure out measurements and then, without even glancing at the carpenter's rule himself, he would cut away at a board, carry it to the pen, and it always fitted perfectly.

Bitsy had plenty of opportunity to watch him while she sorted out the keg of mixed nails that Bruce had handed her. She was no carpenter, but on the farm there always seemed to be work for everyone whether they were skilled or not.

Steve never spoke. Bruce whistled as he worked, and Tim made little hissing noises with his lips as he furrowed his forehead over a particularly difficult connection. They spoke only when necessary. Steve talked when he was alone with Tim, Bitsy knew, but in front of her his silence was an aggressive, positive force that left them all tongue-tied. "Doesn't Steve ever speak?" Bitsy asked when they had done the chores and were walking up toward the pleasant yellow light of the kitchen.

"Oh, sure," Tim said. "He's just shy and queer. A lot of terrific things have happened to him."

"He's not shy when he's drunk," Bruce said grimly. "He'll even sing for you then, if you give him any encouragement. You ask Mother about it. He came up once and sat yodeling on the front steps when she was entertaining the Ladies' Aid."

A few weeks ago Bitsy would have joked with Cousin Bertha about it but not now. For the last fortnight Cousin Bertha had been noticeably jumpy. She was sharp with all three women in the house and even scolded Tim and Stanty without much reason. She's worried sick over something, Bitsy thought, and I'll just bet it's about Bruce.

That very evening Cousin Bert started to ask Bruce bluntly what his prospects with the Army were. Bruce was as evasive as ever and changed the subject before she had a chance to finish her question. "How about going to the movies?" he said. *"Mrs. Miniver* is at Bricklow."

"Boy, can I go?" Stanty said.

"Certainly not." Cousin Bertha's voice was cutting. "At your age on a school night?"

Stanty's eyes reddened but now Mother came to the rescue. "I've got some snapshots to mount into a little book to send Dad," she said. "I wondered if you'd like to help me."

It ended up that Bruce and Margaret went to the movie taking Bitsy with them. It was the first movie she had been to in weeks and it touched her more than any she had ever seen. For days Bitsy went around feeling that the characters in the movie were people whom she had known intimately. The girl who married young Vin Miniver was her own age, Bitsy realized, faced with the heartaches and dangers that might soon be hers. Yes, Carol was her contemporary, but it was of Mrs. Miniver she thought when she was at home in bed. To talk like that, to smile like that, to be able to walk upstairs and downstairs so that it reminded you of soft music.

She turned over in bed, suddenly more eager than ever to have Byrd come back. If he'd only write, she thought. If only tomorrow there'd be a real letter.

But the next day there was no letter, nor in the days

that followed. The days turned into busy, uneventful weeks, but always there was the sharp pang of disappointment when Bitsy found that another day had gone and no word from Byrd.

The work at school stiffened up before midyear. Bitsy felt more at home there now and would have gone out for the school paper but there wasn't time. The roads were so icy that she couldn't bicycle, and the only bus for Bricklow left just after her last class. Besides, there was still plenty of work to be done on the farm. There were always the animals to be fed, and it took longer now that they had to drive out in the old farm truck to bring food to the hogs and the beef cattle who were left out in the snowy pastures.

Even the carpentry became a personal interest. She had had an idea how, with just a few changes, they could reallocate the pens so as to have more space in the middle of the barn. Steve was definitely opposed to the idea, Tim was hard to convince, and Bruce was perfectly ready to let it go for a few more weeks. "But we're doing the woodwork now," Bitsy said. "And if we do it later we'll be wasting more wood and time and everything."

By using a few old crates and grain sacks, she made them a rough model of how it would work, and finally they were won over. Bitsy was still inexpert with hammer and saw, but she hurried out to the barn now as eagerly as Tim himself to see how her idea worked out.

The only thing that was even more important to her was a letter from Byrd. Each day as she turned into the long lane, she was sure that today a thick air-mail letter would be waiting on the hall table and each time she was disappointed. She found herself counting on little superstitions such as the wishbone at Sunday supper and the fact that she had pulled on her sweater inside out, but they brought her no luck. She got one short, breezy postal card and that was all. She answered it immediately with a long, detailed letter about the skating, the carpentry, and the other things that happened on the farm. "Tim's got a Four-H Club entry," she wrote. "A big Hampshire hog that'll probably be judged next month." She went on describing how Tim had taken over the little shoat last summer, how it had been carefully weighed and measured by the Four-H Club leader, and how he was expected to stop by any day now to look over the hog and see how it compared with the other entries he had already inspected. "I hope Tim gets the prize," she finished. "Ten dollars would really be a help toward our day-old chicks this spring."

She didn't hear from Byrd again until the second week in February, when she got a postcard that made her cheeks burn. "Dear Farmerette," it began. "Winter on the farm must be pretty deadly. I think you're a swell sport to put up with it so well. I hope those two Crane oafs don't saddle too much work on you. If they do, they'll have to settle with me. I've got to stay on here three more weeks, but then I'll be back to take care of you."

Bitsy crumpled the card with an angry little grimace and dropped it into the incinerator outside the kitchen door. Byrd was silly. Hadn't he understood that she was having fun? That she liked helping with the carpentry, and that the skating made about the best week she'd ever had?

She set aside the next Saturday afternoon to write to him, but after two stiff, meaningless pages she gave it up. He would be back soon now, and it would be so much easier to explain how she felt when she was actually with him. You had to be a real writer to make someone see the baby lambs, or hear the gay sounds of the skating pond, or feel the minute changes of season that gave the glow to farm life.

Usually on Saturday mornings, when Tim didn't have to hurry off to school, breakfast was not until eight o'clock, but this morning when Bitsy came down the whole family was up and Cousin Bert was grimly cleaning and scouring two long knives out in the kitchen. "What's up?" Bitsy asked. "Can I help do anything?"

Cousin Bert shook her head. "The boys and Steve have just butchered two of the hogs. I was glad you and Stanty were asleep and kept out of the way. It's no sight for women and children."

In the afternoon they were to take the hogs over to Meudon to be dressed, and both Cousin Bert and Mother were going along to do some marketing. They asked Bitsy to go, but she shook her head and started out for a walk instead.

The killing of animals you had fed and worked over was one of the worst parts of farm life. Bitsy had watched Tim kill the chickens and turkeys and geese with one swift blow of a razor-sharp ax, but to watch a hog being stuck would be much worse. Most of the animals from the farm were sold on the hoof, but the hogs they kept for their own use were killed on the farm and then taken away to be cured and smoked. Tim, who hated slaughtering himself, had arranged the time so that she wouldn't be there, Bitsy knew. It was like him to be thoughtful about it, but at the same time Bitsy felt as though she had let him down, and she felt cross and irritated with herself in consequence.

It had turned raw again, and a driving, icy rain made the footing treacherous. After the first five minutes Bitsy wished that she had gone with the rest of the family down to Meudon. Even Stanty was away rehearsing for a school play, and it was a depressing day to walk alone. Just yesterday, when she and Tim had found the first tight shoots of skunk cabbage in the swamp in the glen, it had seemed that spring was just around the corner. But now, as she looked over the sodden fields and the black, wet trunks of the trees, winter seemed to have settled in again for good. She tried to imagine what Byrd was doing at that moment, but as she had no idea of what his work in Washington was like it was impossible to conjure up a picture of him.

Finally she wandered into the barn, but it was lonely and lifeless without Tim. The pigs and sheep comfortable in clean straw seemed smug and self-sufficient, and she turned to look at her geese. She had just two left, fine fat ones, both of them bigger than average, Tim said, because he had domesticated two Canadian wild geese with his flock, and she knew she would get a good price

for them in a week or so. It would be wonderful to get
some new clothes with the eight dollars, but, on the
other hand, if she put it into goslings again or young
turkeys or day-old chicks she would make more money
in the fall. She was still turning it over in her mind when
a sudden noise made her turn and she found herself face
to face with Steve!

His face was streaked with blood and there were thick
dark clots of it on his soiled shirt.

"My God, are you hurt?" Bitsy got out, but he looked
down at her and laughed the queer, guttural laugh that
he used when something went wrong on the farm.

"We keel hogs," he said. "What sort of farmer can't
stand that?"

Bitsy's mind flashed back to Cousin Bert's words earlier
in the morning. She looked up at him with a sudden
gasp of relief and saw his red, dull face still leering down
at her. She realized with a start that he was very drunk.
Bruce paid him every Saturday and today, since he was
going to town, he had probably paid him early. For a
moment she was frozen with fright, but the next minute,
as Steve shuffled off, she gave a little sigh of relief. He
was singing now a strange, unfamiliar melody with words
in a language that she supposed must be Polish. He made
his way out of the barn and, heedless of the rain or the
icy puddles on the lawn, plodded toward his own shabby
cabin.

Bitsy shut the stiff barn door and went straight to the
house. She felt the need of human companionship more
than ever. Margaret was home, she knew, and even if she

were resting Bitsy thought she might go up and sit with her. She turned the corner of the barn and saw that an unfamiliar black sedan had pulled up by the front door. Margaret was standing on the porch talking to the man who had just driven in.

"Bitsy," she called, her face lighting. "This is Mr. Schwed. He's come to look at Tim's hog."

Bitsy shook hands with the county agent. She didn't know exactly what she had expected him to look like, but it was something quite different. She could still be surprised at how citified real country people looked except when they were actually doing farm labor. Mr. Schwed, she decided, looked more like a businessman that she might have seen in the club car of an overnight train than a farm leader. He was neatly dressed in a brown coat and scarf and he looked capable and efficient. "I'll go get the hog right away," Bitsy began. "Tim turned him out in the glen pasture this morning."

"Well, I hate to bother you," Mr. Schwed said. "But with the gas and all I don't know when I could come around again."

"We won't be a minute." Margaret pulled on an old Mackinaw of Bruce's as she spoke. "Would you wait here or would you rather meet us in the barn?"

"Oh, Margaret, you shouldn't," Bitsy began, but Margaret silenced her with a quick gesture of the hand.

"It won't do me a bit of harm," she said as Mr. Schwed left for the barn and disappeared inside. "And I'd hate to keep him waiting. I'm just crazy for Tim to get that prize money."

They separated at the head of the ravine. Margaret was to go to the left where the ground flattened out beside the little brook that led to the covered bridge. Bitsy undertook the hillier ground that cut down to the glen proper. "I'll whistle if I find him," she called. "And then you go straight back to the house."

Margaret nodded, pulling Bruce's big collar up around her head. She moved along slowly, taking cautious, awkward steps as though she were afraid she might slip. Bitsy felt worried about her and hurried down the steep side of the glen as fast as she dared, swinging on the young wet saplings as she went. She was nearly down before she saw the hog.

He looked unpleasantly large and formidable as he rooted aimlessly in the soft mud at the bottom of the glen. For an instant Bitsy hesitated, wishing that Margaret or the Four-H agent were with her. Somehow it took more courage to approach a big animal in winter, and alone, than it did in summer or when other people were around. Even the cows seemed friskier, less docile in winter than they had in warm weather, and right now she herself was so cold that she felt that if the hog charged and ran into her she would break like a brittle stick. She stared down at the hog's black back and then forced herself to whistle loudly to Margaret. She heard a faint whistle in return, and without giving herself another chance to hesitate, started to drive the hog up the hill.

To her relief he went at a gallop. Halfway up the hill he got skittish and darted off in the wrong direction, but now that she had been running she felt warmer and more courageous, and she headed him back into the wide barn door without further difficulty.

Once inside the barn the hog seemed to know what was expected of him. He no longer tried charging this way and that but walked calmly toward an empty pen where Bitsy had spread some food. With the rearrangement in the barn, all the pigs were together on one side and it was possible to keep one pen empty for a sick pig or one that for some reason ought to be alone. The Cranes had been reluctant to make the change, but when Bitsy had finally persuaded them, they were delighted with the way it worked out.

"Bruce told me you'd made some changes," Mr. Schwed said, and his blue eyes behind the square-cut spectacles seemed to take in every detail. "Said it was your idea."

"It makes feeding easier," Bitsy said, and showed him the feedbox that the men had finished the week before. "And we haven't had any trouble with rats since we plugged up the old holes and moved the feed."

She walked around the barn discussing the changes and showing the agent where they kept the old harnesses and the endless brushes and bottles and odd tools that were always being needed. "It's an efficient arrangement," the agent said as she led him back to the Four-H hog. "Cuts down the fire hazard among other things."

They were back at the pen now, and the hog seemed intent on making up for his earlier stampede. He looked at them through small, unblinking eyes and then walked across the pen as though he were just inviting admira-

tion. "He's showing off," Bitsy said, but Mr. Schwed
wasn't looking. His eyes were on Bitsy, and now he
cleaned his glasses while he still looked at her.

"Ever had any farm experience before you came out
here?" he asked, and Bitsy shook her head, wondering
what he was driving at. "Well, you've taken to it all
right," he went on. "From what Bruce tells me, they
couldn't have gotten on without you. I'm making up a
list of high-school boys and girls who might want to
work for different farmers this summer, and I wonder if
you'd like to be one of them? Your teachers at the high
school recommended you and John Larson and several
other farmers who didn't think much of using girls
mentioned your name and said they'd be ready to take
you."

"For all summer?" Bitsy said, and Schwed nodded.

"Certainly," he said. "That's one reason they want you
because you've established a reputation for sticking to
your work. Bruce told me you hadn't missed a day feeding the stock since you started doing chores."

Bitsy felt a sudden wave of gratitude toward the teachers at school and especially toward Bruce. It was like him
in his pleasant, offhand way to give her a good name, and
in her heart she knew she had earned it. She smiled at
the agent but now he was talking again. "We could
guarantee you one dollar and keep," he said. "You'd be
working somewhere here in the county."

"A dollar a day!" Bitsy's breath came in a little
triumphant gasp. A dollar a day meant thirty dollars
a month. One hundred and eighty dollars for the sum-

mer. After nearly six months on the farm it seemed colossal. Her head spun as she thought of what she could buy with one hundred and eighty dollars. But the next minute, as she looked around the barn, she knew she couldn't leave. It was more than likely that Bruce would be off, and even if he stayed, both he and Tim were counting on her help.

"Thanks a lot," she said. "It's nice being asked, but I guess I'll be needed here."

"I was afraid of that," the agent said, and now he turned to consider the hog. "But if you change your mind let me know. From what I hear you'd be worth it to anybody."

Bitsy watched him inspecting the hog through a glow of satisfaction. She had been offered a job—a paying job at work that she loved and wanted to know more about. The sudden unexpected compliment fanned her ambition, and she knew that she was going to buy more geese with the eight dollars she was to get next week. Perhaps she could get a better strain, some that were healthier and easier to raise. She questioned the agent, and he went out to his car to get a few government pamphlets that might be helpful. When he was finally ready to leave, he looked back at the pen and his eyes twinkled. "You send Tim my congratulations," he said. "He's raised a fine hog."

"You mean it's won?" Bitsy said.

Mr. Schwed looked more like a conservative businessman than ever. "I can't say that," he said. "I've got two more hogs to inspect. But I don't mind telling you he's got an awfully good chance."

Bitsy waited until Mr. Schwed had turned his car around and then she tore into the house. "Margaret!" she shouted. "Maggie, where are you? I think Tim's going to win!"

Her words echoed gloomily in the hall. She dashed upstairs, but Margaret's room was empty. She charged down again and into the kitchen and through the dining room to the library. "Margaret!" she shouted, suddenly alarmed. "Margaret, where are you? Margaret!" There was no sound except her own voice and the tick of the kitchen clock. For a moment Bitsy stood rooted, her heart pounding with fear.

XVI

In the Glen

A FEW MOMENTS LATER, when Bitsy was certain the house was empty, she ran outside toward the glen. Was it possible that the whistle she had heard was only an echo and that Margaret was still searching? Was she just walking on and on looking for the hog or had something happened? The remembrance of Margaret's awkward, cautious steps in her black oxfords stabbed Bitsy's heart. It would be so easy for her to fall on this sleety ground. And then if the baby started to come? O God, if she took a bad fall and couldn't save herself.

Bitsy tore at her mind for every scrap of information she had ever had about childbirth. The hygiene course at school, words from Mother and one or two older friends, scenes from novels. It was all less than useless against such an emergency as this. And there wasn't a living soul to turn to. Steve was the only other living human being on the farm, and he was hopelessly drunk. "O God, let her be all right," Bitsy prayed as she ran forward. "O God, let her be all right."

She was down beside the brook when she caught sight

of a patch of blue cloth. The next instant she saw Margaret crouched against the sloping bank of the brook. "Margaret!" she shouted, her heart pumping with terror. "Margaret! Are you hurt?"

Margaret turned so that for the first time Bitsy saw her face. There were great dark slashes on her cheeks and forehead and for one horrible moment Bitsy thought they were blood. She ran forward, and her breath came in a gasp of relief when she saw they were only dark mud. Margaret was lying in mud, must have slipped in it. Why couldn't she get up?

"I'm all right," Margaret got out. "It's just my foot's caught. Under a root, I think."

Bitsy knelt beside her, heedless of the mud. "You're sure you're not hurt?" she said, her voice shaking with fright. "You didn't do anything to yourself?"

Margaret shook her head. "Just gave myself a good scare," she said. "But I'm all right except I can't get my foot free. I guess it's swollen some."

Bitsy turned so that she could get a better look at Margaret's foot. She plunged her hand through the icy mud and felt the tough root that bound the top of the instep. It was clear now exactly what had happened. Margaret had been standing on the top of the little bank when her weight had caused it to cave in. She might have gone headlong into the brook itself if the root that bound her hadn't also given her a toe hold. "I was lucky at that," Margaret said in her quiet, steady voice. "If my foot hadn't held, I'd have gotten a terrific fall."

Bitsy dug furiously, but the root was so tight she

couldn't even get a finger under it. "Try pulling," she
urged, but when Margaret pulled back it only made it
worse.

Bitsy straightened up, wiping the mud from her cold
hands. "I'll have to get a knife from the house," she said.
"Can you stand waiting?"

"Of course," Margaret got out, and she even managed
to smile. "I waited before, didn't I? I figured I'd be here
until Bruce came back and started looking for me."

Bitsy ran until the breath ached in her throat. Finally
she had to walk, but thoughts still flashed movie-like
through her mind. Steve drunk and bloodstained; the
hog; Margaret crouched uncomfortably in the cold not
knowing how long it would be before help would come.
"I waited before, didn't I?" Margaret's quiet voice had
had a proud ring to it. She was like the aviator in the
Saint Exupéry book Bitsy had read that summer who
said, "I stood things no animal could have stood."

Bitsy ran to the hall closet and tore down every available coat and then went back to the kitchen, picking up
one of the sharp knives Cousin Bert had been cleaning
that morning. It was easier going down the glen, and
she made better time getting back to Margaret. "Th-
thanks," Margaret said through chattering teeth when
Bitsy piled the coats around her. "It is cold!"

Cold! Bitsy's fingers were numb as she hacked at the
tough root. The ground was icy and the sleety wind was
knifelike. To Margaret, who had lain there alone and
frightened for over half an hour, it must be perishing.

The root was very thick and the mud made it difficult

to see what she was doing. She worked frantically, but it was impossible to get a real slash at the root without endangering Margaret's ankle. "It's so tough," she got out, but Margaret didn't answer. Her eyes were closed and her lids made a thin blue line on her white face. "Margaret!" Bitsy shouted, and the girl's eyes opened.

"I'm all right," she whispered. "Don't worry."

Bitsy stopped for a moment to try to prop an old coat of Tim's under Margaret's shoulder. The way she was forced to lie half on her side with her leg twisted in front of her would have been agony even without the cold. "I won't be long," Bitsy promised. "I'll have it cut through any minute now."

She cut and hacked as fast as she dared. The white core of the root showed plainly, but there was still a thumb's thickness to cut through.

She worked furiously, her mind moving ahead of her hands. What could she do when she had Margaret free? She would never be able to walk, and how could she possibly get her up to the house? What if the others were late getting back? Should she take a chance on getting Steve to help? Above all her other worries lay the dread that the baby might start to come before she could telephone for help.

She hacked on, but it was slow work. The mud had dulled the edge of her blade and she had to grind off one shaving after another. The sight of Margaret's worn black oxfords wrung her heart. Their ordinary homeliness seemed the symbol of everything that she had scoffed at when she first came to the farm and that she had learned to respect.

She pawed at the mud with tortured fingers when a new idea struck her. If only she had a pair of clippers she might be able to cut at the base of the root. She asked Margaret where they were kept, and with a visible effort the older girl answered her. "Our—study," she said, and then the next minute shook her head. "No use. Bruce has the key."

Bitsy went on cutting and scraping. Her hands were clumsy with the cold and she had a nasty gash on her left thumb. "I won't be much longer," she said cheerfully. "Really I won't."

She glanced up at Margaret, and once more those purplish eyelids chilled her heart. "Margaret!" she called, and now her voice was loud with an almost physical effort to keep her cousin conscious. "Margaret, I think Tim's Four-H hog won."

Margaret managed a smile and for a moment her eyes opened. "Mr. Schwed was crazy about it." Bitsy chattered on as she sawed and cut. "Said he'd call back tonight or maybe tomorrow."

Bitsy was almost through the root. "Pull!" she urged. "Maggie, try once more!"

Margaret strained her foot, and Bitsy clawed at the root with her hands until her fingernails cracked and she felt as though her numb fingers must break. She cut once more and finally the binding root splintered and Margaret's foot was free.

She lurched back and would have fallen if Bitsy hadn't

sprung forward to steady her. "Give me your hands," she ordered. "We're going up to the house."

Margaret put out her hands like an obedient child. Bitsy pulled with all her strength, but it was useless. "Come on," she coaxed. "You push yourself while I pull."

Margaret shook her head. "I—can't," she whispered. "I just can't."

Margaret was half sitting, half leaning against Bitsy when Bitsy heard a shout. It was Tim's voice, loud and clear, calling from the edge of the ravine.

"Tim!" Bitsy shouted, and all her pent-up terror went into the shout. "Here by the brook! Margaret's hurt!"

Tim plunged down the side of the glen with Bruce just behind him. Bruce's face was chalky as he passed his younger brother and reached his wife. "Margaret! Margaret darling, what happened?"

With a sudden terrific effort Margaret got herself to her feet. Her face was lighted now, transfigured, as she put out her arms. "Darling!" she said. "I knew you'd come." She took a step forward and the next instant fainted into Bruce's arms.

It wasn't until two hours later, when Bitsy went back to collect the overcoats that she had piled over Margaret, that she remembered that look on her face. It had been excited, radiant, and yet filled with peace. As though now that Bruce was there no other harm could come to her.

Bitsy bundled up the armful of coats. The mud had frozen on them in ugly patches and she was sure Cousin

Bert would be irritated by the sight of them. She was bound to be if only as a reaction from worry and excitement.

The first thing Cousin Bert had known about the accident was when Bruce and Tim had carried Margaret into the kitchen. She had hardly stopped to ask what had happened before she ran ahead of the boys to open Margaret's bed. It wasn't until just a few minutes ago, when Dr. Craigie from Meudon had left, that she really had a chance to find out what had happened.

Fortunately the doctor had been at a neighbor's, and he had driven up to the farm in a remarkably short time after Bitsy had first telephoned his office. Margaret was suffering from shock, he said, and from the effects of the cold and fatigue, but she was perfectly conscious again and apparently unhurt except for her bruised foot.

Bitsy saw her for a moment when she went upstairs with a hot-water bottle Cousin Bertha had just filled. She lay in the big bed with Bruce sitting in a chair beside her. Someone had washed the mud from her face, but there were still traces of it on her chin and on her mussed hair. "You were wonderful," she said as Bitsy came into the room. Bitsy blew her a kiss and started to leave the room when Margaret turned to Bruce. "You can't imagine everything she did. She was marvelous."

"I believe it," Bruce said, his worried eyes never leaving his wife's face. "Tell me about it tomorrow. Right now you're supposed to go to sleep."

Bitsy smiled to herself in the dark as she carried the armful of coats toward the house. They were all right, those two. The war might put terrible difficulties before them, but they had their faith in each other with which to meet it. Their love was so real and living a thing that even when they were apart the knowledge of it brought courage. "I knew you'd come." Margaret's first words to Bruce still rang in her ears.

Bitsy picked her way carefully over the slick patches of ice. Now that she had time to think about it, she was cold and tired and almost unbelievably dirty. For a moment she wished for the old sheltered days when she could have just sent the coats to the cleaner's and forgotten about them. Right now she spread them out in the damp, musty-smelling library where Cousin Bert wouldn't see them. She would brush them after supper. Before that she was going to have a bath, a deep, deliciously hot bath, even if it used up all the hot water in the tank.

She was halfway toward the stairs when she heard the telephone ring. For the first time in hours she remembered that Mr. Schwed had promised to call and lifted up the receiver expecting to hear his slow, precise drawl. "Hello," she said, and then she heard Byrd!

"Bitsy," he said, and it was unmistakably his voice. "Bitsy, you little sweet, don't you understand it's me?"

"Byrd, how on earth—— But where—where are you, anyway?"

There was a laugh at the other end of the line. "In the railroad station on my way to the Field. I just got in at the Meudon station five minutes ago."

"Byrd, how wonderful!" Bitsy began, but now Byrd was talking again.

"Can I come and see you? Right now, I mean, just for ten minutes before I have to be back?"

Bitsy caught sight of her own torn, filthy hands as she started to answer. She was a sight, muddied and disheveled and in her worst old farm clothes. "Better not today," she said, and then told him about Margaret's accident.

"Golly, I'm sorry," Byrd said quickly. "Of course I won't come when the household's upset. Tell Margaret I'm terribly sorry."

Bitsy hung up with a little sigh of relief. It wasn't until she was finally stretched out in the grateful warmth of the bathtub that she realized that it wasn't the household but the way she had looked herself that had kept her from letting Byrd come straight over. She thought of Margaret with her face streaked and filthy putting out her arms to Bruce. It'd be different if I'd been hurt, Bitsy defended herself. Then I wouldn't have cared how I looked. Somehow, though, the thought took away some of her earlier perfect relaxation, and she got up and dressed for supper.

Mrs. Close, who was walking back from Meudon, hadn't gotten home yet and Tim was helping Cousin Bert in the kitchen. Bitsy started to take some of the dishes into the dining room but he shooed her away. "You've done your share for today," he said. "The rest of this evening Mum and I do the work."

The telephone rang and Bitsy would have answered it if Tim hadn't given her a little push toward the old-fashioned Morris chair that was next to the radio. "Don't you know when to rest?" he asked, and picked up the receiver.

A moment later he charged across the living room. "Bits, it was Schwed," he called. "The hog won. Ten bucks in cash."

XVII

Two Is Company

Margaret got off with nothing worse than a heavy cold, but her accident frightened her into taking care of herself. She had given up her library job after Christmas and now she no longer did the work around the house that she had previously insisted on doing. Bitsy was tempted to ask if she had heard any more about Bruce's getting into the Army, but she decided against it. Bruce was naturally vague and evasive and Margaret had withdrawn into herself in a way that discouraged questions. She was very quiet now but seemed contented and spent most of the time in her own room knitting or sleeping or doing the family mending.

Bitter weather set in during the end of February, and it seemed to Bitsy that she could hardly remember a time when it hadn't been a struggle to keep warm. Getting out of bed on these cold, dark mornings was torture. As Bitsy shivered into her cold, clammy clothes, she longed for the bright, steam-heated rooms in the New York apartment with all her heart. But once she was fully dressed and outside, she enjoyed the vagaries of winter weather. It was strange how much more important the quality of each day was in the country than in the city. It made going out for the first time in the morning a regular little adventure because you really cared what the day was going to be like.

Bitsy was surprised to find that even on the coldest mornings she enjoyed milking. It was an understood thing now that she was to milk the big, gentle Holstein while Tim and Steve fed the other livestock. Bitsy liked the close warmness of the clean animal and the regular rhythmic spurt of the milk against the pail. It was good to have learned anything so thoroughly that she could do it when she was still dazed with sleep, her head nodding against bossy's warm side. Maybe that was the point of farm life, she thought. There were so many things to be done and in the regular doing of them there was the reward of mastery.

During the last days of February it stayed cold and a raw, relentless rain dripped down from leaden skies. There was nothing they could do in the drab fields, and they spent more time than ever before inside the big farmhouse. On several occasions Tim and Steve went down to the wood lot near the glen with axes and heavy clippers over their shoulders to cut out brush. Once Bitsy offered to help, but Tim said gruffly that it was men's work and that she had better go inside.

"Don't be silly," Bitsy said, but Tim's mind was made up and he and Steve trudged off without her. She looked after Tim, square and resolute in his high rubber boots and blue denims bulky with the sweaters he wore underneath, and for a moment she felt cross and left out. She knew that Flossie Larson and Rose Pesky and the other girls who lived on the neighboring farms seldom did outdoor work unless it was for the Victory Club at school, but it was unlike Tim to keep her from trying anything. Probably Steve had put him up to it, she thought, and turned back to the house to thaw out her chilled hands and feet.

Although the living room and the kitchen were the only really warm rooms in the house, Bitsy gradually took to doing her homework in the library where her mother worked on her illustrations. Except for Mrs. Close's little working space directly beside the small oil stove, the library was damp and chilly, but Bitsy preferred to study in her coat and mittens rather than to sit in the living room and hear Cousin Bertha's scolding. Cousin Bert had never been flattering, but now as her inward nervousness increased she was aggressively carping, and Bitsy wondered how Margaret, who was usually her butt, could stand it.

Mrs. Close had a new book to illustrate and she worked on it with a determined concentration that nothing could disturb. A few months ago Bitsy would have resented her concentration, but now she understood the necessity behind it. Cousin Bertha charged them nothing for their lodging, but their board and other expenses came out of Mrs. Close's earnings and the fraction of Dad's captain's pay that he could send them.

During those damp, windswept weeks only Tim seemed really at ease. He was kindly and amusing with his mother and cheerful and open with everyone else. The farm was doing well, his hog had won him an unexpected ten dollars, and things went along smoothly at school.

The only times that Tim seemed off beat was when Byrd dropped in at the farm. Then he usually disappeared and Bitsy often found him afterwards in the barn having one of his long, incomprehensible conversations with Steve. She would hear their voices through the barn door: Steve's deep and monosyllabic, Tim's higher and more cheerful, but the moment she opened the door both voices stopped. Steve sank into a cloutish silence and Tim either whistled or talked to Bitsy about something that had obviously just popped into his mind.

Two days after Margaret's accident Byrd had an afternoon off and came over to take Bitsy to the movies. To be with him again, to feel his strong hand press hers, was almost worth all the cold weeks of waiting.

She bubbled over with questions, but even after he had answered them it was hard for her to understand exactly what he had done in Washington. She had a confused picture of huge government offices, snatches of talk with Captain This and Major That, and gay, sophisticated parties in the evening where Minty Blaine and Josh Asprey had surprisingly appeared.

Now that Byrd was back at the Field, his work had temporarily changed. He was no longer flying but taking the place of one of Colonel Grainger's aides, who was home on sick leave. "It's a sort of staff job," Byrd ended up. "Kind of glorified flunkey for the colonel. It'll last until Oates gets back, and then I'll be in the air again. But now tell me what you've been up to."

"Oh, we keep busy around here," Bitsy began, but Byrd didn't seem much interested. He asked polite, perfunctory questions about Mrs. Close and Stanty, but he seemed bored when Bitsy spoke of Tim's Four-H hog or the trouble they had had with the early lambs.

"I really work hard," she said half defensively. "I know it isn't exactly glamorous, but I guess it's as useful as being a Nurse's Aide."

"Oh yeah, sure," Byrd said vaguely, but it was clear he wasn't interested, and it was a relief when they went back talking about how much they had missed each other.

They went to a teashop in Bricklow village for supper and then about nine o'clock Byrd took Bitsy home to the farm. Bitsy's cheeks glowed as they drove through the moist night air. "I saw a lot of girls in Washington," Byrd had said, "but they didn't come up to you. Not one of them."

Well, nobody came up to Byrd either. He was more successful, handsomer, infinitely more desirable than any other man on earth. Bitsy moved close to him on the seat of the borrowed car. One of the joys about being in love was to put into words what you felt about your beloved. It was as though you had held back these words and feelings all your life and yet now when they came pouring out they were not enough.

As soon as they got back to the farm, the lovely feeling of union and intimacy that had existed between them while they talked of each other or their love disappeared. Cousin Bert sent Bitsy out to the barn to find Tim, and Byrd went with her. When they got near the barn they heard the rumble of Steve's and Tim's voices, but when they went inside the talking stopped instantly. Steve and Tim just looked at them as Byrd rehooked the old-fashioned catch on the barn door. It wasn't until Byrd had walked across the floor with his hand out that Tim finally pulled himself together enough to say hello. Byrd nodded to Steve, but the farm hand only gave his disconcerting laugh and left to go over to his own cabin.

"What's eating the guy?" Byrd asked, but Tim didn't answer, and Bitsy was left to explain lamely that Steve was always unsociable.

The next morning, bicycling to school, Tim was his old responsive self. "Steve can't stand soldiers," he said. "The village he lived in when he was a kid was pillaged and burned and I guess he thinks all soldiers are the same, even Byrd."

"Did he tell you that?" Bitsy looked over at Tim curiously.

"Oh sure," Tim said. "Steve tells me everything about his family, and the red heifer he had when he was a kid, and what he thinks we ought to do on this farm. It's just that he doesn't like talking in a crowd."

As the weeks wore on it became clear to Bitsy that Steve wasn't the only one who resented Byrd. Tim never voluntarily mentioned him one way or the other, but he froze whenever his name was brought up and did his best to keep out of the way when he visited the farm.

Now that Byrd was on staff duty, he seemed to have more time off, and he came over to the farm frequently. It's wonderful he's not flying, Bitsy told herself, and wondered why she so often felt uncomfortable after he left. She was genuinely glad that he no longer had to take the risks he had taken earlier in the winter, but it was disturbing how much more difficult his new work was to talk about. He was no longer concerned with motors, engines, and air speeds, which Bitsy obviously wasn't expected to understand, but with people, and all of them frightening, impressive-sounding people whom Bitsy felt she ought to know but never did. "I was talking about the African raids to Collett," Byrd said once. "You can imagine how he opened up about that." Then he stopped short and looked at Bitsy almost pityingly. "But you don't know Collett, do you? I keep forgetting what a baby you were when you left New York."

Bitsy's cheeks flushed and a quick answer came to her lips, but Byrd didn't even know he had been insulting. He went on blithely in his confident, rather loud voice how Captain This had told Major That that the new men from Kelly Field weren't so good as the ones who had come out earlier in the year.

Mother and Cousin Bert often asked about Byrd, but it wasn't until the middle of March that Bitsy asked him to Sunday supper. Bruce and Margaret went upstairs early, but the rest of the family sat around the living room. Cousin Bert, Tim, and Stanty listened to the radio while Byrd, his long legs stretched out in front of him as he sat on Tim's favorite chair, talked to Mrs. Close about the Field.

"I'm working for Colonel Grainger now," he said. "Probably Bitsy told you."

Mrs. Close shook her head. "Colonel Ben Grainger?" she said pleasantly. "Why don't you bring him around for supper some time?"

Bitsy avoided looking at Byrd, but she could feel the embarrassed red rise up from her neck and ears. Ask Colonel Grainger over for a pick-up supper at the farm! After the way Byrd had spoken about it to him, Mother might just as well have asked him why he didn't bring President Roosevelt or General Marshall in for a little snack. She wanted to say something, but no words came to her lips and now, surprisingly, Byrd was nodding his head.

"He's awfully anxious to see you again," he said politely. "I didn't know until this evening that you knew him. When he heard I was going over to Bricklow, he asked me to give you and Mrs. Crane his best. He said he hoped you'd remember him."

"Remember is good!" Cousin Bert entered the conversation with the grace of an elephant. "He tried his best to marry Katherine for two years before she went East."

Mrs. Close and Byrd laughed and Bitsy lifted her head with a little gasp of relief. "He was stationed out here just after he'd left West Point," Mrs. Close said. "He thought he wanted a wife but he was really married to the Army."

"He still is," Byrd said. "He's the greatest spit-and-polish bachelor in the Army, but his men are crazy about him."

Bitsy thought that the conversation would end there, but the next week Byrd came around with a polite note from Colonel Grainger asking Mrs. Close if she and Mrs. Crane and Bitsy would lunch with Byrd and himself at the officers' club the following Sunday. Byrd was obviously impressed, but the invitation didn't thrill Cousin Bertha.

"You two go," she said with the slightly martyred air that she had worn lately. "I'm staying to get lunch for Margaret and Bruce. I don't want her standing on her feet any more than's necessary. Girls do such foolish things nowadays."

"We'll take Tim," Mrs. Close said cheerfully. "I'm sure Ben wanted three of us."

She left to work in the library, but Bitsy followed her. "Listen, Mum, we can't take Tim," she said. "It'd just be a mess!"

"Why would it?" Mrs. Close asked vaguely, studying the drawing of Ginger that she was using for the cover of a new children's book. "Ben always liked boys, and in the living room just now Tim said he'd like to see the Field."

"Because—because he and Byrd——" Bitsy began, but now Mother was leaning over, rubbing out soft charcoal lines with a rubber and she might just as well have pleaded with the cracked bust of Julius Caesar over in the corner.

Sunday came unbelievably quickly, as dreaded days

always will, and it worked out just the way Bitsy had expected. Tim wearing his outgrown Sunday clothes looked
younger and somehow rougher than ever. He was obviously ill at ease and stumbled over his own feet as they
walked into the long, wainscoted lounge at the officers'
club. Colonel Grainger, immaculate, graying, and even
taller and more beribboned than Bitsy had imagined
him, greeted them and then took Mrs. Close off to have a
cocktail in the bar downstairs. Byrd took Bitsy aside on
pretense of showing her one of the silver skeet trophies
at the far end of the long room. "Why on earth did you
bring that oaf?" he asked. "He looks as though he might
start picking the hayseed out of his ears at any moment."

Ordinarily Bitsy would have stood up for Tim, but
today she was too annoyed with Mother for bringing him
to do anything but agree. "Mum would bring him," she
said. "I told her it'd spoil everything, but she wouldn't
listen."

Byrd would have said more but just then Tim joined
them. "What's that plane that's just taxiing over the
Field?" he asked. "The one that looks like a P-40?"

"P-38," Byrd said without even turning around to look.
"I thought every fool knew those."

Four young pilot officers, their wings gleaming on perfectly pressed tunics, came into the big room and stopped
to speak to Byrd. He introduced them to Bitsy but ig-
nored Tim as though he had been part of the furniture.
It was a moment before Bitsy realized that he had really
left Tim out on purpose. She knew that she could have
introduced Tim herself, but by the time she was aware

of what was happening, it was too late. The pilots had nodded politely and now strode off toward the dining room, consciousness of their wings reflected in every inch of their broad backs and well-scrubbed necks. While Byrd moved after one of them, Bitsy turned to Tim, who looked thinner, more insignificantly civilian than ever. "Don't you say a word," he said before she could even open her mouth. "I'll get even with that guy if it's the last thing I do."

More and still more groups of officers and ladies were coming into the club. On the pretense of seeing the planes better, Bitsy moved out onto the deserted porch that overlooked the huge Field. It's all Mother's fault, she fumed. She shouldn't have brought him. I knew it would spoil everything.

In a few minutes Mrs. Close and Colonel Grainger had joined them and the colonel was methodically explaining the use of the warehouse and the repair shops that looked like solid concrete blocks at the far end of the tan field. Tim stood beside them and Bitsy moved over closer to Byrd, hoping to take his mind off Tim. "Those are bombers," she said, pointing to the big glass-nosed walruses that were lined up to the right. "And I know those are transports, but I never can separate the pursuit planes."

"Oh, it's easy really," Byrd said. "You see these are the 38's, and those are the 40's of course, and these are the little Piper cubs. You can't miss once you get the hang of it."

"Oh no?" Tim had edged his way in beside Bitsy and

Byrd. "Well, that was a 40 we saw from the lounge window. The colonel just said so."

Byrd tried to shrug it off, but Colonel Grainger was looking at him and already beginning to laugh. "I guess he caught you short that time, Lieutenant," he said. "Even a good bomber pilot can make a mistake on these new pursuits."

Byrd managed to laugh it off, but Bitsy knew that he could have cheerfully killed Tim right then and there.

The wind whipped across the open field onto the uncovered porch and after a few more minutes they were forced inside. Their table was ready for them, and Colonel Grainger led the way into the crowded dining room. Even after they were seated more people came into the dining room, and several of the officers stopped to speak to Colonel Grainger. Each time Byrd snapped to his feet with Tim shuffling up less confidently after him.

If Byrd had lost face out on the porch he scored back on Tim during luncheon. Colonel Grainger was mostly occupied by talking over old times with Mrs. Close while Byrd chatted with Bitsy. Tim was left out in the cold. His confidence waned perceptibly and by dessert he was almost crimson with discomfort.

The colonel had ordered Camembert with their coffee and the rushed waiter brought it to them in one single round with a cheese knife. "You cut it, Lieutenant," the colonel said, and Byrd in turn passed it to Tim.

"You're used to dairy products," he said, and pressed the knife into Tim's unwilling hand. Tim's hand shook with embarrassment and he would have sliced the cheese the wrong way if Mrs. Close hadn't come to the rescue.

"Oh, this is woman's work," she said, and in another moment she had the cheese cut the right way and passed it around.

The uncomfortable meal was finally over, and when Byrd and the colonel went to the officers' cloakroom to get their coats Mrs. Close stopped to telephone to a friend who was living at the Field. Tim and Bitsy were left alone in front of the bulletin board. Bitsy knew Tim was going to say something and began ostentatiously to read aloud the notices of a skeet shoot, but Tim began talking anyway. "Your mother's like Mrs. Miniver," he said slowly. "She just walks in beauty like the night. She couldn't even imagine people being mean."

Bitsy started to giggle, but something about Tim's tense face made her stop. "Mum's O.K.," she said lamely, and let it go at that.

She thought about it again when she sat between Tim and Byrd on the way home. Mother was beautiful. And it was true that she was so completely generous herself that she couldn't even suspect other people of meanness. Probably she'd never wanted to hang onto a beau who every day seemed to grow more desirable and unattainable. Bitsy gave a little sigh as Byrd turned down the lane toward Bricklow. Perhaps Mrs. Miniver was sometimes too good to live with in actual life.

The colonel got out in the snowy driveway the minute Byrd stopped the car. "Won't you come in and see Bert?" Mrs. Close asked him, but he shook his head.

"I'd love to come another time," he said. "But we've

got to get back to the Field. I have a staff conference at five o'clock."

Byrd made a grimace behind the colonel's back and squeezed Bitsy's hand, but when Mrs. Close and the colonel turned he saluted smartly, and a few moments later they had driven off.

They went into the farmhouse and for a moment Bitsy thought that everyone had gone out. The radio was turned off and the Sunday paper unwrinkled and unopened lay on the table in the living room. "Stanty!" Mrs. Close called. "Stanty! Where is the boy?"

"They've probably all gone out for a walk," Bitsy said, and just then they heard a sound in the kitchen.

They looked in and there was Cousin Bert with her sleeves rolled up kneading bread as though her life depended on it.

"Why, Bert," Mrs. Close said. "I thought you never worked on Sunday afternoons."

Cousin Bert turned, and for the first time Bitsy caught sight of her face. It was about the color of the dough she was kneading and tears had made deep furrows down her cheeks. "I like to keep busy," she said uncertainly. Then, as Mrs. Close moved toward her across the kitchen, she straightened her shoulders and kneaded harder than ever. "Bruce got a telegram this morning," she said fiercely. "He's been accepted as a flying cadet to go into the service April 15th."

~~~~~~

XVIII

Trouble in a Jeep

Even before she got up the next morning Bitsy knew that something unusual had happened. She woke up during the night to the sound of footsteps and whispering voices. She wondered, vaguely, if Stanty had a stomach-ache, and then pulling up her blankets she fell asleep again. When the alarm clock rang she lay still for a moment, nerving herself to get up out of bed and cross the cold floor to her clothes. She heard her mother humming a tune as she went into the bathroom, but there was no clatter of pots and pans nor the whirr of Cousin Bert's egg beater downstairs.

Bitsy got out of bed wondering if Cousin Bert could possibly have overslept. She pulled on her clothes and hurried down to the kitchen, but there was no sign of Cousin Bert. Mrs. Close, who was usually the last one down, had already started to get breakfast. She held a coffeepot in one hand while she searched hopelessly for the coffee. "Bert must be asleep," she said. "Poor lamb, after yesterday's news I guess she needed the rest."

Bitsy got out the coffee and turned on the small elec-

tric range beside the big coal stove. Cousin Bert had been
superb. The thing that she had dreaded had come to
pass, and all her natural stoicism rose to meet the inevi-
table. Except for the look on her face when they had first
seen her kneading bread she had acted as though Bruce's
going off were as much a part of farm life as an early
frost. She had spent more time than usual on getting
their Sunday supper, but when she came into the dining
room her face was cheerful. She had barely tasted the
delicious Parker House rolls or the Welsh rabbit herself
but she had been unusually considerate to Margaret, and
her martyred attitude had entirely disappeared.

"Cousin Bert was swell last night," Bitsy said, but now
Mrs. Close was inexpertly breaking eggs into a mixing
bowl and didn't hear. Bitsy had just started to say it again
when Cousin Bert herself walked in—a Cousin Bert looking weird and unfamiliar in pigtails and mannish wrapper at half-past seven in the morning!

"Why, Bert!" Mrs. Close gasped, but Cousin Bert was
already talking.

"It's come!" she burst out. "A seven-pound boy, and
Margaret's splendid. They—they're naming it Vinton!"

"No!"

"When?"

"Bert, how lovely!"

"When did it happen?" Tim asked, coming into the
kitchen from the barn.

Just then Stanty bounced into the kitchen from the
hall. "Wh-what's going on?" he demanded when he

saw them all clustered around Cousin Bert. "Is there a f-fire?"

"Margaret's got a new baby boy," Mrs. Close told him, but Stanty didn't seem much impressed.

"Is th-that all?" he said, and then another idea struck him. "Where is it?" he asked. "Can I see it right now?"

"He's over at the Meudon Hospital," Cousin Bert told him, and her tired face looked happier, gentler, than Bitsy had ever seen it. "I'll take you over next week."

"Not till then?" Stanty said, and looked around the kitchen. "Well, then, when do we eat?"

A hungry boy was always a challenge to Cousin Bert. She took charge of breakfast, and her small pigtails whisked this way and that as she bustled around the kitchen. "We ought to have something to celebrate," she said, whipping the egg whites to a towering mass. "I meant to get up early, but Bruce only came back from the hospital about an hour ago, and after he told me I went to sleep."

"How's Bruce?" Tim asked. "Did the father bear up well?"

Cousin Bert shut the oven door on a pan of muffins. "He'll live," she said. "But he needs sleep. He took Margaret over to the hospital at twelve and the baby was born at half-past four."

Even with Cousin Bert running things it was a late meal. There were too many questions to be asked and all of the family felt too much like celebrating to treat this like an ordinary Monday. Tim and Bitsy didn't take the school bus and had to bicycle hard against the stiff March wind. At that they were late, and Bitsy felt as though she spent all the rest of the school day hurrying to catch up.

For the first time in weeks she was struck with the impersonality of the enormous high school. Except for the Larsons, whom she saw at lunch hour, there was no one there who would be interested in the news. She knew most of the people in her class by name, but except for the handful who lived around Bricklow she didn't know them any better than she had at the end of the first few weeks of school. It was partly the size of the classes but also the fact that as soon as school was over they went back to different sections of the countryside that were too far apart to be easily visited during gas rationing. The students who lived right in Meudon saw a good deal of each other, Bitsy knew, but those from the outlying communities were swallowed up by their unknown outside lives as completely as she and Tim were absorbed by the farm.

The wind was at Bitsy's back going home and she made excellent time. She thought about Margaret as she pedaled, and a feeling of curiosity mixed with shyness came over her. She wanted terribly to see Margaret right away, to know firsthand that she was all right, and to hear just what she had gone through. Equally surely Bitsy knew that she didn't want to hear Cousin Bert and Mother discuss labor pains as matter-of-factly as though they were talking over floor wax or a new door for the stove. It wasn't that Cousin Bert, or Mother certainly, was coarse or hard-hearted. It was just that all older people who had been through childbearing long ago chilled you somehow so that the very mention of pain was frightening. Perhaps it was like the trip out on a ski train when the mention of spills and hairbreadth escapes was terrifying, whereas on the way back, when you had been down the runs yourself, you gloried in talking of every hairpin turn and obstacle.

When Bitsy got back to the farm she found the army jeep that Byrd sometimes drove when he was on errands for the colonel parked in front of the door. Byrd himself came out before she was off her bicycle. "Boy, am I glad to see a friendly face!" he said. "Stanty told me about his new cousin and then he went off to visit a friend. Your mother's out, Mrs. Crane's asleep, and Tim doesn't like my face and has gone out shooting."

"Did Tim say he didn't like your face?" Bitsy asked, but Byrd looked down at her with a grimace.

"Actions speak louder than words," he said, and kissed Bitsy's cold cheek. "He took one look at me sitting alone in the living room and then picked up his gun and ran. He didn't shoot me, but I have an idea he'd like to."

"Tim's swell really," Bitsy said, but she giggled in spite of herself. "It's just that you make him feel like a dope."

"Which he is," Byrd said calmly, and pulled Bitsy toward the door.

"He is not," Bitsy said hotly, but it was impossible to argue with Byrd.

"Listen, honey," he said, his voice suddenly pleading. "I'm a dashing young officer A.W.O.L. just for the sake of your blue eyes. Quit trying to sell me your cousin and give me something to eat instead. I've only got a few minutes more, and I've been so lonely I even went up to the barn to see if the cows felt sociable."

There was a shot in the glen to the south of them, and Bitsy jumped at the loud report. "Tim's shooting all right," she said. "But I guess he'll get back on time so that he and Steve can do the chores."

"Even the Pole's away," Byrd said lightly. "But that's just too bad for Uncle Timothy. I'd love to see him really have to hump himself for once."

"Tim works harder than you do," Bitsy said, but Byrd wasn't listening. She made them both some hot chocolate and then as she set out the cups she asked Byrd how he had gotten there in the first place.

"My big boss is on his way to Washington," Byrd said. "He goes in a plane, but Man Friday takes his foot locker down to the express office for him. Funny thing how much time you can spend at a railroad station."

"Byrd, you're terrible," Bitsy said, but her voice was anything but shocked. "You mean you stopped off here on your way back from town?"

"Haven't even been there," Byrd said calmly, buttering himself a thick wedge of homemade bread. "The colonel's best becomes are sitting outside in the jeep in his own little suitcase. I've got to take 'em down to the station in ten minutes."

They had just begun to drink their hot chocolate when Tim came in, his face red and wind-burned from the cold. "Can I have some?" he asked, and when Bitsy nodded helped himself from the saucepan on the stove.

Byrd made no effort to make room for him at the table, but Tim seemed determined to be polite. "I see you're going off again," he said pleasantly. "Saw your baggage out in the car."

"You don't want to jump to conclusions," Byrd said shortly as his hand reached for Bitsy's under the table.

Tim looked at him, his ears reddening, and then clumped out of the kitchen, his hot chocolate untouched.

A few minutes later Byrd had to leave. Bitsy stopped to pick up a coat and followed him outside. He was just beside the car when she heard him cry out. "Who's been at this?" he demanded. "Where's that fool cousin of yours?"

Bitsy's heart thumped as she ran forward. Byrd's voice was shaky with anger and his face was scarlet. "Byrd," she said. "Byrd, what has happened?" The next minute her shocked eyes saw the mess in the back of the jeep. Papers, uniforms, underclothes, were scattered everywhere. One suitcase and the foot locker were entirely empty. The other bag was apparently locked, but on top of it lay a dead squirrel, the red blood oozing down over the initials B. G.

"Wha-what in the name of——" Bitsy began, but now Byrd had hold of her shoulders and was almost shaking her with rage.

"I'll scalp that cousin of yours within an inch of his life!" he shouted. "I'll just kill him for this!"

"But, Byrd," Bitsy got out. "How'd you know he did it?"

*B*yrd never stopped to answer. Tim had come down now on the way to the barn, and Byrd crossed over to him in three short steps. "You—you lout!" he said, and for one terrible moment Bitsy thought he was going to hit Tim full in the face. Instead he picked him up as though he had been Stanty's size and half dragged, half carried him toward the car. "What is this?" he roared. "A joke? Can't you understand I could be court-martialed for this, broken?"

Tim's face went absolutely white. For what seemed like ages he didn't say anything at all but just looked at the car, his mouth a thin, tight line. "It's fierce," he said finally. "But I didn't do it."

"You lie!" Byrd said, and shook Tim so that his cap rolled in the mud. "You sneaking, lying, cowardly pup. If you were half my size I'd lick you within an inch of your life."

"Try it!" Tim said. "Go ahead and try it."

Luckily just at that moment Stanty tore around the corner of the house on his bicycle. "Hello, Admiral," he called, and for an instant Byrd turned to look at him.

Stanty jumped off his wheel and ran to the jeep. "Wh-what's happened?" he asked, and then he, too, saw the shambles in the rear.

"G-golly!" he got out, and even the hair on the back of his head seemed to stiffen with curiosity. "W-who did it?"

"That sweet cousin of yours," Byrd said fiercely, but now for the first time Bitsy found her voice.

"We've got to get it cleaned up," she said, and flung

the dead squirrel out of the car and a moment later Ginger ran off with it. "Stanty, go get a brush. Tim, get some hot water. Byrd, you'd better start fixing these papers before they blow away."

Byrd was already crouched in the back of the car, sorting out the papers. "Is everything there?" Bitsy asked, her voice dry in her throat.

Byrd nodded. "Seems to be," he said gruffly. "But by God I'd like to kill that kid."

"Byrd, he said he didn't do it," Bitsy began, but her words lacked conviction. Byrd knew and she knew that he knew that the farm had been deserted except for Tim. "I'll get even with that guy yet." Bitsy remembered Tim's words, even the tone of his voice that miserable day at the officers' club. She began to fold the shirts and underwear with shaking hands. The squirrel's blood had made an ugly smear on one suitcase, but nothing else seemed to be injured. Even so, it would be impossible to get things back exactly the way they had been, and Colonel Grainger didn't look like a man who would appreciate a practical joke on himself.

Bitsy thought of her first day on the farm when Tim had let her believe that he was Steve's son. He had pulled a practical joke then, but this one was infinitely worse. "What will happen?" she asked finally. "What will the colonel say?"

"What will he *do*, you mean?" Byrd said, and now working with his overcoat and tunic off and his barracks cap pushed back on his worried forehead, he looked terribly young and cold and pitiful. "He can do almost anything. Even get me kicked out of the service with a dishonorable discharge!"

"Oh, Byrd!" Bitsy said, and her heart flooded toward him as it hadn't since the day of their bicycle accident. "Byrd darling, he just mustn't! He can't!"

They worked in silence for several minutes, and by the time Tim and Stanty came back with brushes and hot water, Byrd had himself more under control. "Did you or did you not shoot this squirrel?" he asked Tim, and his voice was steely.

"Yes, I did," Tim said, his eyes avoiding Byrd's. "But I just left it up at the barn."

"And then it ran down here and jumped on the suitcase, I suppose," Byrd said bitterly. "And took great care to pop right onto the B. G. that you thought were my initials."

"Well, it won't hurt them," Tim said stubbornly. "Your darn old bag's going to be as good as new."

"It isn't my bag! It happens to belong to Colonel Ben Grainger, and what he's going to say about this kind of a joke I wouldn't like to guess."

For an instant Tim only stared. "B. G.," he said, his eyes on the bag. "You mean—you mean this isn't your suitcase?"

"No!" Byrd snapped, but Bitsy didn't hear him. Her eyes were on Tim, and there was a cold, gone feeling in her stomach. This proved that Tim had done it. He'd thought the bags were Byrd's because of the similar initials. "Tim, how could you?" she began, but now Byrd had gotten into the jeep to leave.

"Good-by, Bitsy," he said. "I'll telephone you to tell you what happens."

For the first time in her life Bitsy went out of her way to be demonstrative to Byrd in front of Tim. She reached up and, putting her arms around his neck, kissed him on the lips. "Good-by, darling," she said. "It's got to turn out all right."

In another minute Byrd had gone and Bitsy was left standing face to face with Tim. "Bitsy," he pleaded, "Bitsy, I didn't know——"

"You fool!" Bitsy cut him short. "You poor, simple fool!"

Bitsy was never quite sure how she got through the hours until her mother came home on the late bus. During suppertime she pleaded a headache and stayed in her room. Cousin Bert, still thrilled and companionable over the new baby, brought her up a tray of delicious creamed eggs and muffins without asking a question. "You just get a good rest," she said when she came back for the tray. "Tim wasn't feeling up to the mark either. Maybe I've been so filled up with my own worries I've driven you all a little hard lately."

Bitsy felt a sudden twinge of remorse, but there was nothing she could say or do. She couldn't sit opposite Tim that night if it was her last meal on earth. "I'm all right, thanks," she mumbled. "I'll feel fine tomorrow."

She tried to do her homework, but at the end of three pages she realized that she hadn't understood a single word. She took a hot bath and spent the rest of the evening puttering around in a pretense of tidying up her room.

Finally she heard the creak of the door, and she dashed down to find her mother coming into the hall. Before Mrs. Close even had a chance to take off her hat or coat, Bitsy pulled her into her own little room and began to tell her the whole wretched story. "It was such a rotten trick," she finished up, her bitterness against Tim suddenly rising. "I—I could have cried for Byrd."

"How about Tim?" Mrs. Close said. "You don't honestly think for a minute that he did it, do you?"

Bitsy could have stamped her foot with irritation. "But, Mum," she said. "I just told you Byrd accounted for everybody on the farm. He happened to find out about everybody because he was bored before I got home."

Mrs. Close got up and put her hands on Bitsy's shoulders so that her deep violet eyes looked straight into Bitsy's. "Bitsy," she said. "You know Tim's terribly in love with you, don't you?"

Bitsy's eyes shifted slightly. "Yes," she said. "I know he likes me anyway. But Byrd, but Byrd and I——" She wanted to tell her mother that she and Byrd were engaged, but she couldn't. Not now, when she still felt furious, filthied almost, by what had happened.

"Then think a moment," Mrs. Close said. "And try to be fair. Since Tim loves you, would he do anything to make you like Byrd more? Even granting that he thought the suitcases were Byrd's, would making trouble for Byrd be likely to put him in a better position with you? Anything that you would be bound to know about that would get Byrd in trouble or even make him uncomfortable would be a stupid move for Tim to make, and he's not stupid."

Bitsy pulled herself free from her mother's hands and moved over to the window. She looked out at the big barn, dark and massive, silhouetted against the moonlight. It had seemed so obvious that it must be Tim that she hadn't even stopped to think that it couldn't be. "He said he didn't do it," she said slowly, and Mrs. Close nodded her head.

"Of course," she said. "And can you imagine Tim telling a good lie? It'd be about as easy to imagine Cousin Bert lying."

"Or Rip or Ginger," Bitsy said, and smiled for the first time since she had come home from school. "But if he didn't do it, who did?"

"We can't find that out tonight," Mrs. Close said as she took off her hat and coat. "It's frightfully late already."

"Don't go," Bitsy pleaded, but now Mrs. Close was firm.

"I've got to," she said. "I've got to get up early to work tomorrow and I've had a long, hard day and so have you."

Bitsy went to bed, but the minute the lights were out she felt more wide-awake than ever. She still could see the awful picture of that littered jeep and then Byrd's angry face and finally Tim's. It had been white and drawn and strangely unfamiliar. Tim, sturdy, reliable

Tim, with tears in his eyes and his voice shaking. Tim, the person who always understood things and now so terribly misunderstood himself.

She twisted and turned so that the sheets pulled out and her bed was an itchy, uncomfortable mess. She switched on the light and straightened up her bed, but when she lay down again, she felt chilled. She decided to go and see how much hot water was left, and putting on her wrapper and slippers she padded down the hall. She was just turning into the bathroom when she saw Tim, still dressed in his work clothes, coming up the stairs.

He saw her at about the same moment and started to back down, but on a sudden impulse she called out to him. "Tim, don't go. Please don't. I want to talk to you."

He came up slowly, his face red and sheepish-looking. "I forgot to feed the animals," he said. "First time in my whole life."

He looked so wretched and humble and woebegone that Bitsy's last crust of pride melted. "Tim," she said, "I was a dope. I know you didn't mess up Byrd's car. But it's so frightfully puzzling who did do it."

"Bits!" Tim said, and now his face looked as though he had suddenly seen sunlight after years of blindness. "Bitsy, I knew you'd believe me. I was sure you would when you stopped to think."

XIX

Visit to Margaret

For the next few days the March wind howled down the chimneys and a cold, disagreeable rain dripped from the bare branches and left the fields sodden and homely. Inside the farmhouse it seemed to Bitsy that they were all living on such different planes of happiness that they could hardly communicate with each other. She herself felt nervous and irritable and jumped each time the telephone rang, thinking it might be Byrd with word from the colonel. Cousin Bert was happily preoccupied cleaning and rearranging the farmhouse for the baby's homecoming. As for Bruce, he seemed almost lightheaded with pleasure and relief. He was the one now who passed up his plate for second enormous helpings and made the simple, earthly little jokes that Cousin Bert loved, while Tim sat silent and haunted-looking with his blue eyes on his untouched food.

Mrs. Close was more abstracted than ever. She drew a great deal and spent every spare moment in banging out letters on her old portable which she mailed herself. Even Stanty was different. He seemed to sense that something was wrong with Tim and followed him around with a devotion that was at once touching and irritating. Tim never mentioned the trouble with the jeep again and actually avoided Bitsy as though he were afraid she might change her mind about his part in it. With Bruce definitely out of the picture for farm work that spring, he was busier than ever and spent every available moment going over the farm machinery and getting ready for the first plowing.

Once Bitsy caught him alone when Stanty was at school and he was starting up to the barn to milk. "What d'you really think will happen?" she started in. "About Byrd's jeep, I mean."

Tim's face had grown thinner and there were dark shadows under his eyes. "I've thought about it ever since it happened," he admitted, and his hurt eyes avoided Bitsy's. "But no matter what they do, Mother's bound to hear. And it'll come just when Bruce has to leave. It couldn't have happened at a worse time."

Byrd didn't come out to the farm again but he telephoned occasionally, and his voice sounded cold and impersonal. "I'm on ice until the colonel gets back," he said, and then added with a sarcastic laugh that sent cold shivers down Bitsy's spine: "But even if they shoot me at sunrise I'll see that Tim gets his."

"But, Byrd, I'm positive he wasn't the one," Bitsy protested. "Mother convinced me it couldn't be. If you could only come out here and let me tell you."

"You couldn't tell me a thing about that dope," Byrd said harshly. "I'd send him to a reform school if I had the power. He's never done you any good either, if you'd like my opinion."

"Oh, Byrd, listen," Bitsy began, but it was useless to try to convince him over the telephone, and a few minutes later he hung up.

Bitsy turned away from the telephone feeling depressed and insecure. Byrd had always hated her affection and respect for Tim. It was the part of her character that seemed to him babyish and dull and made him act as though she were still the old Sea Cliff Bitsy who had been so young and stupid as to be beneath his notice.

For a few minutes Bitsy stood irresolutely looking out of the window of her room. It really couldn't do Tim any good to stand up for him to Byrd. The colonel was the one who would actually decide what would happen to him. Why irritate and alienate Byrd by defending Tim when it couldn't help anyone? Bitsy stared through the rain at the muddy barnyard, and the miry homeliness of it reflected her mood. Life without Byrd as a beau seemed as bleak and dun-colored as the sagging fences and the rain-soaked outbuildings in front of her. If Byrd turned her down she would be back where she had been in September before the Labor Day week end. The very feeling of that cold, hard bench by the Sea Cliff pool came back to her. Loneliness. Insecurity. The feeling of being tongue-tied in front of a gay crowd whose jokes you couldn't join. She remembered arriving at the pool almost praying it would be deserted and at the same time hoping with a shameful, humiliating eagerness that any boy she met would want her for his girl.

She was just turning from the window when she saw
Tim open the barn door to lead the Christmas lamb out
to the pasture. Even now a little flicker of amusement
went through Bitsy at the sight of the absurd, leggy little
creature frisking after its dam. She watched as the coal-
black lamb, suddenly adventurous, dashed off toward the
first patch of green and got caught under the board
fence. She saw Tim stoop and patiently work the lamb
free and then give it a friendly little pat before he set it
down beside its mother.

Bitsy turned and hurried over to the table where she
kept her books. She pulled out her writing paper and
began a letter to Byrd without giving herself time to
change her mind. It wasn't fair. It simply wasn't fair of
Byrd not to listen when she tried to explain to him about
Tim. She had cheated Tim by blaming him herself.
Setting him right with Byrd was the only thing she
could do to make up.

"Dear Byrd," she wrote. "You've simply got to try and
let me tell you about Tim. He couldn't have done it. . . ."
She wrote on and on, her pen scratching across the paper.
When it was finished she stamped the letter and took
it down to the post office and mailed it herself.

She never got an answer, and on Thursday, when Byrd
called up again, she asked him if he had gotten the letter,
half hoping he would say no. "Of course," he said. "And
I hope you don't mind my saying it was a very foolish,
excited letter. I don't think you grasp just how serious
this thing is."

"Oh, Byrd——" Bitsy began, but he was talking again.

"The colonel gets back this afternoon late," he said coldly. "I'm going to explain the whole thing to him the first chance I get."

The tone of Byrd's voice haunted Bitsy for the rest of the day. That afternoon after school she was going to see Margaret and the new baby for the first time. She had been looking forward to it for days, but now her mind was so occupied with Byrd and Tim that she hardly knew what she was doing until she had crossed the tiled, ether-smelling hall of the hospital and the nurse behind the desk asked her whom she wanted to see.

Margaret had dark circles under her eyes but she looked well and there was a peaceful pride about her that Bitsy had never seen before. "Oh, Bitsy, it's good to see you," she said. "I thought they'd never let me see you or show you Vinton."

Bitsy laughed as she took off her coat and mittens. "I feel as though I'd seen him already," she said. "Bruce talks about him as though he were old enough to go out and plant the corn." She looked at Margaret, and the shyness, the ostrich feeling of wanting to hide her head that Cousin Bert and even Mother gave her was all gone now. "Maggie, how was it really?" she asked. "Did you have a terrific time?"

Margaret was as earnest and direct as when she had explained one of Bruce's drawings months ago. "People only tell you the bad parts," she said. "But even the pains are bearable. And there's so much more. A sort of a power-and-glory feeling that I've never had before. It was much worse for Bruce."

"Bruce acts like a two-year-old now though," Bitsy said, and for once Margaret giggled.

"He's been acting Stanty's age ever since it happened," she said. "The morning the baby was born he went home and nobody was up except his mother and Steve. So after he'd told her, he went out and told Steve and gave him the day off and paid him a week ahead."

"He did what?" Bitsy asked, and Margaret repeated what she had said.

"He gave Steve the day off and paid him his wages ahead. Why?"

"Because, because what Steve did that day may be terribly important." She told Margaret what had happened to the car and finished up half out of her chair. "If Steve got all that money he'd be sure to get drunk. And messing that car'd be just the kind of thing he'd do! Margaret, he must have come back to the house when Byrd and I were inside and seen the jeep the first thing!"

"It sounds possible," Margaret admitted, "but he'd never confess to anyone but Tim, and Tim wouldn't ask him if it would get him into trouble. I guess you know that." Her quiet eyes looked steadily at Bitsy, but now Bitsy looked away from the high hospital bed out of the window over the red roofs of Meudon.

"I thought Tim did it at first myself," she admitted. "I feel like crawling when I think about it."

Margaret would have said something but now a starched nurse looked in and beckoned to Bitsy. "I think perhaps Mrs. Crane has visited long enough," she said. "Would you like to come and see the baby?"

Bitsy said good-by to Margaret and followed the nurse down the long hall to the nursery. The nurse disappeared inside and a moment later appeared pushing the baby in a little crib in front of her for Bitsy to see through the glass door.

Vinton looked much smaller than Bitsy had expected and infinitely more fragile and flowerlike. He wasn't red or grotesque in the least, and the small relaxed hand lying over the top of the sheet was such a pale, shell-like pink that you felt you could see through it. He was sound asleep and his eyes were closed, but his neat little button nose and the generous ears reminded Bitsy of Tim. "He's sweet," she said, and the nurse nodded through the glass before she rolled the baby back to the nursery.

Bitsy left the hospital thinking hard. If Steve had done this thing she owed it to Tim to find out and set him right with the colonel. And it would be important for Byrd, too, terribly important, that Colonel Grainger should have the true facts when he first heard the story. Bitsy pedaled as fast as she dared over the wet road toward the farm. The day was rainy and slushy underfoot, but brilliantly clear and soft overhead. It was after five and still quite light, but for once Bitsy was oblivious of the weather. She had a job ahead of her, a difficult job, and the sooner she got it over with, the better.

By the time she got to the barn Steve had just finished bringing down clean bedding for the mules and Tim had started to mix the pigs' food. It was all routine to Bitsy now, and she carried the full pail to the troughs at the far end of the barn with her mind still on what Margaret had said. "It was a break your coming here just when Bruce has to go off," Tim said once. "We wouldn't be able to get through this summer without you."

At any other time Bitsy would have been pleased and touched by his words, but right now she hardly heard. When the chores were done and Tim went down to the house she was going to have to follow Steve up to his cabin and ask him straight out about the mess in the jeep. Steve was never easy to approach, and to get him to talk about a crazy thing he had done when drunk would be next to impossible. She looked over at him as he stood by the door to let the sheep in. He was as big as a giant in his blue work clothes and high boots and his broad face was absolutely expressionless. He's just got to admit it, Bitsy told herself. I've got to make him understand that somehow.

Finally Tim was ready to go down to the house. "Coming?" he asked, but Bitsy shook her head.

"I'm going to brush off Caesar," she said, giving the hog the name that Stanty had given it weeks before. She did stop to brush off the animal with an old brush that she kept on a window sill of the barn. The hog was to be sold the following week and Tim had told her it would bring a better price if it was in perfect condition. The hog was completely over his lameness and his coat was in better shape than any other hog's on the place, but Bitsy was hardly aware of him as she brushed. "You do good job with hog," a voice said suddenly, and Bitsy jumped. She looked up to see Steve looking down at her over the high side of the pen.

For a moment Bitsy only stared with surprise and then, forcing herself as though she were diving from a high board, she plunged into speech. "Steve," she began. "You know the day Bruce's baby was born there was a lot of trouble with Lieutenant Gaylord's car."

The man's small eyes moved shiftily. "What of it?" he said. "I know nothing of soldier or his car."

He was lying, Bitsy knew, and a sudden wave of frustration and anger swept over her. If he lied, Tim and Byrd were just as badly off as before. The fact that she and Margaret and Mother all believed that Tim was innocent would not be enough to satisfy the colonel. "You did it," she flared suddenly. "And now you'll let Tim take the punishment."

"Teem?" The man wheeled on his big boots. "What he got to do with it?"

"The lieutenant thinks Tim did it," Bitsy said quickly. "The colonel, all the other officers will think so too. They'll do something to Tim, you see."

Steve's face changed to a dull red. "Teem know nothing," he said. "I pick up squirrel and put heem in car. Maybe mess up soldier things a leetle. I was plenty drunk."

Bitsy didn't wait to hear another word. She was out of the pen and beside Steve almost before he finished speaking. "You'll stick by that?" she pleaded. "Even if you had to say it in court?"

Steve looked cornered. "Teem know nothing," he repeated. "I say that to any man."

Bitsy hurried out of the barn and toward the house.

Tim met her by the empty clothes yard. "What's the big rush?" he asked. "Supper won't be ready for quite a while."

"Steve messed up the car!" Bitsy said. "He was drunk because Bruce paid him early. He probably wanted to do something to Byrd. You know how he hates officers."

"So that was it!" Tim said, and he looked more as though Bitsy had slapped him instead of bringing him good news. "When we were in the barn one day I let out that I couldn't stand Gaylord, and Steve probably thought he was doing me a favor. He's just that simple."

Bitsy didn't even stop to let him finish. "Where's Mum?" she demanded. "We've got to get her to call up Colonel Grainger right away."

"She's not home," Tim said. "She had to go to New York unexpectedly. Mother says she left a note for you on the hall table."

Bitsy dashed into the house searching for the note. After the months on the farm, Mother's suddenly going off to New York without a word ahead of time seemed as wild and improbable as though she had suddenly flown to Russia or out to Africa to meet Dad. The letter was short and surprisingly non-committal.

"Bitsy darling," it ran. "I'm off to New York on a short, unexpected business trip. I just got the telegram this morning and they wired me to come at once. Bert is driving me over to the five-o'clock train. I'll be back Thursday and tell you all about it. Love, MOTHER."

Bitsy's heart contracted into a cold, uncomfortable ball. Ever since she had left the hospital it had been at the back of her mind that if she could get Steve to admit what he had done, Mother would fix it all up with Colonel Grainger. And now Mother wasn't there, and by the time she got home it would be too late.

For a minute Bitsy just stood with the note in her hand, and then the next minute she began peeling off her clothes. She rushed into her green skirt and coat and then hurried out through the kitchen. Cousin Bertha looked up from the stove with a surprised face. "Going out now? And in those clothes? Supper's nearly ready."

"I've got to go out," Bitsy said, and looked up into Cousin Bert's face as though by the sheer intensity of her pleading she could make her understand. "It's terribly important. To—to Tim and to everybody."

"But you haven't had supper," Cousin Bertha began, but Bitsy was already out of the house and over at the barn. Bruce had taken the sedan to the hospital. The old Ford hadn't had any gas in it for weeks so there was nothing for it but to bicycle. She jumped on and began to pedal down the drive just as she heard Cousin Bert call to her from the kitchen window: "Bitsy! Bitsy, where are you going? Supper's ready!"

Bitsy pedaled furiously. She felt as though she were being chased. As though Cousin Bert might suddenly summon a car out of the blue and come after her down the road before she could reach the Field. Bitsy kept on until her legs and thighs hurt and even then she wouldn't allow herself to coast. Byrd was going to report to the colonel at once. So the colonel knew now and was probably just deciding what to do. She had to get to him

right away before Byrd could throw all the blame on
Tim.

Each time Bitsy had been to the Field she had been
there with Byrd, and she had entirely forgotten the gatehouse and the armed guard. Before she was really up to
the gates the guard came out and stopped her. "I want
to see Colonel Grainger," she said. "It's terribly important."

"Sorry, miss." The guard shook his head. "Can't let
you on the post without a pass."

"But I've got to get in! I've got to see the colonel
right away!"

"I might call him and see if he'll admit you." The
guard relented a little. "What name, please?"

"Elizabeth Close," Bitsy said. "Mrs. Kenneth Close's
daughter. And tell him it's frightfully important."

The man's uniformed back was non-committal, but
beckoning to another guard he stepped into the little
gatehouse and picked up the telephone. "Lady to see
you, sir," Bitsy heard him say. "Short and slight with
brown hair. Name of Coes."

"Close!" Bitsy shouted. "Elizabeth Close. Please tell
him the right name."

"Close," the sentry corrected himself. "The name's
Miss Elizabeth Close." The colonel said something at the
other end and the guard nodded. "And you'll be re-
sponsible for her, sir? Yes sir. I'll send her right up."

Bitsy was already back on her bicycle by the time the
first guard got out of the gatehouse and motioned to

the second to let her pass. "Third quarters on the left," he called. "After you pass the officers' club."

Bitsy nodded and began pedaling up the long roadway that led past the post hospital and the exchange to the officers' red-brick quarters that bordered the flying field. Her heart pumped hard as she walked up the neat brick steps and rang the bell under the sign reading "Colonel B. Grainger." She was suddenly lost, groping for just the right words. She had been so concerned with getting to the Field that she hadn't had time to think just how she was going to tell the colonel.

A maid let her in and showed her into a living room just beyond the door. "Bitsy!" Byrd's voice sounded in her ear. "How'd you get here?"

"Biked," Bitsy said, and the next moment she was shaking hands with Colonel Grainger.

"My dear young lady," he said, taking Bitsy's coat. "This is a most unexpected pleasure."

While he put her coat in the hall, Bitsy had a moment to look around. It was a stiff, conventionally furnished room. One end was half filled with a big, official-looking desk with Byrd standing rigidly beside it. "It's all out," he said in a low voice. "I'm lucky if I'm not busted. But Tim's going to get his too. The colonel's furious."

The next moment Colonel Grainger came back into the room and Bitsy turned toward him. "I've come about the awful business of your suitcases," she said. "It wasn't Byrd's fault and it certainly wasn't Tim's."

"What do you mean?" Byrd exploded, but the colonel motioned to him to be silent.

"It was Steve Kolinchak, our hired man," Bitsy said. "He was drunk, and he's got sort of a grudge against army men. You see he isn't entirely right in his mind and he's just crazy about Tim."

Slowly at first, and then more and more rapidly, Bitsy told the colonel just what had happened. She told him what Steve was like; what she knew of his childhood; and his almost doglike devotion to Tim.

"This clears young Crane, of course," the colonel said. "I'm delighted because it would have been terribly upsetting for his mother. From what you tell me about Kolinchak I don't think we need do anything about him." He turned back to Byrd, and for the first time in days Bitsy's heart melted toward him. "And it wasn't Byrd's fault either," she said. "Really, Colonel, you do see that, don't you?"

For a moment Byrd's face lit up, but the colonel's next words brought back the frozen expression it had had before. "On your part it was a serious offense, Lieutenant," he said, and looked at Byrd as though Bitsy didn't exist. "For an aide to leave his superior officer's equipment where anything could happen to it is a grave infraction of duty."

"Yes sir," Byrd said, and Bitsy's heart ached for him. Byrd the confident, the dashing, was so humbled now. She wanted to say something, but the colonel was speaking again.

"Captain Oakes reported back for duty this morning, I understand?"

"Yes sir," Byrd said, and Bitsy stared at the colonel.

"That means your duty as aide would normally be over, isn't that true?"

"Yes sir!" Byrd's answer might have come from an automaton.

"You would naturally expect to rejoin your unit which will be leaving shortly?"

"Yes sir." Byrd's voice was fainter, and for a moment the colonel didn't speak. He considered some papers on his desk and then he looked back at Byrd.

"Your record except for this episode has been extremely good," he said. "And we need pilots. You will rejoin your unit at once."

"Oh, sir——!" Byrd began, but once more the colonel stopped him. "You will proceed to quarters immediately," he said, and just the flicker of a smile crossed his face. "I will see that Bitsy gets home safely."

"Yes sir," Byrd said. "Thank you, sir." In another moment he had saluted and was gone, and Bitsy was alone with the colonel. "He's a nice boy," the colonel said, taking out a pipe. "And a smart flier. But he's always had too high an opinion of himself."

Bitsy didn't trust herself to say a word. She was glad for Byrd, but it was for Tim that she really rejoiced. Tim, white and haggard and yet determined not to get Steve into trouble. Tim, terrified as to what would happen and still generous enough to grieve because it would upset his mother.

In spite of anything that Bitsy could say, the colonel insisted upon sending her home in an army car. "It's worth it, my dear," he said as the orderly lifted the bicycle into the back. "It doesn't help anybody to get the wrong person into trouble." He helped her into the high seat and then looked up at her, smiling. "You were a good sport to come over," he said. "If I wasn't such an old man, I'd envy Lieutenant Gaylord, or is it young Tim Crane?"

~~~~~~

XX

Unexpected Decision

BY THE TIME the orderly had taken Bitsy's bicycle out of the back of the car and driven off, Cousin Bert had come out of the kitchen door. Her arms were folded and her whole solid body was rigid with disapproval. "And just what have you been doing?" she asked as Bitsy came up the steps.

Her voice was even colder and more thoroughly disapproving than it had been that fall evening when Bitsy had first come to the farm. Then it had seemed terrifying, but now Bitsy understood the warmth that lay behind that forbidding exterior. "Everything's all right!" she said, and flung her arms around the older woman's neck. "It's turned out marvelously!"

"I do not understand!" Cousin Bert began, but just then Tim appeared on the steps beside her and Bitsy launched into a flood of explanation. Now that Tim was completely cleared, there was no reason Cousin Bert shouldn't know the whole story.

"How'd you first dope out it was Steve?" Tim asked when Bitsy stopped for breath. "I was sure, but I thought it'd be impossible to prove it. Besides, I know he'd break up if it ever came into a court."

"He told me!" Bitsy said, and then she told him about her talks with Margaret and with Steve himself.

"That Pole!" Cousin Bert said, but now her voice sounded older, worried, as though Steve were one more problem that she couldn't face alone. "If I only knew what to do with him. After Bruce goes——"

"Leave him to me," Tim said quietly, and for the first time Bitsy noticed how much he had grown that winter. "I'll handle him, Mum, and there won't be any trouble."

"Well, you work with him," Cousin Bert said with a little sigh of acquiescence. "And I always said a woman had no call to be managing farm hands."

The next morning Tim had a long talk with Steve. Bitsy didn't know exactly what he said but she knew he must have told him that she had gotten him out of serious trouble. Steve never mentioned the matter, but his whole attitude perceptibly changed. He didn't turn silent when Bitsy came into the barn now, but went on in his strange, deaf-sounding monotone talking about the plowing and the stock and the little hillside farm in Europe where he had lived as a boy.

Even the weather seemed to express Bitsy's mood and turned suddenly springlike. The red buds thickened on the maples; the crocuses and hyacinths to the south of the kitchen bloomed into welcome dashes of purple and yellow; and the fields that sloped away from the house were a rich emerald green.

Inside the main barn the changes were as noticeable as outside. It was no longer necessary to shoulder the stiff door closed against a maddening wind. The watei pails weren't frozen stiff, and the hogs and cattle could be left out at night.

Most of the sheep had either just lambed or were nearly due, and these were still kept inside. Bitsy never got over the thrill of surprise and pleasure in the baby lambs. On two separate March nights she had helped Tim with the lambing. At first it had been a strange, unreal sensation to follow Tim over to the dark barn where the nervous ewes shoved and stumped and the baby lambs bleated with high, babyish bleats. She felt woefully aware of her own inexperience and inadequacy, but gradually the very necessity for her help gave her confidence. Like everything else on the farm, lambing had a variable pattern that gradually became clear. She learned exactly the moment to begin heating water over the rickety oil stove and when to go for more clean straw in the shed next to the barn.

It was hard, exhausting work, and Bitsy's eyes stung with sleep at school the next day. She felt limp with fatigue, but the work had been satisfactory beyond anything she had ever done. It was good to see the tired ewes clean and comfortable on the new straw, and the lambs were entrancing.

She gradually lost the dread of doing the wrong thing that had petrified her on Christmas night and worked efficiently and quietly beside Tim and Steve. The day after she went over to the Field the last of the lambs were born and Bruce brought home the hundred day-old chicks they had ordered in February. The big barn was a nursery now of small, appealing animals. Even the old gray cat reappeared, gaunt and thin, but arched with pride over the two black kittens that padded along behind her. Stanty nearly exploded with excitement. "B-boy!" he got out. "B-baby animals everywhere!"

Bitsy smiled, glad that it was Saturday and that she had the whole day on the farm. There was so much to be done that as you did one job you found yourself planning the next one. Cousin Bert was taking over the chickens and the turkeys and Bitsy was going to manage the truck garden that Tim had kept in the past. With Tim's help she had ordered the seed, and today, when the ground was soft and warm and the sun shone through the budding trees, was a perfect time to start planting.

She hurried to get at the spading, but it turned out to be slower work than she had expected. She liked it though. It was good to feel the fork cut in under her foot, and the smell of the moist earth as she turned it over was rich and fresh.

It was slow, steady work, and she thought of a remark that Byrd had made once that all farming was just dig and sweat. The thought of Byrd brought back her hopeless conversations with him over the telephone, and her forehead wrinkled with irritation. She tried to forget it and just give herself up to the soft, balmy air and the sound of the birds singing in the lilac bushes beyond the kitchen door. It was spring, and the farm stirred with new life, but the soft, pulsing feel of it eluded her and she found herself arguing in her mind with Byrd. Tim isn't a clod, she defended him.

Oh yeah? She could hear the very tones of Byrd's drawling, confident voice and see the supercilious twitch of his straight nose.

He's got vision. Bitsy tried again. He understands things. But the Byrd in her mind was even more evasive and mocking than the real Byrd when she disagreed with him.

By noon Bitsy was still digging at the earth and still arguing and twisting in her mind. Even the smell of the moist earth and the good heave and haul on her shovel had escaped her. She could feel only the dull ache in her back and the tenser, more poignant frustration in her mind. Tim brought the mules back to the barn after the morning's plowing, but it wasn't until he picked up another spading fork and began to work right beside her that Bitsy was aware of him.

The greater part of the garden was still tight and untouched and covered with the blackened stalks of last year's pumpkin vines. "I've got a lot to do yet," Bitsy said, and stopped to look at the surprisingly small patch of broken earth. "It'll take all afternoon."

"I wish I could help," Tim said. "But Bruce is going over to see Margaret and I've got to finish the plowing."

"It's O.K.," Bitsy said, and kicked the caked earth off her heavy shoes. "We might as well get used to running this farm without Bruce."

"That's right!" Tim said, and the gratitude on his face was almost as plain as words.

After a lunch of Cousin Bert's rich, savory beef stew and newly baked muffins, Bitsy felt surprisingly better. She picked up her spading fork and started toward the garden. She was at the sagging picket fence when she saw how much of the earth had been turned for her. "Why, who——" she began, and then she heard Steve's familiar laugh and saw him starting toward the barn with Tim's fork over his shoulder.

"Oh, Steve!" Bitsy said. "Thanks just loads."

The man stopped for a moment and looked at her gravely and then nodded his head. "It O.K.," he said briefly. "Teem says you help farm all summer."

Bitsy dug up the last rows with a light heart. Steve's acceptance of her was as complimentary as Mr. Schwed's offer of a job. Besides that, it augured well for their teamwork during the coming months. She and Tim and Steve would be able to manage on the farm. Bitsy smiled to herself as she remembered how even a few weeks ago the Pole had seemed threatening and ominous just because he wouldn't talk.

She raked the ground carefully, straightening out the rolls and bumps that came when she hurried. Finally she went up to get the battered garden line and the hoe with the packets of seeds that she had left at the barn that morning. She had just finished her first row of beets, the rough seeds sticking to her fingers, when Stanty came around the house with Ginger behind him. "Golly," he said. "That looks f-fun. Let me do it."

Bitsy showed him how to drop the light little carrot seeds into the shallow rows that she had made beside the beets. "How d'you get to know so much?" Stanty asked, and his voice was genuinely admiring.

"Oh, I'm just a born dirt farmer," Bitsy joked, but by four o'clock, when the first twelve rows of the garden were all neatly seeded and marked with stakes, she really felt like one. To actually have the seeds in the ground was a rich, prosperous feeling like having money in the bank.

The next morning she was quite stiff, but by the time she had pumped the sprayer for an hour so that Tim could spray the apple trees the stiffness had worn off. Mrs. Close was coming home that afternoon and Cousin Bert and Bruce had told Bitsy she could take the car to meet her. It was the first time she had driven in weeks, and she found herself looking forward to it enormously.

When she got to the station she learned that the train was an hour and a half late and she decided to go for a walk. It was delicious to be able to move around without having to hurry to keep warm or having it wet or slippery underfoot. Bitsy found there was a lovely feeling of freedom in just sauntering along that she had never experienced before. Spring was welcome anywhere, but in the country, after a long, cold winter, it was bliss.

She passed a row of cramped, ugly little houses with littered yards and peeling paint. She wondered, suddenly, what it would be like to live with Byrd in a house like one of those. To live there indefinitely, without the hope of moving away. Beside the sagging stoop of the house in front of her a blooming forsythia bush seemed

to give off actual warmth and light to its seamy sur-
roundings. That bush's blooming would be the high spot
of the year, Bitsy thought, and Byrd's voice, familiar and
cocky, began arguing in her mind's ear. "Some high
spot! If I lived there I'd sell it for the first fiver!"

Bitsy walked a little faster, trying to escape the inward
argument that began now each time she thought of
Byrd. It was as though all the arguments that she had
glossed over or stifled when she was with him rose up
to taunt her when she was alone.

She turned finally and headed back toward the station.
An outgoing train whistled in the distance and the
sound, wailing and melancholy, filled her with a loneliness that she hadn't felt since those first nights on the
farm way back in early September. She pushed back the
damp curls from her forehead and let the warm breeze
blow through her opened sweater. Spring was so many
things. The change in the trees, the sweet freshness in
the air, and the vague, indefinable restlessness that left
you lonely and aching.

Soon after she got back to the station the train roared
in. Among the soldiers and civilians that crowded off
Bitsy saw her mother in a new flowered hat struggling
with a suitcase and a big artist's folder. "Bitsy!" Mrs.
Close called when she saw her. "How are you, darling?
And how's Stanty?"

"Fine!" Bitsy took her mother's bag as she spoke.
"And there are two letters from Dad waiting on your
bureau."

"Wonderful!" Mrs. Close said, her face sparkling. "It will be good to get home."

They talked hard all the way. Mrs. Close had seen old friends and relations who had sent messages to Bitsy. She had been to several art exhibitions and to a play and she had had long, satisfactory conferences with two publishers who wanted her to illustrate further books.

"Was that what you went for?" Bitsy asked, but Mrs. Close shook her head and put her hand on Bitsy's.

"Don't go home yet," she said. "Couldn't you turn off somewhere? I've got too many things to tell you."

Bitsy nodded, turning down the lane that led to the covered bridge, and parked when she got to the brook. She was only too glad to have Mother to herself for a moment before they got into the mill run of family life. She had plenty of things to tell her about, too; Byrd's jeep; her call on Colonel Grainger. Mother had asked about Byrd already, but Bitsy had said only that he was well and let it go at that. The new uneasy feeling that came into her mind whenever she thought of him was something she couldn't discuss with anyone.

"Miss Fair sent for me." Mrs. Close plunged into her news. "She wants me to teach art there next year."

"Mother!" Bitsy turned to look at her, but Mrs. Close's eyes were on the small pasture vivid with new green that lay on the far side of the brook, and she went right on talking.

"She wrote to me about it some weeks ago. I wrote to Dad and got a cable from him saying to do whatever I thought best. The next day I got a wire from Miss Fair asking me to come on at once at their expense."

"Then we'll be living there?" Bitsy said, and her voice sounded like a stranger's. "You and Stanty and I."

"Not Stanty," Mrs. Close said, and her hands nervously wove in and out of the handle of her purse. "We could afford only a tiny apartment and there wouldn't really be room for him. Cousin Bert's crazy to keep him, though. She suggested it the minute she saw Miss Fair's telegram. You know how she loves little boys."

Bitsy nodded. She knew all right. It seemed as though she knew and understood everything that happened on the farm. It was New York that she was struggling to conjure up in her mind. She had a picture of the bright, sunny rooms at Miss Fair's with the sound of the river traffic coming through the windows; of rainy nights with the streets gleaming like patent leather; of the click of the subway stile as you dropped down your nickel and hurried through. Yes, she remembered the look and sound of New York, but she had lost the feel of belonging, of having it the place where you lived and worked and made your plans. "I wonder what I'd do if you want to go back to New York," she said aloud, and Mrs. Close looked at her curiously.

"Bert thought you'd jump at the chance," she said. "I wasn't so sure. I know you've come to love the farm——"

Bitsy turned quickly and looked straight into her mother's eyes. "D'you want to go?" she demanded. "I mean really want to go for yourself?"

Mrs. Close shook her head. "No," she said. "Living there without Dad would be awfully hard. It's easier somehow to bear loneliness in the country."

"Why do we do it then?" Bitsy asked. "We can both be useful out here."

Mrs. Close's eyes were back on the brook pasture. "You're awfully honest," she said. "And awfully quick. It took me almost a week to find out my own mind. But I could do it. After talking it over with Miss Fair I know I could do it."

"And loathe every minute of it," Bitsy finished. "Teaching dumb brats to draw when you could be out here with Stanty and drawing things like this." Her hand swept toward the small pasture that Mrs. Close was looking at. Except that the trees in the distance were black and leafless and that the grass had the rich greenness of early spring the place looked much the way it had when Bitsy had come upon it that first day she had walked home from school. In early spring as in late autumn it had the same remote, individual quality that set it off from the rest of that broad, uninteresting landscape.

"Look at that," Mrs. Close said suddenly, and there with majestic dignity the three fat gray geese walked across the field toward the dark water.

Bitsy looked at the geese and then shut her eyes tight. It would be superstitious, insane, to take them for a sign that she was to stay, and yet she knew in her heart she didn't want to go. It would be fun to go back for a visit, to be able to buy clothes and see plays and visit her old school friends, but that would be all. She couldn't imagine living there now when so much seemed to depend on her at the farm.

"I don't want to go," she said slowly. "I know I don't."

"Oh, Bits," Mrs. Close said, and her eyes were soft with tears. "I never thought you'd say that and mean it. I've tried so hard to work it out in my mind. To plan to give you a chance to go back if you felt you wanted it, and yet to leave Stanty here and be in New York without Dad back in the old whirlpool, fighting expenses and trying to force myself into being a teacher——"

She didn't finish the sentence, but Bitsy understood. She looked at the geese, and a little sigh of relief came to her lips. "Let's not talk about it," she said. "Let's not even think about it again. This is home really. You said so ages ago in Sea Cliff and you were right."

Mrs. Close squeezed Bitsy's hand as she let the gear-shift into first speed. "Darling, I want to see Stanty," she said, "and get those letters. We've settled everything, and we won't have to fuss about it again. You're a good girl!"

Mrs. Close was lighthearted and gay on the short drive home, but Bitsy still felt uncomfortable and disturbed. It wasn't that she regretted her decision about New York. It was just that when she thought of her life there and Minty and Mabs and the old gang who had gone to Sea Cliff every summer she thought of Byrd, and now she knew with a sudden stabbing clearness that she was nearing a decision about him too. You couldn't go on loving a person and wanting to be near him and at the same time arguing and fighting with him in your mind.

As she stopped the car she unconsciously sighed, and

Mrs. Close looked at her with eyebrows raised and questioning. "You haven't changed your mind, have you, darling?" she said. "If you want to think about it longer, I'll wait before telling Cousin Bert."

"You mean New York?" Bitsy said. "No, I'm absolutely sure about that!"

"I'm glad," Mrs. Close said. "Though it means your giving up a lot." She turned and kissed Bitsy on the forehead. Bitsy smiled at her and carried her suitcase inside and then went up to the barn to help with the chores. Mrs. Close stood for a minute looking after her with a worried expression in her eyes before she went inside herself.

XXI

Stand Fast and Reply

T̲HE WARM WEATHER HELD, and Tuesday Bruce brought Margaret and the baby home from the hospital. Vinton looked almost too small and frail to be human, wrapped up in a blue woolly blanket in Bruce's arms. Bruce would have stopped to show him to Stanty and the rest of the family who had come out on the porch, but Mrs. Crane gave him a little push. "Bring that baby right inside," she bossed. "Do you want him to catch his death of cold?"

Usually Margaret looked upset when she heard her mother-in-law scolding Bruce, but now she never even noticed, she was so intent on the baby. Vinton's little mouth opened and he yawned a wide, stretching grimace that knotted his face. "He's cr-crazy," Stanty giggled.

Margaret bent over the baby with joy in her face. "He's just sleepy," she said. "I'm glad we've got him home."

Bruce himself was livelier and more outgoing than ever before. At first Bitsy had thought his exuberance was sheer relief over the baby's safe arrival, but gradually she realized how much of it was renewed confidence at being accepted by the Army. "No man wants to be told he's unfit," Tim said one day when Bruce had left them to take the old tractor out to the cornfield. "And Bruce had his heart set on being in the Air Force. If it wasn't for leaving Margaret he'd be on top of the world."

Tim was absolutely right. Bruce was more gentle and loving with Margaret than ever before. When Bitsy had first come to the farm he had been quite content to let Margaret wait on him, but now he sprang up to take a dish out of her hands or to do some chore ahead of her. Once as Bitsy was feeding the chickens Margaret came to the side door to say good-by to Bruce before he went off plowing. Bruce's face when he turned away was white and set, and Bitsy had the feeling that he was steeling himself for the infinitely harder leave-taking that was just ahead of them.

He was natural and charming with the baby, but it was Margaret on whom his mind and heart were set. He took her off to the study as early as possible, but even when there were other people in the room or when she was busy with the baby, Bitsy had the feeling that he wasn't aware of any presence but hers.

The baby's bassinet was in the tiny hall bedroom next to Margaret's and Bruce's. Most of the time he lay cozily asleep, but sometimes when Margaret was fixing his formula he cried, a harsh, dry little wail that rang through the house. "Margaret takes good care of him," Cousin Bert said one day as she and Mrs. Close washed the luncheon dishes while Margaret fed the baby upstairs. "It's a wonder when you stop to think she's an orphan and an only child."

Mrs. Close didn't say anything, but when Cousin Bert went back into the dining room for the last of the dishes she looked over at Bitsy and smiled. "I'm glad that's established," she said. "It's going to make it a lot easier for Margaret after Bruce has gone."

Bitsy nodded over the saucepan she was wiping. It was true that Cousin Bert's mind worked in fixed categories and that once Margaret was set as a successful parent she would stay that way. It was the unexpected generosity, even subtle understanding, that Cousin Bert had shown lately that was surprising. She got up uncomplainingly to feed the baby at six so that Margaret could sleep. She slaved and schemed so that Margaret and Bruce could have every available minute together without acting martyred or imposed on.

Once when Bitsy found her ironing crib sheets in the kitchen late at night, she offered to help. "Can't you see I like it?" Cousin Bert said fiercely. "Helping to take care of that baby boy gets me almost cheerful."

A few months ago Bitsy would have been hurt or bewildered, but now she understood what was behind the sharp-sounding words. As she left the kitchen she paused to give Cousin Bert's shoulder a loving little pat. "You're a good girl," Cousin Bert said with one of the rare, sudden smiles that made her broad, middle-aged face look like Tim's lean young one. "It was a weight off my mind when your mother said you'd decided to stay. I don't know how Tim and I would manage without you."

Bitsy flushed with pleasure. She was glad that both Tim and Cousin Bert wanted her. And it was good to know deep in her own heart that her work was worth solid cash to a perfect stranger. Schwed's offer had meant even more to her than she had at first realized. To know that you were doing a job that could command a decent price gave you a feeling of independence, of freedom, that grew as you experienced it.

But even in the midst of her new feeling of elation and pride Bitsy realized that the brunt of Bruce's work would fall to Tim. She would do the best she could, but there was plenty of heavy man's work that was beyond her physical capacity which he and Steve would have to shoulder.

Tim had grown taller during the winter, but since the trouble over Byrd's car and the news of Bruce's acceptance he seemed to have taken on added years as well. He was as friendly and companionable with Steve as ever, but now it was he who made the decisions as to which field was to be plowed and harrowed and what stock was to be turned out and where. In everything connected with the farm he had an air of quiet authority which was new to him, and even in things that were purely social he seemed more mature and poised.

On the occasions when Byrd came over to the farm Tim spoke to him pleasantly enough and didn't go off to the barn until Byrd and Bitsy had made their plans for the afternoon. Once, in the first week of April, he even offered to show them the way to walk over the back part of the farm. Bitsy had never taken that particular path in the fall and it had been impassable in the dead of winter. "He's really been quite decent," Byrd condescended when Tim had showed them the way to go and then gone back to do his milking. "A lot of kids would have stayed sore."

Bitsy said nothing, but she knew that it was more than generosity on Tim's part. It wasn't just that he was ready to let bygones be bygones, but since the day Bruce had received his orders he had felt himself to be the head of the farm with a host's obligations to anyone who came on it.

Bitsy noticed him the morning Bruce was to leave. Steve had suggested that he plow the south meadow while Tim was at school, but Tim shook his head. "That'll flood again," he said. "We always get a heavy rain in April and it's likely to wash. Better start with the north piece."

Steve shook his head, but when they went toward the house, Bitsy saw that he headed the mules toward the north field. Inside the farmhouse the morning seemed to have started like any other. Cousin Bert was in the kitchen. Mother was upstairs making beds. Stanty chased around the living room looking for the map he had made last night and muttering what he would do to the person who had taken it.

Bitsy put down the milk can and Cousin Bert turned to her with a sharp request to put it in a handier spot. Bitsy was on the point of saying it was the same place where she had put it every morning for months, but she held her tongue. A few moments later, when she passed the dining room, she was glad that she had not spoken. It was a school day, but breakfast was all laid out on the best Sunday tablecloth and all of Cousin Bert's precious hyacinths had been cut and carefully arranged in a bowl in the middle of the table.

A little while later, when they were seated, Cousin Bert pressed ham and waffles and the special butter rolls that Bruce liked upon them in an endless profusion, but she herself never even sat down to eat. Bruce was pleasant and agreeable, the way he had always been, but there was a suppressed excitement, a bubbling aliveness, about him that Bitsy had not seen before. He can hardly wait, Bitsy realized with a little stab of pain for Margaret. He's been wanting to leave the farm for years, and this is his chance.

Margaret herself was like a person in a dream. She spoke and passed things just as she would have done any other morning. She helped herself to food and made an attempt to eat it. Even Mother standing mute and frozen on the station platform after Dad's train had left had not moved Bitsy more. She's swell, Bitsy thought. She knows it's right for Bruce to go not only for the war but for himself. She's going to behave if it kills her.

Her mind was on Margaret, and the school day dragged endlessly. It was only in the English class that she came upon something that appealed to her present mood. She had decided to learn Amy Lowell's *Patterns* for her English assignment, and as she reread the words in the book in front of her, they flamed into new meaning. "In a pattern called a war." "Christ, what are patterns for?" Bitsy said the words under her breath. "Christ, what are patterns for?"

Margaret was back from seeing Bruce off when Bitsy and Tim got home. She was upstairs, and Bitsy could hear her singing, her voice clear and true, as she settled Vinton for the night.

"Everything go off all right?" Tim asked, and looked around him as though he expected to see some actual physical change in the old stove or the worn linoleum.

"Of course!" Mrs. Crane snapped. "Margaret only had to take Bruce to the Field. You didn't expect her to break down, did you? She's a sensible girl!"

Her last words had a sudden proud ring to them. Cousin Bert and Margaret were going to be all right. Their ways of facing Bruce's possible going had been different before it had been an established fact. Now that he had actually gone, their need of him and their pride in the baby had turned into solid bonds of affection and respect.

The only time that Bitsy saw Margaret openly upset in the days that followed was when she was packing away Bruce's civilian clothes. She was as careful and systematic with the newspaper and moth balls as ever, but when Bitsy looked at her face she saw that it was streaked with tears. "Oh, Margaret, I'm sorry," Bitsy said impulsively, but Margaret only mopped at her tears and went on folding and sorting.

"I'm all right," she said. "It's right for Bruce to go and I know it. It's just—it's just that I wish I could have seen him in his uniform before he left." Her words ended in a little wail and she put down her head and sobbed.

"Maggie, Maggie dear," Bitsy said, more touched than

she could say by this small, utterly feminine wish in someone who was so eminently sensible.

"I'm all right really," Margaret said, the tears pouring down her face. "It's just that after you've had a baby you —you cry easily. Your mother and Mrs. Crane said they felt that way too."

Bitsy had nothing to say to that, and she began to help fold and wrap the two woolen suits and the piles of blue denim work clothes. "I'm a lot better off even than Bruce's mother," Margaret said. "No matter what happens we'll be together again somehow. Nothing could really keep us apart, and it's silly to worry about things that don't matter."

It was true, Bitsy knew, and she felt humbled and somehow inferior as she worked beside Margaret. They understood each other, Margaret and Bruce. They were totally different, one the dreamer, the other so practical, but they fitted together. They were a pattern in themselves, a perfectly resolved chord.

Margaret hung up the blue serge suit that Bruce had given to Tim and then fixed the water for Vinton's bath. When Bitsy left her she had the small towel-wrapped baby gurgling on her knees. She's all right, Bitsy realized; she knows what she's doing and why she's doing it.

She had just finished setting the table when the telephone rang. She wondered, vaguely, if it could be Bruce, but when she picked up the receiver it was Byrd's voice at the other end. "Bitsy, I'm off," he said. "I heard by a fluke that we'll be leaving tomorrow night. Can you get over to say good-by?"

"Of course!" Bitsy's heart was in her answer. "I could meet you at the entrance to the Field at half-past four."

"Good girl!" Byrd's voice was husky. "I knew you'd get there."

Bitsy went to bed early that night, but it was a long time before she went to sleep. There were so many things that crossed and recrossed her mind. All the arguments that she had thought but never spoken to Byrd seemed destined to torment her when she was alone. They were such ugly thoughts, waiting and hovering like vultures to edge in upon her when she tried to rest. Byrd's attitude toward Tim. His boredom about the farm. His half-amused, half-contemptuous attitude toward Bitsy's work.

Bitsy was wide-awake, her body tense and cold, her tired eyes twitching. She switched on the light and saw that it was after one o'clock. She flung her coat over the foot of her bed and then lay down again and began to repeat poetry to put herself to sleep. *The Ode on a Grecian Urn. Patterns.* Finally, "Let us not to the marriage of true minds admit impediments." She said it over twice, and Margaret's half-sobbed words came back to her. "Nothing can keep us apart really. It's silly to worry about things that don't matter." It meant the same thing. Margaret and Bruce! Bitsy's set lips relaxed into a smile as she thought of them sitting together in their study, walking hand in hand across one of the big fields; of Margaret's face when she had first seen Bruce after her accident. Bitsy's hand that gripped the edge of her pillow gradually relaxed. Margaret and Bruce. Just to think of them brought comfort to her heart. "Let us not to the marriage—of—true—minds." "Love—is not love which bends with the remover to—remove." The great words came more and more slowly. "It is an ever-fixed mark." Bitsy was asleep.

It was still dark when Bitsy woke up the next morning. She lay still for a moment, listening to the sleepy chirping of the birds. She felt tired and spent but somehow relieved and made whole. A decision that yesterday she hadn't even dared face was now resolved in her mind. She lay back huddled against the pillow, her mind on Byrd. She couldn't let him go away thinking they were engaged, pretending to herself everything between them was happiness and peace.

She was ahead of him at the Field and left her bicycle at the far side of the road. She made no attempt to go past the guard's hut but stood outside the forbidding gates on the main road. "Blaine Field—Gate No. 3." Her eyes perceived the words without her mind understanding them. It was flat and open around the Field and the wind was cold. She walked up and down trying to keep from shaking, but she was chilled from nerves as much as from the wind.

Four enlisted men off duty came through the gates and walked past her toward the bus stop further down the road. "Waiting for a soldier?" one of them kidded her, but she never even heard him.

She was toying with the idea of not telling Byrd. Why couldn't she just say good-by to him and then tell him later that she couldn't marry him? Byrd was going off to fight, perhaps to be killed. The finality of the thought numbed her so that she couldn't walk. "It would be so much kinder not to tell him," one voice inside of her said. "And so much easier."

"It would be a rotten coward's trick," a second voice answered. "You owe him more than that."

Bitsy had begun to walk again when Byrd suddenly appeared beside her. "Good girl," he said, and gave her arm a tight squeeze. "I knew you'd turn up."

For a moment Bitsy said nothing at all. It seemed so horrible to tell him in this bleak, windy place. Behind them cars roared by on the main road and in front of them was the open plain of the post littered with the ugly rubble of new buildings. She looked around desperately. If there were only a diner, a drugstore, any place where they could be warm and facing each other across a little table. "You're frozen," Byrd said suddenly. "And you look tired out. Have those fools been driving you again? Really, Bitsy, your doing that farm work is too absurd."

It was now or never, Bitsy knew, and she looked up at Byrd with pleading eyes. "Byrd," she said. "Byrd dear, you just don't understand. I like the farm work. I could have given it up, but I honestly didn't want to. It's my job just the way flying's yours." She struggled now for the right, the honest words as she told him about her mother's offer and her own immediate decision.

Byrd had let go of her arm as she started talking and he looked at her with a stranger's eyes. "Good lord, girl," he said when she had finished. "You may be on that farm for years. What are you going to do with yourself, without friends, contacts, interesting things to do?"

"The farm is interesting," Bitsy said stubbornly, but Byrd wasn't even listening.

"In a couple of years you won't even be the same person," he said angrily. "You'll just be a country hick like that precious cousin of yours. And he'll probably get himself drafted and leave you flat!"

With Byrd's words a chilling fear of loneliness numbed Bitsy's heart. Newcomers were rare on the farm. Suppose she never met anyone she loved more than Byrd. Suppose that for months, for all her life, this sickening inner loneliness held her prisoner? Why couldn't she compromise, meet Byrd halfway before it was too late?

"I want my wife to be a reasonably sophisticated person," Byrd went on. "I want her to be smart and amusing and able to meet people."

Suddenly Bitsy saw the Sea Cliff pool as though she were sitting hopelessly beside it at that very moment. Byrd loved her for the person he wanted her to be, not for what she was! Out here, far from his home, she had come to represent the sophisticated country-club girl whose pattern she had just learned to escape. It was ironic that just as the farm was teaching her to be herself, to choose what she wanted out of life instead of what other people thought she ought to have, she had attracted him as being the very type she no longer wanted to copy.

With understanding came new courage. "Byrd," Bitsy

said, and her voice was very gentle, "I guess you know it as well as I do. I couldn't ever be your wife. We're not the same kind of people at all really."

For a moment as she looked up at Byrd's face she thought he was going to make a scene. Then slowly his expression changed, and she wasn't sure whether it was relief or amusement that was uppermost. "You're a queer one," he said finally, and pushed his barracks cap back off his forehead. "For a girl who's lived in New York and Sea Cliff to choose the corn belt!"

"People are terribly different," Bitsy said, and now relief made her feel released, affectionate. "And I'll always like you an awful lot."

"And so let's just be good friends!" Byrd mocked, but he wasn't really angry, and he pulled Bitsy's arm back through his and led her toward the gate.

They talked on for a few moments directly in front of the gate where they could see past the unfinished storehouses to the raw new barracks beyond. Their words were only shadow talk now, with no real meaning to any of it. As she struggled for something to say, Bitsy thought of Margaret and Bruce parting at this same spot only yesterday. As she thought of them the last vestige of a desire to compromise left her. She could almost laugh now at the wave of self-pity that had just engulfed her. She was only giving up a beau, a dancing partner who had meant more to her pride than her need for companionship. Why, even Tim, young and coltish though he seemed, had always been more her true companion than

Byrd. To think of Byrd's leaving on the same plane as the agony Margaret must have suffered was almost laughable.

She looked up at Byrd with a new light in her eyes, and just then he took her by the shoulders as though he meant to shake her. "Is it that fellow Tim?" he demanded. "I've been wondering ever since that day at the club."

"No!" was on the tip of Bitsy's tongue, but she hesitated, searching her own heart. She had cheated Byrd enough by slurring over the things that really mattered. She owed it to him to be honest now. "I don't know," she admitted finally. "We like the same sort of life and we look at a lot of things the same way. But he's still such a kid, and besides he'll be going into the Army in a few more months if he's not deferred for the farm."

"Then I give up," Byrd said, and shook his head. "I just don't understand what it's all about. Bitsy, think! Think hard! In six months what will you be doing?"

In six months it would be the end of September. The season when Bitsy had first come to the farm. There would be the haying then, and the corn to husk, the last of the garden—terrific back-breaking work if Tim were called away. "I guess I'll just be working on the farm," Bitsy said, and she managed to grin. "There'll be plenty to do!"

"But what'll you be feeling?" Byrd asked, and his voice was more earnest, more really interested than at any time since she had known him. "What'll you really be thinking about and hoping for?"

"I don't know," Bitsy said slowly, and now she talked as much to herself as to Byrd. It was when she thought of life on the farm without Tim that the cold, hopeless loneliness closed in upon her. She fought it off as she would have a net that snared her feet. "I'll probably just do the thing that's right ahead of my nose," she went on. "But at least if it's work that I feel I was meant to do, I won't be cheating anyone and I won't go around arguing and fighting in my own mind."

"I get that," Byrd said slowly. "But it sounds like awfully cold comfort."

Just at that moment there was the long-drawn, commanding call of a bugle in the distance. Byrd listened to it, unconsciously squaring his shoulders. "This is it," he said finally. "I've got to get back to quarters."

Bitsy held out her hand, but now Byrd took her face in both hands and while the gaping sentry watched he kissed her coolly on both cheeks. "You're a queer kid," he said. "But we've had a lot of fun."

"Oh, Byrd! Byrd, we have!" Bitsy said, but now he had turned away and was gone.

She watched him with tears in her eyes as he passed through the big gate. The sentry presented arms and then with a rattle of his rifle straps stood at attention as Byrd snapped back a salute. The next minute Byrd was swinging down the road that led to the officers' quarters. He's all right, Bitsy thought, and now that it was all over she felt tired and almost sick. Byrd had been surprised and a little hurt, but at heart he had felt the same way himself. She watched until his smart military figure was out of sight and then she picked up her bicycle from the gutter. She had just moved it onto the road when a sign inside the field caught her eye. *"Answer when challenged by the guard,"* it read. *"Stand fast and reply."*

She reread the last words, and a little flicker of amusement crossed her lips. That's just what I'll be doing, she thought, and there was a certain wry comfort in seeing it expressed in those impersonal military words. No matter what happens from now on I'll just have to stand fast and reply.

When she got back to the farm she saw Tim's slim, blue-jeaned figure waiting for her outside the barn. "I thought you'd never come," he said. "I've got something to show you in the garden."

More than anything Bitsy wanted to go up to her own room to sort out all the thoughts and feelings that had crowded over her in the last twenty-four hours. "I want to go upstairs," she began, but Tim wasn't to be turned down so lightly.

"Oh, come on," he said, and his face was gay, almost mischievous. "It's something that belongs to you."

With an irritated shrug of her shoulders she followed him toward the shabby picket fence and through the gate. She was just inside the garden when she saw the little dotted rows of fresh green. "Tim!" she said. "It's all up! My garden's really begun to grow!"

"Of course it has," Tim said, and there was approval in his voice. "But that isn't all. Look over there."

She looked where he pointed to the new clearing beyond the garden and across the glen. Only this morning it seemed to her there had been a forest of saplings and spindly second-growth trees shutting out the view. Now a broad, open swathe, wide and beautifully curving like a river, led the eye over intervening fields to the covered bridge and the little emerald pasture. "Tim!" Bitsy got out, and the boy nodded.

"It's ours," he said. "I bought it after Steve and I finished clearing. We worked on it on and off all winter, but we left the growth nearest the house until today so you wouldn't notice. That's why we didn't want you along when we were clearing brush way back in February." Bitsy gazed at the lovely view without speaking. Tim's Four-H prize money, his savings, every available cent must have gone into that land. It was folly, madness, but of an indescribably touching sort. The whole farm from the tree-guarded house to the pleasant apple orchard and the sweeping fields was ennobled, beautified, by this sudden, unexpected view.

She looked at Tim and his blue eyes smiled back at her. "I know it's crazy," he said quietly. "But if you haven't anything to look at when you're farming, you might just as well work in a store or a coal mine. Besides, the place was this way when my Great-Great-Uncle Bert built the house. The saplings just sprang up after my father sold the pasture by the covered bridge."

"It's beautiful," Bitsy said, and now her eyes were back on the soft green. Now, as when she had first seen it in the fall, that little separate spot of lush green was an oasis between acres of plowed utilitarian fields. She searched over it and there, walking calmly toward the water, were the three geese. "Tim," she called, her heart suddenly lifting. "There, there! My good-luck geese!"

"Of course," Tim said matter-of-factly. "I bought them with the land. I planned it way back last fall when we were talking about Kim."